The Funeral Bride

Part I of
The Autobiography
of Empress Alexandra

by

Kathleen McKenna Hewtson

ISBN-10:   1519238010

ISBN-13:   978-1519238016

'The Funeral Bride: *Part I of The Autobiography of Empress Alexandra*' is published by Taylor Street Books and is the copyright of the author, Kathleen McKenna Hewtson, 2015.

Dedication

To Tim, who has made, and continues to make, my own story the happiest on earth.

To my family, both in the United Kingdom and the US, thank you for your love and support, because saying I could not have done this without you is not an overstatement, merely the truth. I love you all.

And to the great expertise and beyond-the-call caring natures of Drs. Rosenberg and Kornguth in San Francisco who saved my husband, Tim's, life this last year.

Part 1

The Funeral Bride

1884 - 1894

Chapter 1

I have undertaken to write the truth because it has become apparent to me that I may be in death, as I was in life, completely misunderstood.

Much has been said of me, nearly all of it lies or distortions, that I was mad, bad, hysterical, deluded … and finally a saint. While I appreciate the latter sentiment and find it closest to the truth of my life and times, it still does not paint as accurate a portrait of my strivings as one might wish, so I have decided to end once and for all the sayings of others.

Now *I* shall say.

To begin with, I need to make it clear that I was born to save Russia, and I very nearly did. This is not to be vainglorious, which is yet another of the un-truths spoken of me; I am not a woman given to flights of fancy. It is, in fact, the central core of my existence. So few now can remember the circumstances by which I came to be Tsarina, a term I prefer to 'Empress' as it embraces the mystical portions of my position as well as the rather more practical applications, by which I mean power, the limitless power that was the lifeblood of an empress such as my grandmother, Queen Victoria. No, to be Tsarina is to be divine, to be the earthly incarnation of our mother in heaven.

That is who I was, not who I chose to be, but who I became, as destiny had marked me for this role and I humbly bowed to its will, by which I mean, of course, the will of God. Never may it be said that I have tried to impose my own will over His.

This brings me to yet another specious accusation – the most damning to my mind. It has long been said, and written, that I did indeed impose my will upon my husband, Nicholas II, Emperor and Tsar of all the Russias, but to do so would have been beyond even my abilities, for, you see, Nicholas, my darling Nicky, had no will at all and, without mine, all of us – Russia and its peoples – would have perished. That we did so in the end is simply because at last my enemies succeeded where they had so long failed and drove me to my knees. By doing so they destroyed a family, and an empire, but none of it ever needed to happen ...

I was born into an unusual position in life. By title alone my advent into the world did not seem particularly auspicious – or at least not to those who glanced but casually at it – yet my mother, Alice, was one of nine children born to the great Victoria, Queen, by the Grace of God, of the United Kingdom of Great Britain and Ireland, and of the British Dominions beyond the Seas, Defender of the Faith, and Empress of India, and in her time the most powerful woman in the world, as well as being, to my humble mind at least, the greatest woman of her age.

She had married for love and raised a relatively obscure German princeling to the lofty position of being her Prince Consort, having understood that, with his beauty and his gifts of mind, he, Prince Albert of Saxe-Coburg, would – indeed could – be the only man suited to help her carry her burdens as the sovereign of such a mighty realm.

She loved him with an abiding passion, the sort of love that I have noted seems to run through the women of our family and is only exceptionally to be evidenced in less exalted natures. This is both a fine thing and a terrible burden, as when it should happen that one is disillusioned in one's love, or, as in my grandmother's case, devastated by the premature death of one's one-and-only. We do not recover from such misfortunes, as say one might if one were less sensitive and evolved towards the highest state of love. To love, it is said, is human; to love without boundaries, is, I feel, divine.

My dearest mother, while not born a boy, was the favorite child of both her parents, my dear uncles proving to be considerable disappointments to their parents, and my sweet aunts appearing singularly lacking in any of the gifts of beauty and intelligence that were characteristic of my darling mama from an early age. Indeed, Mama's beauty and gifts of the mind made her the dearest companion of her papa, the Prince Consort, as his own adored spouse was necessarily dutifully occupied by the affairs of state, and so it came to pass that, being the much-loved child of a great love match, when Mama's mind and heart became settled upon the man who would become my papa, her parents – the Empress and the Prince – found it impossible to deny her wish, despite poor Papa's relatively humble place in the world.

Papa was born Ludwig of Hesse-Darmstadt and was, until his marriage to Mama, a mere Grand Duke, a situation that was corrected when my grandmamma, the Empress Victoria, elevated him to royalty by according him the title of 'His Royal Highness Prince Louis of Hesse-Darmstadt' upon his marriage to Mama, sadly a title not recognized by the ignorant German states surrounding our small kingdom of Hesse-Darmstadt; they unkindly continued to refer to poor Papa as mere Grand Duke Ludwig IV for the whole of his life. That is, of course, unimportant, as are all titles and designations except those given by our Lord. I only mention this in passing to illustrate the source of potential misunderstandings of Papa's status in the world of European monarchy.

As Mama used to say, "Papa is not a great man in the world, so it falls to me to ensure that he be a very good man," quite an irony as I, her daughter, would one day marry a truly good man who, by birth, was destined to be a great man and yet who, without me, would have failed utterly to achieve his God-given role here on earth.

Forgive me. Oftentimes now, when I think of poor Mama, I am drawn to an appreciation of my own sufferings, as I should not, for her earthly sufferings were as nothing to my own. No, Mama was allowed to marry the man she loved, my poor papa, and despite a rather unfortunate beginning – the loss of her own dear papa right before her wedding and the commensurate grief of her mama, the Empress – the young couple was able, at first, to live in a state of near-perfect happiness. This felicity did, of course, diminish over time but through no fault of either Mama or poor Papa.

Papa, who was under great pressure from both financial sources and the not far distant annexation of Hesse by Prussia, was not always available to Mama for the companionship that she so sorely and naturally needed, having come to live in a strange country whose people and customs were unfamiliar to her. Given poor Papa's schedule, Mama was forced to rely more and more on her own thoughts and abilities to embrace her new role as wife of the Prince of Hesse-Darmstadt, and though at times she felt overwhelmed, she remained guided by her own Papa, Prince Albert, who began appearing to her in ghostly form soon after her arrival at her new home. That poor Papa could not, or willfully refused to, believe in the presence of Mama's beloved late father rather began to drive a wedge between them, marring the first bliss of their marital love.

Still, Mama, having been raised to be first a wife and then a princess, remained ever dutiful and loving towards her chosen one, and produced seven children for him, of which I was honored to be born sixth, following three older sisters, my adored brother, Ernie – or as the world would know him, Grand Duke Ernest of Hesse-Darmstadt – and my younger brother Frittie After my own, I suppose, rather uneventful arrival, Mama would go on to have one more blessed cherub –my darling baby sister, May.

The birth of so many healthy and beautiful children should have brought Mama and poor Papa closer together than ever, but alas, with the children came great heartbreak, as is often the case. My dearest brother, Frittie, the light of Mama's life, was cruelly taken from her following a freak fall out of the window of Mama's boudoir. Then the dread disease diphtheria visited our poor family and, naturally, Mama took it upon herself to nurse first poor Papa, when he fell ill, and then all of her remaining children. All of us suffered terribly during the fearful course of the disease, but it was May, the smallest of us, who was the one to succumb.

Shortly thereafter, poor Mama was also taken from us, no doubt dying of a broken heart, leaving us as survivors of a shipwreck, wandering the echoing halls of the new palace, the beautiful home Mama had ordered to be built for our family in Hesse-Darmstadt despite poor Papa's protestations that we had no money for such a place, and that, further, the old nobility would be insulted by the conspicuous extravagance of such a modern, and relatively English, home in their midst. However, following the irreparable loss of his dear wife, I must say that poor Papa grew to be forever grateful for Mama's insistence on building the new palace, which remained an oasis of English peace and taste in his increasingly dark life.

I was only a very small child at this time, being a mere six years of age when God chose to remove the sunshine from my life, my adored, irreplaceable Mama, of whose comfort I had already been much deprived due to her wretched mourning of the death of little May and the consequent chronic invalidism that had been visited upon her. Nevertheless, in her tribulation, she had managed to remain a constant, if unseen, force for love and wisdom for me, as daily – and sometimes as often as hourly – my much-loved Nanny Orchard would gift me with small notes from Mama lying upstairs in her boudoir.

After her death, all my toys and dresses were burned to mitigate the continuing threat of diphtheria in the palace, and along with the loss of my dolls and my little girl treasures, all Mama's notes disappeared, and, to me, a small girl, it was as though she and little May had never existed, though this dreadfully confusing state would soon be brought to an end by the appearance in my life of my dearest grandmamma, Her Royal Majesty Queen Victoria.

Grandmamma, of course, had been understood to have existed by me, as Mama made constant references to her both in person and in my daily notes, but until Mama's death the Queen was a figure almost of imagination to me, like the Christ Child and Father Christmas. After Mama's passing, Grandmamma, roused from her continuing grief at the loss of Grandpapa Albert, came to the rescue of we orphaned Darmstadt children, declaring herself intent on being "as a mother to us."

Oh and she was, she was indeed, the kindest, dearest mother-grandmamma any child could wish for.

At first she confined herself to including special notes just for me in her daily letters of instruction to poor Papa. As this was so reminiscent of my relationship with darling Mama during her lifetime, I began to miss Mama much less, and following an abbreviated three year mourning period in deference to my tender age, I was sent off to England to meet the great monarch in person.

Chapter 2

It has been said, by the much-lauded Count Leo Tolstoy, that all happy families are alike whereas each unhappy family is unhappy in its own way. While I do not feel that I can wholly endorse the writings of this noble gentleman of letters, I might have been able to do so with some enthusiasm when I was younger, at Osbourne with darling Grandmamma, where Grandmamma, a great Queen-Empress, had succeeded, despite all being against her, to create a small, secluded oasis of private family life.

She had begun this endeavor in order to share the sweetest hours of her life with her adored Prince Albert, my departed – though never to be forgotten – grandpapa, and had, following his untimely death, tried, for the sake of her dear children and then grandchildren, to maintain this tradition of cozy, even perfect, family togetherness and joy in the homes she had once lived in with her lost beloved one.

It was to Osborne House that I was first sent to her. Later, I would share prolonged holidays with her at Balmoral Castle, the modest but enchanting palace she had purchased with her dear prince, and it was during my times there that I became decided upon my vision of what entailed a truly happy home life, and I used the ideal of Grandmamma and Grandpapa's great love as my secret hope for my own future happiness, should God so grant it to me.

Grandmamma once, in a fit of the grief which could still assail her at her loss, showed me a passage she had written in her diary on the first morning of her married life.

> *I NEVER, NEVER spent such an evening!!! MY DEAREST DEAREST DEAR Albert ... his excessive love & affection gave me feelings of heavenly love & happiness I never could have hoped to have felt before! He clasped me in his arms, & we kissed each other again & again! His beauty, his sweetness & gentleness – really how can I ever be thankful enough to have such a Husband ... to be called by names of tenderness I have never yet heard used to me before was bliss beyond belief! Oh! This was the happiest day of my life!*

I was an innocent wee child of eight when I read these profound sentiments of love and, dare I say, of *la grande passion!* But I was not too young to understand, nor to contemplate, their meaning and to apply the hope to my untried girl's heart that I would one day wish to make such utterances to another. Oh and I did, I did, I did. Nicky, wee one, sunshine, Huzzy, did not we have such love, and even more so than any other mortals?

We did, and yet ...

But I must postpone discussion of such things, and indeed at the time I could only imagine such lofty feelings as they applied to Grandmamma and her lost one. I found that it was when Grandmamma first took me to her great palace of Windsor that I knew, knew completely, what one should hope for in life, in love, and in matters of the heart.

For, if love can survive in a garret, only imagine how it can flourish and grow in one of the world's great palaces. In no way do I mean this to indicate that I ever did, or shall, find any sort of pleasure in material objects – of course, I have no interest in such trinkets – I mean only to say that, if one's loved one is a personage of importance, then doesn't that show all too clearly that God's especial grace and care is visited upon him? And if that is true, and it is, then it would stand to reason that the one most loved by God, the one set by Him on earth to rule over others, would be a person of a particularly sensitive and exalted nature, and therefore must also be somebody specially blessed with all the gifts that our Creator can endow him with.

I came to see this deepest truth after first arriving at Windsor, and in my small girl's imagination I naturally liked to think of dearest Grandmamma and Grandpapa as having lived and loved there when they were young and beautiful. It was also at Windsor that I first knew that to be able to rule a vast empire one must have a small life as well, for if a monarch has no rich, cozy, enduring family life and support, she will naturally become lost in all her vast palaces and lost to herself in all the flattery and beguilingly false admiration of the sycophants who surround castles and those who live in them.

That is who and what my dear grandpapa had been to my grandmamma. In him the mighty Empress found a hearth to return to after her endless days spent governing her realm.

Following my first visit to Windsor, my tutor, Mr. Elson, a tedious little man who understood nothing of importance, attempted to explain to me that England was a constitutional democracy and that my dearest grandmamma, the Empress, was its constitutional monarch, little more than a figurehead, there only at the pleasure of the British people, and someone who could neither make laws nor determine the day-to-day governance of those peoples she had been set above by God to rule. She could, he said, "advise and influence," but that, as far as actual power went, she had none.

Mr. Elson was soon let go by my own poor papa, who was naturally affronted to hear that his children were receiving propaganda rather than an education, but I will say this much for that poor misguided soul: He left me with much to consider, and I did, drawing, as one will, my own conclusions upon the matter, which were that if only God can set a ruler upon a throne, and this is a widely accepted truth, then doesn't that mean that God has then chosen that personage to rule over His earthly kingdom and its peoples until such time as we are all called home to our heavenly reward? Well, of course, no other interpretation can make any sort of sense. And if one accepts that, then one must also accept that democracy is the tool of those who do not accept the rule of God, Our Father, who created us all in His image to varying degrees.

I did not then, and do not now, blame Grandmamma for allowing her God-given rights to be eroded over time. She was young when she began her reign and then suffered the impossible loss of her one-and-only, but the rotten state of England has long proved the truth of my understanding.

If one views my own choices through the honest eyes and childlike faith of the child I indeed was when I came to make them, one can better understand the heavy burden I chose so willingly, and why I made it my life's mission to see that my own one-and-only, God's anointed on Earth, must never forget that it is not for we humble servants of our Creator to try and usurp His will. God set my grandmamma, and then my husband, on thrones to rule, and to rule, if that is what we are called to do, is what we must do. Burden or no, we must be obedient to His will. If a simple English shepherd can grasp this, as does every Russian peasant, then we, who have been given so much more, cannot fail to do so either.

These feelings and their ramifications were, of course, all in the future. I was a young girl and much more preoccupied at that time with family matters than with those things unseen and yet deeply felt.

This is not to say that my feelings for my family were ever less than paramount in my life, which is why the year 1884, my twelfth year, was to loom so large for both my present and my future.

Since my beloved mama's untimely death, and the further tragic death of two of my small siblings, our much reduced family had grown even closer in defense of our great losses. In the year of 1884, we in Darmstadt were the most united and happy; this a nod, yet again, to Count Tolstoy's observation on family circumstances. Our dearest papa watched over us with tender care, and my older sisters – Victoria, Ella and Irene – watched over me, their small Alix, and my darling, my dearest brother, Ernie, as second mothers.

Given Ernie's and my tender ages – fourteen and twelve respectively – we hoped, and indeed were right to hope, that Victoria, Ella and Irene would stay and watch over us and act as comforts, and at times of need consorts, to poor Papa in his burdensome role as the Grand Duke of Hesse-Darmstadt … but it was not to be. Both Victoria and Ella had fallen in love and had accepted marriage proposals. Naturally, poor Papa was consulted and asked for their hands by Prince Louis of Battenberg, in the case of Victoria, and by Grand Duke Sergei, for Ella, and despite his doubts in both cases, he gave his reluctant consent to the matches and weddings were planned.

Papa was greatly attached to Victoria, and with good reason. My oldest sister was so very like darling Mama, a force for calm and good sense, that his reservations about her romance with darling Louis might, I am forced to say, have had more to do with his own sadness at losing her than with anything relating to Louis himself. Louis, it is true, did not have a great deal in the way of titles or wealth to commend him, but he did possess the most loving heart, the entirety of which he had given into the care of my dear sister. And besides, Grandmamma liked the match and so forward it went with great happiness on all sides, except, of course, on the part of Papa, myself and Ernie, though we wished the bridal couple well and valiantly tried to conceal our own natural sadness at our upcoming loss.

The case of my dear Ella was somewhat more difficult. Ella was, as is her nature, I am sorry to say, rather selfish and unthinking in her choice of mate. She had long been considered the beauty of our family, and because of this, and because too of her especial care of we orphaned Hesse children, darling Grandmamma had taken a particular interest in her marital prospects, an interest, I fear, that Ella, in her headstrong way, disdained. At the first, Grandmamma proposed that Ella marry Frederick, the Grand Duke of Baden, whom she always referred to as "good and steady," which were high accolades coming from Grandmamma. Ella declined his suit, to Grandmamma's considerable displeasure, thus creating bad feeling in the family, and not just with Grandmamma, as Frederick's own mama, the Empress Augusta, was so infuriated by her rejection of her son that she refused to speak to Ella for years.

Ella's next suitor was our first cousin Wilhelm, a boy so disagreeable that even Grandmamma could not object to Ella's adamant refusal of his hand, of which honesty commands that I must unkindly add he had but one, his having been maimed during a disastrous birthing process. Still, Ella would have become Empress of Germany had she accepted his offer, and maybe then all the troubles that would subsequently afflict the entire world from Germany's corner could have been averted.

Ella never cared about the ramifications of her decisions; she always wanted what she wanted and had no regard for any duty but to herself, which is how she came to accept the suit of the Grand Duke Sergei, the younger brother of the reigning Tsar-Emperor Alexander III of Russia. In fairness to Ella, and of course to my own later choice, I feel obliged to mention that Grandmamma disliked Russians in general and the reigning Tsar-Emperor Alexander in particular. The Emperor, a very large man himself, was once overheard at a state dinner dismissively describing Grandmamma as a "belly woman," going on to compound this remark by opining that she looked like a fat round ball on shaky legs and was, besides, a selfish ruler.

These were, of course, terrible and cruel things for him to have said – and quite untrue – and naturally they were terrible and cruel things to hear spoken of oneself, and poor Grandmamma was quite devastated at first, particularly so since she had so nearly become engaged in her youth to his father, Alexander II. However, Grandmamma was, it must be said, somewhat fiery in nature, and after learning of the present Russian Emperor's feelings toward her, she hesitated little in retaliating by referring to him as "that great clumsy Russian bear who occupies an increasingly shaky throne."

Therefore, long before Ella's engagement to Sergei, Grandmamma's sentiments towards the Russian royal family had been causing a certain amount of discomfort around her, for my Uncle Bertie, the Prince of Wales, was married to Princess Alexandra, who was the sister to Empress Marie, the Tsar's wife. The two sisters were extremely close, so it was naturally somewhat distressing for Aunt Alex when Grandmamma would insist on communicating her deeply negative feelings towards the Tsar over family dinners, something she did with regularity as Grandmamma was not a woman to forget, or indeed to forgive, any perceived insult, which in this case, of course, was not merely perceived but real.

Still it was uncomfortable and became yet again a daily topic of discussion when Ella said yes to Sergei.

Sergei had been a frequent visitor over the years as he traveled often to Germany to observe the Kaiser's military training encampments, and for my own part I quite liked him, as did Papa and Ernie. To my young girl's eyes he seemed like a fairytale prince. He was very tall and slender and had such pretty green eyes, and he favored me with a great deal of attention and said, with what others considered teasing, though I did not, that he wished I was old enough to court instead of Ella, as he believed that I, not she, was the true beauty of the family.

Grandmamma did not like Sergei, however. She sniffed that he wore a corset under his clothes and that he was a "perfect Prussian of a prince." Being "Prussian" was not a compliment from Grandmamma, nor had she really forgiven Ella for refusing her choice of Frederick of Baden.

And so it was a bit tense during the engagement, and afterwards Grandmamma and Ella never did regain the close relationship they had shared.

I, however, was beginning to forget my upset at Ella's departure in the anticipation of my own, for Papa had accepted Sergei's invitation for himself and Victoria and Irene and Ernie, and even for my small self, to travel to Russia to attend their wedding. Better still, I had been asked to participate in Ella's wedding party as a junior bridesmaid. I was really beside myself at the prospect of such a journey. I had, of course, visited Grandmamma a great deal, but had never traveled otherwise, and the prospect of a trip to the hidden land of the tsars, with all its ensuing mystery and grandeur, loomed large before me.

The six of us began our journey from Darmstadt at the end of May, using the Tsar's own imperial train which he had kindly loaned his younger brother for the occasion of his wedding. I had been on trains before, yes, but this one was a small traveling palace: the rooms were hung with blue and gold velvet and there were more servants on board than I had ever seen, even at Windsor. I was given my own room on the train. It was so small but pretty, and the walls were covered with a pale blue satin, and at night I lay contentedly upon my feather mattress and watched as the familiar countryside, filled with spring flowers and myriad dwellings dotted with happy, waving people, gave way to something altogether alien, quieter, emptier.

There are many who have tried to describe Russia, some with accolades, others with distaste, but the only proper word for the landscape, if one must choose, is 'vast.' We traveled for three days over a land where I seldom saw a single dwelling or, for that matter, a tree. It just went on and on and on, this land of endless empty grasses blowing in an unseen wind, and I felt puzzled: Was the Tsar the mightiest of emperors because he had more land than I had ever imagined existed or was he the least of rulers, as Grandmamma had intimated, for if there were no villages – let alone cities – then were there any people to rule?

These were only the ponderings of a silly little girl of course, for when at last our train pulled into the royal enclosure of the great city of St. Petersburg, my speculations vanished as if into dust. Here was a city, the like of which few of us could ever have imagined.

It's rather hard to describe St. Petersburg as I viewed it then, against how I came to see it, but I will try. In the interests of all truth and justice, I will try.

To begin with, it has often been said that St. Petersburg itself should never have existed: it was a swampland, a place of rivers and marshes that led to the Gulf of Finland. Ancient and enormous beyond the comprehension of any but God, Russians had always inhabited small primitive villages and their tsars had lived in the ancient Muscovite city of Moscow, home to the Kremlin and to 'seventy times seventy' Orthodox churches. But when Peter the Great ascended the throne, the long beard and scepter and knout of his ancestors were not for him. He was the first of the Romanovs to travel widely, and Europe, with all its beauties and cultural advancements, made a deep impression on him.

He decided to create his own Rome, his own Paris, his own Venice. But despite his admiration of these remarkable cities, he still remained Russian, and moreover he was a Romanov, and that meant that what he dreamed of for himself must humble every other city, and every other palace within that city, that had yet been created. If Rome was a city of architectural wonders, he would order his aristocracy to build monumental edifices grander and more powerful than the world had yet seen. If the Sun King had Versailles, he would have Peterhof and the Winter Palace, which would be the largest royal structures ever built. St. Petersburg, with its swampland and the River Neva, resembled the disposition of Venice, so Peter would fashion a city built to reflect and enjoin the water. The palaces were enormous and designed by the greatest French and Italian architects money could buy, and because Russians adore color – possibly because for so much of the year they live only in whiteness – the palaces were painted exactly to reflect a tradition all their own, the great Russian Easter eggs.

So while the Mall in London had astounding stone and marble mansions, those of Peter's city did too, but etched in deep reds and pale greens, and oceanic blues or bright, happy yellows, and further lavished with copious and sumptuous gold decoration. In the brilliance of the June sun, which in the Russian summers never sets, it was almost too dazzling. And as if all of this beauty wasn't more than enough, it was all constantly reflected back to one's admiring eyes by the waters of the great Neva River which bisected the city and could be crossed by a hundred ornately gilded bridges.

We were met at the train with great fanfare before Ella was escorted away from our party by a brigade of what were called Cossacks. These were tall men in high black boots, enormous black fur hats and fancifully designed red coats. On foot they were impressive enough; when I later saw them on horseback, I thought they resembled figures from Russian fairytales.

Ella was led over to a stately carriage, which I later found out was occupied by the Empress Marie who, I must note for history's sake, did not bother to bestir herself to leave it and come over to welcome us formally, this despite our party being made up of Ella's own dearest papa and sisters and only brother. No, not for us a formal greeting and the courtesy of shared carriages. I suppose to Empress Marie's august eyes, she having been born into the lofty ruling house of Denmark – a country so small that I could never properly find it on a map during my geography lessons – we terribly unimportant Hessians could wait for another occasion to be publicly honored by our imperial hosts.

Thus it was that poor Papa, who must have been quite overcome with humiliation at this slight, along with his poor motherless remaining children, were gathered together some minutes later and stuffed into another not quite-so-gilded carriage to be driven the short distance to the Winter Palace where our small group was to be lodged until the ceremony.

At that time, during my first visit as a fragile wee childy of twelve, the Winter Palace was an almost frightening edifice. It was then, and I believe remains, the largest single dwelling upon our Earth. It stretches as far as the eye can see and towers a hundred feet into the air, as intimidating a testament to the power and wealth of the tsars as is conceivable. Somewhat amusingly, it kept burning down, but the tsars remained undeterred and kept building it right back up again. The existing monstrous palace was finished by Empress Elizabeth and then added onto by Catherine the Great, who I must add, was also a "poor, insignificant German Princess."

In truth, the may-I-say proud, or perhaps over-proud, Romanov dynasty to all intents and purposes probably ended with the Great German Catherine. Her unfortunate husband, the Emperor Peter III, was a complete madman who preferred to spend his days court martialing rats in his rooms rather than learning statecraft, and though a son was born to Catherine – who became the Emperor

Paul – she is said to have admitted that her son's true father was her lover Sergei Saltykov. The then-Emperor Peter was in fact so certain of his wife's infidelity that, when her second child, a girl, was born, he declared, "It's none of mine and may go the devil." I believe that Emperor Paul, who was in due time assassinated by his own officers, doubted his legitimacy as well, since his only memorable achievement as tsar was to enact the dreadful 'Pauline Laws' that would come to haunt my own life terribly.

These laws, introduced by Emperor Paul, who as I have mentioned was probably no emperor at all, barred once and forever any female Romanov from inheriting the throne, so that if the reigning tsar has living daughters at the time of his death, but no son, the crown will pass to his brothers, then his nephews, then his cousins. This incongruous, might I even propose unconstitutional, ruling allows any male Romanov to inherit in precedence to a legitimate daughter, and this despite Russia's greatest ruler having been the Empress Catherine.

For my part, since I was a proud granddaughter of the greatest Queen-Empress that England has ever known, including another great queen, Queen Elizabeth the First, this proclamation seemed offensive, though it would not be until later that I found it personally sinister and oppressive. Those days awaited me, but at the tender age of twelve I had no way of knowing this. No, I was but a little girl still, and all that the Winter Palace and the mighty ruling family represented to me was an undreamed of panoply of wealth and beauty.

When we arrived at the Winter Palace, Irene, Victoria, Ernie and I were taken to our rooms. To get there we trailed slippered servants through endless marble corridors and up staircases so grand and lovely and gilded and baroque that it seemed as though heaven itself could not be more glorious. I was given my own astounding suite of rooms and six maidservants to cater to the every need of my one little self. They unnerved me a bit because, while I was quite well educated for a mere girlie, I did not speak Russian and naturally that was all they spoke. Also they seemed puzzled by, if not judgmental of, my modest wardrobe, and I felt that when my back was turned they were probably tittering over the simple little muslin gown that I was to wear at Ella's wedding.

Our humble clothes were all poor Papa could afford. This naturally did not apply to Ella. Oh no, for Ella money had been found, or borrowed, to create a magnificent trousseau suitable to her wedding a Russian Grand Duke, which turned out in the end to be a complete waste of time and money, for from the day we arrived in Russia I never again saw my sister in the same gown; nor in fact did I see her in any of the dresses our poor little Hessian seamstress had labored over so lovingly and Papa had struggled so hard to provide. Sergei had no doubt presented her with a secret wardrobe of trunks filled with couture from Paris along with the dozens of velvet boxes crammed with the dazzling jewels that she received from him during their engagement. In Ella's defense, I will say that Sergei had a keen, even rather odd, interest in Ella's apparel and this had manifested itself even during their courtship.

Naturally I did not lower myself to inquire after these matters, even to satisfy my innocent girl's natural curiosity about new clothing.

That very first night, in fact, we humble Hessians were invited to dine with the mighty Tsar, *en famille* as it were, to find my dear Ella, my own beloved older sister, clad in a magnificent gown of what I later learned was *Valenciennes* lace, and even that pretty garment was barely visible under the layers of diamonds and pearls she wore in abundance. I could not even compliment her on how lovely she appeared, however, as she was seated next to the Empress Marie, whom Ella addressed as 'Minnie,' while I was seated with my sister Irene and brother Ernie far down the table, towards its middle. As a, I suppose, courtesy to his brother's fiancée, the Tsar had seated Papa to his immediate left, but then proceeded rudely to ignore him by confining his remarks to some aged, much-beribboned general who was seated to his right.

Still, I was fascinated by the sight of the great ruler … fascinated and, I must admit, a tad disappointed. He was enormous; that much greatly impressed me. I had never seen such a colossal human being and it was immediately apparent that Grandmamma's description of him as a large bear was indeed unnervingly close to the truth.

It was then that I got myself into a bit of trouble. I was thinking he looked much as a stuffed bear I had once seen, and then thought how funny it was that a bear should have on clothes, and then I noted that the clothes, at least the odd puffy blouse that he was wearing, was badly stained by what appeared to be beet juice. I was in fact certain it was beet juice, for to my growing dismay and hunger, everything I had been offered thus far at dinner was either a beet or was covered in beets, with the result that the whole became stained an appropriately royal purple.

I let my eyes follow the trail of juice from the Emperor's blouse right up to its point of origin, and there, to my horror, I noted that one whole side of his reddish beard was colored by the stuff.

Desperate not to laugh out loud and disgrace myself and my entire family, I cast my eyes around the table and met those of a boy whose own bright blue eyes twinkled merrily right back into mine, and whose handsome face smiled towards mine as though he were in on the joke and found it delightful ... found me delightful.

And that was it – the first time I ever encountered Nicky.

Chapter 3

I claim not to have noticed him already, although I had when we entered the dining room at the Winter Palace, the smallest one, since it was just ourselves and the Tsar's immediate family who were to dine there, and Ernie nudged me a tad rudely and said, "There's the heir, the Tsarevich as they are called here, and he's rather puny, don't you think, Alicky? I mean, if one considers that great giant of a father of his."

I was, as I nearly always was, both amused and scandalized by my darling brother's frank observations of people, and while I agreed with his comments regarding the Tsar's size, I did not like hearing Nicky criticized. You see, even then my little girl's heart must have been calling out to his own boyish one. Oh Nicky darling, sunshine, agoo wee one, my Huzzy, how could it ever have been otherwise?

Of course, I did not in that night, in that never-to-be-forgotten moment, think of him as a boy. He was sixteen and I but a tender twelve. To my eyes he was a man, a fairytale prince, and this impression was only heightened when, after dinner, he and Ella performed an impromptu skit from a delightful French play.

This entertainment had been kept a deep secret by both Ella and Nicky, the better to surprise us all. Ella's French, it must be said, was rather clumsy, but Nicky's was perfection. I do not mean to imply here that my linguistic skills were superior to those of my dear sister. In point of fact I do not like the French language and have never chosen to develop more than a passing familiarity with it. I consider it vulgar and find it unfortunate that the Russian court has always preferred to converse in French rather than in its own mother tongue.

Forgive my lapse into the subject of languages; I was speaking of Nicky as I saw him that night. He was certainly not "puny," as Ernie had so unkindly described him, but I had to agree that he was far from tall. In fact he and I stood eye-to-eye then and later I came to grow several inches taller than him. But if he was a trifle less statuesque than his father, brother, cousins or most other men, he was a thousand … no, a hundred thousand … times handsomer.

Nicky was still under the instruction of his tutor at that time, but he was indeed the heir, so unlike other schoolboys, he was accorded a degree of sartorial license. Indeed, my dearest one was, it must be conceded, a bit of a dandy. His heavenly head of thick brown hair was in curls and he sported a jaunty mustache which added miles of maturity to his otherwise still tender face. My Nicky's eyes were always his most captivating feature, being a deep, pure blue of a hue seldom seen on earthly beings, but then a Tsar is never a completely earthly being, having been placed in his singular position by God alone, though I must say his father, the great Tsar Autocrat Alexander, seemed more animal than divine, but possibly my impression of him remains colored by dearest Grandmamma's frank speeches to me on the matter, which she favored me with on numerous occasions.

Ah, but Nicky, he was as finely made as some of the best works of art produced in the Dresden china factories

I had once toured with Ernie, having inherited to a degree, I suppose, some of the celebrated *finesse* of his mother, the Empress Marie, known to her family and intimates, and now to my sister Ella, as "Minnie." I say this because whereas they shared the same coloring and facial features, and were nearly of the same height, there the resemblances end, as I, even then, found the Empress-Tsarina to be a somewhat frivolous and self-willed sort of woman.

Grandmamma had warned me prior to our great trip that I might find her so, cautioning me that, in some women, power combined with the adoration of faceless millions could act as a corrosive influence upon their souls and lead them to forget that we are all daughters of Christ, whatever our stations in life, and must therefore act accordingly, as Grandmamma did in such an exemplary manner all the days of her long and blessed life.

I found that while I did not feel any particular warmth for – or it must be said from – Empress Marie, I liked Nicky's siblings, each and every one of them, enormously. There was his next youngest sister Xenia, a very pretty girl, who was kindness itself to me and who passed complimentary remarks on my complexion within minutes of our introduction. Then there was Nicky's darling brother George, a sweet, quiet boy, and his youngest brother, Michael, a little monkey of a fellow whom his mama the Empress called by the silly name of "Flopsy." Lastly, there was the baby, little Olga, a fat, physically unprepossessing little girl, who made up for her lack of esthetic charms by performing like a perfect comic imp and who was clearly her father's favorite child, as he addressed her lovingly as "Baby" throughout our stay there.

However, it was not upon that night, that very first night when a tiny childy of twelve's eyes met those of a beautiful boy just at the threshold of manhood, that we first spoke. That came during the days leading up to the wedding.

Ella was most terribly occupied with the attentions of both Sergei and the Empress Marie, who seemed nearly as in love with my sister as did her own dear fiancé, and who would monopolize Ella's every conscious moment with one frivolous demand, disguised as a request, after another.

"Oh Ella, dearest, do come and meet General Who-knows-who-he-is and his dear wife, Princess Senility."

Or, "Ella, I simply must have you by my side this afternoon while I have my rubies weighed."

I must beg your forgiveness for any poetic license I might employ in my descriptions of Empress Marie's needs, but really her conduct was remarkably selfish as her tireless series of requests kept Ella apart from our tiny family circle and we were, after all, the ones who were losing her forever to this family of nearly limitless wealth, power and whim. I fancy that even Sergei was feeling a bit deserted, although, if so, one could not have guessed at it, since he was the absolute soul of charm and kindness to us, Ella's small "unimportant" family.

He was what young people nowadays call a "dab hand" with children, arranging one joyful excursion after another for Irene and Ernie and me, and naturally the Tsarevich and his younger siblings were included in all our entertainments. We played bowls and hoops in the Winter Palace's children's gardens; we were taken by enclosed carriage to a grand indoor arcade on the Nevsky Prospeckt for cream ices; and he even arranged for a troupe of players to come to the palace to perform a private Punch and Judy show for us that left us all breathless with gales of laughter. He seemed just instinctively to understand the hearts and minds of young people and he was continually setting up small competitions for us, such as who could run up the Jordan staircase and then slide down the banister first. The winner would be given a bag of sweets and, of course, triumphal honors. My own much more sedate upbringing, both with poor Papa and dearest Grandmamma, who did not enjoy any amount of noise one bit, had poorly prepared me for such japes and high jinks, but I was quickly caught up in the spirit of all of the fun and my natural shyness began to evaporate.

As it turned out, Nicky was almost as shy and reserved as I was, despite being the eldest boy in a family bubbling with terribly loud and energetic siblings and cousins, so it was not any one moment, or adventure, or event, which caused us to become comfortable with each other. Rather it was the whole of the times of play and joy we shared as part of a, at first, somewhat nervous, divided group that became, over that enchanted week, a family of simple children, herded and overseen by our dearest Uncle Sergei. If I felt … if he felt … if we knew then … it was not spoken of or acknowledged until Ella and Sergei's wedding, an event etched so clearly into my mind, more clearly – and isn't that odd? – than my own wedding would ever be.

The long-anticipated great day began for me when I rose early to watch the pearlescent sky over the Neva compete for attention with the sunlight that so lovingly caressed the brightly painted and gilded castles edging, and indeed competing with, the river itself for glory and admiration.

I was not normally, I must confess, an early riser, but St. Petersburg in the summer with its "white nights" made longer sleep less necessary. And anyway, that morning there wasn't a soul alive who could have slept past dawn, as the bells of the great Orthodox churches in the city had all begun to peal joyously by 5am.

I crept into Ella's room and found her still abed but awake. She wordlessly held out her arms to me, and I ran to her, and she clasped me tightly against her, and we both cried, I can't say why really. I suppose it was a case of bridal nerves for Ella but for me it was something … oh, I cannot describe it, truly I can't. I felt somehow exultant, as though it was for my own wedding day, and not Ella's, that the bells rung, but I felt something else as well, a sense of horror, of someone or something awful, indescribable, as though right outside Ella's chamber in the corridor, the one I had just passed through, just beyond the portal, there might be a terrible thing waiting for me.

I told Ella this and she laughed and wiped away her own tears and mine.

"Darling, there's nothing frightening out there, unless you count the footmen whom I can barely understand, or maybe you are simply scared of Daria, my new maid of honor, who even I'll admit is a bit scary."

40

I snuggled against my sister, the one who had been as a mother to me, for the last time and let myself be comforted for a few moments until that self-same Daria entered the chamber and drew back Ella's curtains to begin her wedding day.

It seemed to my young eyes that there could not be a single person in St Petersburg who had not come to line up outside the Winter Palace to cheer the bride and the groom. I felt so moved on behalf of my dear sister to see the great love and veneration that the Russian people felt for their Tsar and, by extension, for his family.

The Tsar was just as generous in his own love of his subjects because, though Sergei and Ella were to be married in the Winter Palace where Ella was already installed, he had arranged for a golden carriage to carry the bride to the Cathedral of Peter and Paul where she would meet Sergei for a blessing and then, together, they would ride back to the Winter Palace so that the people would be able to gaze upon the bride a second time.

I must say that Ella was a rather divinely beautiful bride that day. I fancy that even the Empress Marie was a bit taken aback at what a fine showing a little German princess from an "unimportant duchy" could make.

In point of fact I know she was, because Romanov royal family weddings all follow a long set protocol, and in that protocol tradition demands that the reigning Empress be the one to set the bride's veil upon her head as soon as the hairdresser is finished. Ella's dress was a magnificent white brocade gown so stiffened with diamonds that she could barely move an inch without help. She joked with Irene and me that she thought this must be how Romanov brides maintained such a stately posture on their approach to the altar. We both laughed a little through our tears, but truly, with the dress and the long ermine cape and the lace veil, and the enormous diadem of emeralds over that, she appeared almost otherworldly and not our own Ella at all anymore.

The Empress was wearing a dress that I felt was designed to overshadow our Ella, if possible. She was clad from head to toe in a silver brocade so covered with diamonds that it hurt one's eyes to look at her, and I must say in all honesty that, given her lack of height, the ensemble was not the best, and if indeed her intention had been to outshine the bride, she managed it literally but not figuratively.

Once Ella and Sergei had returned from their blessing, we all followed the bride in her slow and solemn procession up the Jordan staircase and into the great hall where the priest and her own dear Sergei awaited her. The ceremony was silent except for the somewhat droning voice of the priest, as in Russian Orthodox weddings the bridal couple does not exchange vows, they just stand there somewhat awkwardly holding a candle for ages, and when it's finally over they walk three times around a small table.

It looked a bit silly, given their grand clothes, but any desire I had to laugh was stilled by my twin concerns. I was losing forever my sister and also I knew that Nicky, who was standing just beside Sergei at the altar, was staring at me. I could feel the heat of his blazing blue eyes upon me and I am certain that I blushed fiercely, a thing that happens to me whenever I feel the slightest bit uncomfortable.

Still, I had to be certain, and finally, steeling myself, I chanced a look, and he was … he was gazing at me. Oh the expression in his unforgettable eyes … such longing.

I must have looked startled because his own dear face flushed greatly and he nervously cast his eyes down, but for the rest of that seemingly endless ceremony I was in a state of ecstasy, which I do believe is unusual in one as young as I was, but you see, I knew, I did know, that God on that day, the day of my sister's wedding, had shown me a glimpse of my possible future if only I could reach out my hand.

Two nights later, our very last in Russia, I was doing exactly that – holding out my hand to Nicky.

You see, Nicky had arranged a ball just for me. I think all of us children, both Hessian and Romanov, knew that, but of course we pretended that Nicky had done it as a familial goodbye gesture. But that wasn't true: he had done it just for me so he could hold my hands in a dance; the rest were there merely to see our love become the future.

The ball was held at the Alexander Palace in Tsarkoe Selo – that means 'the Tsar's village' – and as for the Alexander Palace, well given how large that small precious palace would loom in my future, I cannot believe that it was simply a coincidence that led Nicky to choose that as the setting of our night's entertainment. No, he must have felt … sensed it all, as I did. But on that wondrous, entrancing night, the park of Tsarkoe and its palaces were all unknown to me and fairness demands that I describe my first sight of them.

43

Tsarkoe Selo is a short train ride from St Petersburg, being but twelve miles from Peter's great city, but it might as well belong to another world, an enchanted world, a better world, free from all of life's ugliness and concerns. It is aptly named 'the Tsar's village' as it is a small, perfect village built around a park and protected by tall, decorative wrought iron fences and the high fur-hatted Cossacks who patrol its perimeter day and night.

I will admit that the use of the word 'park' is a bit disingenuous since Tsarkoe itself, the private part that belongs to the Tsar's family, is a rather large area encompassing some enormous amounts of acreage – who can say how much? Within the park itself is the enormous blue Catherine Palace, which is so perfect, if perfectly gargantuan, a structure about which the Italian architect who built it said to the Empress, "All your palace needs now, Your Majesty, is a glass dome to put over it,"

There is a very old church there, one built by Peter the Great's wife, as Tsarkoe was originally a gift to her from him, thus establishing, to my mind at least, that it was always meant as a place of love and family. Then there is a small lake that can be filled and emptied like a bath, and an island with a teeny house just for children on it. There is also the royal family's private zoo, and hundreds of paths and hand-smoothed, pretty roads that travel through lime and cherry trees, and there are dozens of fountains and follies, even a Chinese Pagoda. It's a veritable fairyland where, in every conceivable place that the eye can fall, there is a sight to delight it and to soothe and exalt one's soul with the beauty and peace of the place.

Then, best of all, there is the Alexander Palace. Empress Catherine built it for her darling best-beloved grandson Alexander so that he could have his own sweet little dwelling place in her perfect park. It's not very large, being only a hundred rooms, which might sound large but not if one considers that the Winter Palace has some fifteen hundred rooms and that even the Catherine Palace, a mere weekend home of the tsars, has some four hundred or so rooms, but what the Alexander Palace loses in size it makes up for in its simple charms. It's a round, yellow palace with intimate, sunny rooms and numerous balconies, that retains a cozy feeling at all times, even in the great Rotunda Room, the palace's largest formal space and the room where Nicky chose to host our small ball.

I wasn't quite prepared for a ball, I must say, being just a little girl of twelve and ages away from coming out into society, a thing that does not happen for a girl until she turns sixteen and can put her hair up. So there I was that night, wearing the only real party dress I possessed, which was my bridesmaid's gown from Ella's wedding, and with a large pink bow in my long curls and no ornamentation except a rose that Nanny Orchard had pinned to my child's breast, and yet I was the guest of honor at a ball in a royal Russian residence and the especial partner of the heir to the throne of all the Russias!

That night, despite the fact that Nicky and I had spent so many easy days and evenings together romping with our siblings and Uncle Sergei, we were uncomfortable with each other and seemed unable to meet each other's eyes. So, when I danced a quadrille with him, he rather

45

clumsily tried to express his feelings to me and ended up creating a most distinctly awkward social *faux pas*, the memory of which we would one day cherish but which, that night, caused me agonies of embarrassment.

Nicky, it seems, had decided that he had fallen in love with me. I'm not certain when this occurred to him; it might have been during one of our games of bowls on the lawn at the Winter Palace. There had been a day when I had so fully forgotten myself that I had run about as freely as if I were that little hoyden Olga, to the point that one of my pink hair ribbons had become so loosened that it had fallen to the ground.

Later, when I was searching for it, little Xenia came up to me and laughingly offered, "Alicky, you ought to ask Nicky where your hair ribbon is."

I didn't understand her at all and said so, and she looked down at her feet and mumbled that she had seen him pick it up and kiss it before putting it in his pocket.

Naturally, wondering if it could really be so had preoccupied my thoughts for the rest of that day, but when I tried to speak of it first to Ella, she snapped at me haughtily and told me to go off and find something to do as she had a fitting in a few moments, and when I addressed my sister Irene about it she only sighed and said, "Another of our House's beauties draws attention. I, of course, never do and suppose that after this wedding I must plan to resign myself to a life of good works and devotion to poor Papa."

I do think that if Victoria had been with us on Ella's wedding trip she could have advised me best, but she had remained at home in Darmstadt, occupied with the pressing matter of her own upcoming wedding.

46

I, in fact, ended up having to remind Irene of this and to comfort her by pointing out that no one had ever considered Vicky any sort of beauty and that someone was marrying her all the same.

She didn't brighten much at my encouraging remarks, nor did she bother to thank me by offering me advice on what to do about Nicky, so at the age of twelve I was left alone with my dilemma, and after worrying to bits about it, decided to remain quiet and pretend it had not happened, since, after all, I hadn't seen it happen and Xenia might have misunderstood what she saw, being but ten and quite a child herself.

Nicky, in the meantime, did have all sorts of loving and interested family about him with whom to discuss the new feelings his boyish heart was experiencing, and had gone, as a boy must, to his first dear one, his own mama, to ask what was best to be done. As I have been forced to admit, the Empress was a rather frivolous woman and not given to looking seriously at matters, though, to be fair, she may well have been quite preoccupied that afternoon by the upcoming wedding and her choice of jewels for the great day.

This is doubtless how it all happened: I imagine that the Empress Marie was sorting through her great trays of jewels, looking for one in particular, when in came her darling Nicky to speak of his new-found feelings. The Empress, probably feeling that this was a mere schoolboy crush and not the stirrings of a love so powerful and unshakeable that all the world would come to sigh at our story, must have carelessly tossed him an unwanted, old-fashioned brooch from her vast collection and said something like, "Here, darling, here's a pretty trinket. Why don't you give this to that little Hesse girl, Ella's sister – what is her name again? – I can't think, but never mind, she might like this as a parting souvenir. Now run along, dearest. Mama's busy, as you can see."

The "trinket" she had tossed to Nicky was in fact a brooch with a rather large central diamond of ten carats in weight that was surrounded by fifty or so smaller diamonds, none being less than two carats, but that this piece of discarded decoration could have fed a thousand of her subjects for a year was apparently lost on the Empress who did not concern herself with such matters, and certainly my darling Nicky did not know its worth. As the heir to all the Russias, he had been surrounded with such wealth and grandeur since birth that he couldn't have acquired the least idea of monetary value. He doubtless just thought it was pretty and shiny, and that the object of his new and tender affections might like it.

So it came to pass that on the evening of the ball, right after our quadrille, Nicky, blushing furiously, asked if he might speak to me "privately" for a moment. Of course, he did not intend the word "privately" to suggest that we hold a conversation in a room where there would be no others in attendance, but merely that it should take place in an area where we might not be so closely observed. I must add though that, being Nicky, the heir and the hope of all of his people, such privacy to act and speak naturally could never be his, and I felt the collective eyes of the partygoers burning into my back as I walked with him rather nervously over to a window embrasure in that Rotunda Room.

When we reached there, Nicky rather comically tried to hide himself behind the drawn back *portières* and motioned me closer, an offer that I declined as I was feeling desperately self-conscious and quite aware that people were watching us. Do try to remember that I was but twelve years old.

Feeling, I imagine, completely undone by then, Nicky fished hastily around in his pockets and sort of thrust the brooch at me, saying, "Here, this is for you. Mama said I could give it to you and so I am. I hope you like me … I mean the brooch … and well, um … I well … You will take it, won't you?"

As, in his nervousness, he had indeed thrust it at me, I had no choice but to take it, and for a moment I was so lost in admiration of the beautiful object that I completely forgot my own shyness and smiled my gratitude right into his eyes. At that, Nicky's face cleared and such an expression of joy came over it that I fear we were both lost.

Of course, awareness of one's surroundings will always intrude upon even the most sacred of moments, and so it was with us, and within a second I felt that I should say something, so I mumbled "Thank you," and that seemed to release in Nicky an ability to speak more clearly than I had ever heard him do before.

"Oh please, Alix, dearest sweetest Alix, don't thank me. Why, having you here … I mean, having your family here … I mean, they are all such fun and I wanted to say… I mean, to show that I thought … well, that I had … well, um … am having the best time and to … well, I mean, I asked Mama what to do … you know, to

49

say … to show how much I liked all of you, and she gave me this, so I …"

He had run out of breath at the end of this remarkable recitation and somehow his dearness and confusion added years to my girlish soul and I felt able to tease him a bit by replying, "Well, it's so kind of you … but then, Nicky, if you wanted to thank my dear family for coming here and for being such fun, hadn't you better give Papa the brooch? After all, he is the head of our family …"

Nicky looked quite startled, as I do not think he had before that moment guessed at my rather sly sense of humor, but he quickly collected himself and grinned at me so happily that it was my turn to fall into blushing confusion.

Noticing this, he nobly rescued me, saying, "Here, look, diamonds are deuced … oh pardon me, Alix … I meant, diamonds are terribly useful as cutting tools. They are much harder than steel and things. Did you know that?

I merely shook my head and smiled at him.

Emboldened, he carried on. "No, it's quite true. They can even cut through glass. Here, I'll show you. Might I borrow back the brooch for a minute?"

I handed it to him, our fingers just touching, which caused us both to shiver – a funny thing, I thought – but then he quickly turned towards the window with the brooch and, shielding me from his actions with his back, did something against the window.

When he had finished, he turned to me triumphantly and said, "Here, look at this then."

I did, and what I saw caused my little girl's heart to flutter madly in my chest. He had carved out a clumsy little heart against the glass, and inside it he had put our initials, *N* and *A*.

I was so taken aback, so overcome by the romance of it all, that I couldn't speak a word. Seeing this, Nicky gently handed me back the brooch and said quietly, "I mean it, you know. I do. I think you're the best girl I've ever seen. Well, of course, I haven't really seen many girls, except my sisters and Mama, but even if I had, I'd think you were the best one."

I began to cry, and he, feeling he had distressed me, reached out for me, but I was off, running through that beautiful room without meeting any of the startled glances I was unwillingly conscious of, and I didn't stop in my wild flight until I had raced up the stairs and into the room I had been given for the night and into the surprised but loving arms of Nanny Orchard.

I can't say why I cried so heartily and for so long. The inner workings of a young girl's heart are impossible to fathom, even to oneself. My tears were, I think, of gratitude, for so often I was simply one of many of poor Papa's children and one of dozens of Grandmamma's grandchildren, and no matter how kindly people behaved towards me, no one had ever before said I was the best of them.

I think my tears, too, were of anxiety. The feelings Nicky had incited in me were too large for such a small girl. And then, well, there was this: I felt fear, a terrible nameless fear, but of what I cannot say, or could not say then. I later learned that in certain very sensitive and exalted natures lies the gift, or better to say the curse, of premonition, so possibly I experienced a shadowy intuition of what lay ahead, I do not know. I only know I cried terribly in Nanny's arms.

She did not say anything much beyond her usual patented soothing. "There, ducks, there-there my own sweet girl, it will all come out in the wash, and in the morning we will have forgotten the events of this night."

Given that we were in Russia in the summer, where there is no night to speak of, the latter didn't make much sense, but I responded to her warmth all the same and let her undress me and tuck me up into bed, as she had since I was a wee infant. And if I dreamt that night, I cannot remember doing so.

When I arose hours later, Nanny told me that I could not keep the brooch as it wasn't proper for a young maid to accept such a fine gift, no matter how heartfelt and innocent the giver's intentions, and so after breakfast I pressed it wordlessly back into Nicky's hand, mumbling. "I'm sorry, I cannot ... forgive me. Here, you must keep it ... thank you."

He was so obviously put out by my returning the brooch that he did not even accompany our party to the railway station to say goodbye. Later I learned he had given it to Xenia, who, having no use for the thing, decorated one of her doll's hats with it.

Chapter 4

No sooner had our little party returned home to Darmstadt than we were plunged into preparations for yet another wedding. This was something of a saving grace for me as it stopped me from thinking too much about Nicky and Russia. For poor Papa, though, it was a truly difficult time. He was very close to Vicky, much more so than he had been to Ella or was to Irene. Of course, he loved Ernie and me very much but we were far too young to be companions to him, or, in my case, to act as his hostess, as Vicky often did.

My sister Vicky, or as the world knew her, *Victoria, Alberta, Elisabeth, Mathilde, Marie of Hesse-Darmstadt,* was Mama and Papa's first born and I believe, although of course no parent will ever admit to this, that being first makes that child always rather special, as Vicky was to my own parents. I never begrudged her this because Vicky herself was so cheerful and clever and capable, and not very pretty. Vicky would have been the first to agree with my assessment and was indeed so lacking in any sort of personal vanity that she would have been surprised if one had commented on her appearance, favorably or otherwise.

Grandmamma, however, was nothing if not pragmatic about such things, which is why she had urged poor Papa to accept the suit of dear Prince Louis of Battenberg for his daughter. Grandmamma knew that in the tiny narrow world of royalty in which she and her family existed, the heirs of great houses tended to marry the daughters of equally grand families and we humble

Hessians were, rightly or wrongly, not considered to be a dynasty of any great moment.

Then, too, there was the matter of money. Poverty is somewhat relative, and I suppose, to one of modest birth, our lovely new palace seemed a grand edifice and our little cotton-frilled gowns were gorgeous garments. But in the *milieu* we lived in, it was all seen as rather low key and second rate.

If one wasn't born into a great ruling house directly and one wasn't a boy who would at least inherit one's papa's title – as my darling brother Ernie would – then a girl would have to hope to marry into one. Grandmamma was called the 'Grandmother of All Europe' because she so loved, and took such an interest in, all her grandchildren, whether we were descended from the sovereign rulers of world powers, like England or Germany, or from obscure grand duchies, like Hesse-Darmstadt, as we poor orphans were.

This is why she was so bitterly sad about Ella's choice. Grandmamma felt that, with Ella's beauty, a grand match was possible and she in no way considered the younger brother of a tsar of a country whose throne seemed to be on the verge of tottering a wise choice.

With our dear Vicky it was different. Vicky had, as they say in fairytales, neither face nor fortune and, sadly, being clever isn't much of a consideration with girls. But dear Louis loved her and Grandmamma adored Louis, and when poor Papa showed reluctance about the matter, as Louis was rather impoverished himself, Grandmamma was forced to become rather stern and maybe she did argue him into it, as he later said, which is possibly why he created such a terrible scandal at his own dear girly's wedding.

After it was all over, after the smoke had cleared, as peasants say when they have finished preparing a field for harvest, I could see how many clues I had missed, how much we had all missed, but at the time I think we simply dismissed poor Papa's odd behavior as excitement, or possibly grief, over Vicky's wedding and her upcoming departure for England, for England was where it had been decided by Grandmamma that Vicky and dear Louis would reside.

Louis, as I have mentioned, was a younger son of a small Austro-German dynasty, and although he was royal, he had neither money nor prospects to speak of. Grandmamma, however, loved Louis very dearly, since he was related closely to her own great lost love, her late consort, Prince Albert. It was Grandmamma who had introduced Louis to Vicky, and Grandmamma who had argued down Papa's doubts, and it was Grandmamma's own great country of Britain to whom Louis now belonged.

He had long since lived in England, having enrolled in the Royal Navy at the age of fourteen, and Grandmamma, having such affection for him, had granted him small but beautiful grace-and-favor homes at both Windsor and Balmoral, and it was to these that the happy young couple would depart after the wedding, and to the British Navy that Louis would return following the modest honeymoon that Grandmamma had planned out for them.

Poor Papa had most naturally hoped for a greater match for our Vicky and so his reservations can well be understood, though his way of expressing them was somewhat wrongheaded. For example, when our little family was inspecting the tables of gifts that had arrived for the young couple, Papa laughed somewhat rudely when he saw the lovely silver tea service for fifty that Grandmamma had bought for them.

Shaking his head, he said to Vicky, "Service for fifty, my girl? Is it likely that you and young Louis will be able to afford to feed more than five at a time?"

Vicky, who has always been the very soul of tact and kindness, and who was particularly devoted to Papa, acted as though he had made a funny joke and simply laughed and answered, "Well, I don't know, Papa, as though you aren't correct. I expect that Louis and I might be able to feed more than five, but shall we? After all, I have not engaged a cook as yet, and if our poor future guests are ever subjected to my culinary talents, then I imagine that you are all to the right in thinking that Grandmamma's wonderful gift might be far too adventurous for us."

Papa responded by pinching Vicky's cheek affectionately, but Louis seemed affronted and strode out rather hastily to the gardens, probably to avoid saying something untoward and ruining Vicky's last days with her family.

That Louis and Vicky loved each other most tenderly was never in doubt, even to Papa, it is just that Papa had a natural concern about their future security. I'm certain that was it. Still, it did become more and more uncomfortable during the last days leading up to the wedding as Papa's sense of humor seemed lost on Louis.

On the day before the ceremony, Papa sent Louis a secondhand uniform from one of our guardsmen, with a note attached suggesting he don it for his groom's attire if he didn't have anything else to wear. Louis, in his turn, complained to Grandmamma, who had arrived for the festivities, and she, I fear, berated Papa rather harshly, or so I was informed by Nanny Orchard, who had been told by cook, who had heard it from one of the servants who had witnessed the scene. According to Nanny Orchard, Grandmamma unkindly reminded Papa that the very palace that he was living in was paid for from his deceased wife's dowry and that if poor husbands were a deterrent to marriage, then many a royal girl, my own Mama included, would be barred from marriage for want of suitable husbands.

I must say that this sort of unpleasantness had a tendency to mar the dinners and picnics and the small ball leading up to the wedding, and led to the most unfortunate sort of gossip in Darmstadt, and I think that is why none of us noticed that beneath Papa's ill humor there also lurked a sort of flushed excitement.

I must speak now of this and then lay it to rest, for it remains in my mind and heart the one memory I have of my dearest darling Papa that is less than perfect.

Papa had, one must remember, long been a widower, darling Mama having died years before while both she and Papa were still young.

At our modest court there served a former lady-in-waiting to Mama, one Alexandra de Kolemine. After Mama's death, Madame de Kolemine continued to reside at our court because her husband was the Russian emissary to Darmstadt. Madame de Kolemine was very young, being nearer to Ella's age, and very pretty, and a close friendship formed between her and Ella.

When Ella and Sergei, newlyweds themselves, arrived in Darmstadt for Vicky's wedding to Louis, the two friends took up their happy chatter right where it had been left off, but Madame de Kolemine, despite her beauty and seemingly sweet nature, was a woman with a clouded past, for she was newly divorced.

Divorce is, of course, frowned upon by the entire Christian world, and though I liked Madame de Kolemine very much, I had felt uncomfortable around her since her divorce from the Russian minister, but it was in fact Papa who had used his influence to help Madame de Kolemine obtain her recent divorce from her husband, a man whom Papa described as a "drunken, brutal fellow."

Following the divorce, Papa implored his new son-in-law Sergei to use his influence with the Tsar, his brother, to have this appalling man re-assigned to a new post. Sergei did so and Monsieur de Kolemine was duly packed off to the Orient, leaving his former wife behind him in Darmstadt with us.

Under normal circumstances, no divorced woman would ever have been permitted to reside in close proximity to members of decent society, let alone our ruling family, but Papa and Ella were both so fond of Madame de Kolemine, and so sympathetic to her sufferings in her former marriage, that they urged us all to show her Christian love and not to judge the poor creature.

I, being merely a small girl, did not pause to wonder how, or rather I should say *who*, was providing for the young divorcee's home and clothing but merely accepted the dictates of my elders and treated her with the same kindness I had shown her before her terrible disgrace. In truth, I was far too pre-occupied during that year, what with Ella's wedding, my travels, meeting Nicky, leaving Nicky, coming home and preparing for Vicky's wedding, missing Nicky, and all of the strange new feelings that consumed me, to give much thought to the life and times of a woman who seemed, to my young eyes, to be rather old and uninteresting, and who, in any case, was not a member of the nobility and not someone with whom I had much interaction.

I should have been paying more attention – we all should have been – but even the sharp-eyed Vicky was too busy and too caught up in her own private happiness to notice much of what was happening around her that did not concern her directly, and it is just at such times in life, times when one's betters are busy and not keeping watch, that those of lesser birth are given to taking advantage of the situation. It is their nature and, I suppose it cannot be helped ... but neither should it be condoned.

The disastrous *denouement* unfolded on the night of Vicky's wedding, Vicky's "sweet, small, homespun wedding," as Ella described it, Ella, it must be said, having grown rather grand and supercilious since marrying into the mighty Romanov dynasty.

I suppose Vicky's wedding was rather small and homey as compared to Ella's, but the oddest thing happened to me as I was watching Louis and her as they left the church in their modest open landau on their way back to our new palace for their wedding breakfast.

It was so strange. One moment I was seeing Vicky, her sweet plain face wreathed in smiles in the carriage, and the next I had a vision of Ella in the golden carriage that she had ridden down the Nevsky Prospect following her ceremony. I squeezed my eyes shut and opened them again, but it was still there, the grand carriage leading all the other almost-as-grand carriages, the glittering palaces and the great river as a backdrop, and yet when I looked closely at the bride, hoping to dispel this vision and see once again my own true surroundings, instead of Ella in the carriage, I saw myself, and sitting beside me on the tufted velvet seat I saw Nicky, and then I fainted right there at the foot of the church steps.

When I awoke, I was in my own room in our small palace, and both Nanny and Ella were fluttering around me speaking comforting nonsense about the cold and the excitement, and did I feel well enough to attend the wedding supper or should a tray be brought up to me?

I didn't disclose what I had seen before fainting and merely thanked them for their concern and agreed that, yes, it must have been the excitement and that maybe it would be better for me to stay in bed and just rest for the night. I told Ella to please rejoin the others and to give Vicky and Louis my best love, and then I think I must have fallen back to sleep, for when I awoke I was alone but for Nanny Orchard who was sobbing into her handkerchief.

Naturally I felt quite alarmed, as I could only think that poor Nanny's grief had been brought on by worrying about me. She did nothing to dispel this misapprehension because, when I spoke her name, she gave a terrible start and stumbled to my bedside and, taking me into her arms and sobbing harder, called me her lamb, her dearest lamb, her poor lamb.

I then became agitated, fearing that a surgeon might have been called as I slept, and having been summoned had found that I was much sicker than I had thought; that in fact my faint and vision had been a precursor to, given Nanny's hysterics, what could only be a fatal illness.

I trembled in her arms and, drawing fully upon my courage, took a deep breath, pulled back and said rather imperiously, I'll admit, "Tell me, Nanny, if there is terrible news. I have the right to know. Just say it and have done."

Nanny appeared somewhat taken aback at my firmness of spirit, but was clearly strengthened by my own resolve and so blew her nose, straightened her shoulders, and spoke.

"I will tell you, darling, although you're far too young to hear this, but hear it you shall, and it is better that it comes from Nanny, who loves you most, than from some terrible gossip in your poor papa's household."

Now I was terribly confused. "Nanny, why would someone in Papa's household tell me if I were dying? Wouldn't Papa want to tell me himself?"

"Dying? *Dying?* My lamb isn't dying. You merely had a faint, possibly brought on by the wedding and a slight chill you took –"

"Nanny, please, if I'm not dying, why are you acting like this, and what news is it you want me to hear from you, and would you please get on with it before I die of old age."

"You're not near old enough to speak to Nanny in that tone, young lady. In fact –"

"Oh Nanny, please just tell me!"

She shot me a warning glance, which I returned meekly, and my response apparently appeased her sufficiently for her to relate the dreadful events of the previous evening that I had mercifully slept through.

It seemed that, despite my family's natural concern for me, the wedding breakfast had gone off well and that afterwards the family and guests, Grandmamma included, had dispersed to various rooms in the new palace to nap or to read, and thus pass the day until the hour set for the wedding supper that Papa and Grandmamma were jointly hosting to honor the bridal couple. But Papa hadn't gone off to nap or to read or to stroll, he had instead gone off to find a minister in order to marry Alexandra de Kolemine on the spot, with just her sister in attendance as a witness.

My shock and horror at this terrible and shaming news was such that I began to cry, and indeed cried for so long and so hard that Nanny was forced to call for both Ella and the surgeon, although it turned out that Ella was no longer available to be summoned. I found out later, much later, after everyone had left the palace, that Grandmamma, upon hearing of the wedding, ordered Papa to have the marriage annulled immediately, upon pain of having his income from her discontinued, and that Papa, sobbing and broken-hearted, had agreed to her demand, being more in need of the income than of a wife.

The seductress Madame de Kolemine was consequently bundled off hastily in a closed carriage and ordered into exile on the understanding that, if she were to choose to linger in Darmstadt instead, she would be arrested. Only Ella saw her off and further disgraced herself in front of Grandmamma by imperiously declaring that "love was not a crime."

She was taken away by Sergei at first light, just as Grandmamma was leaving with Vicky and Louis for England. They had all simply left, and without a word of goodbye to me, a frightened little girl; left Papa and Irene and Ernie and me all alone in our sad little palace, a palace now filled with more ghosts than people.

Yes, it is true, there were ghosts. Many a time I caught glimpses of shadows and I once saw the specter of my poor dead mama as she wandered the stairs, wringing her hands. More frequently, out of the corner of my eye, I would espy the small ghosts of my lost little brother and sister, and even sometimes the shades of the living who were no longer with me – of Ella, of Vicky, and of that scarlet woman who had destroyed poor Papa. They all revealed themselves to me in the long, empty halls and over the longer, emptier years. On occasion it seemed as though they wished to address me, but, if so, I could not hear them and I do not know what information they wished to impart to me or why they were haunting me. I only knew that, no matter how lonely they were in their graves or in their faraway lives, their isolation could never have begun to match my own.

During the desolate years that followed, I could see them, when the skies outside were gray and filled with rain and snow and I had nothing to do but to sit in the empty, dusty rooms, and wonder whether my life would ever be other than this.

Chapter 5

There isn't a great deal to be said about that four year period of my life that took place between the years 1884 and 1888. It seemed to me, even as I was living through it, that nothing much was occurring and, looking back, I see no reason to alter my opinion.

Irene, Papa's remaining child who was of age, took up the duties of matriarch, as had Ella and Vicky before her, trying to fill Mama's empty place at Papa's side. It was, I suppose, easier on her than it had been on my other sisters as, following Papa's contemptible attempt at remarriage, he had fallen into a morose silence, one that did not involve a great deal of entertaining. Still, there was the occasional ambassador who would stop over in Darmstadt on his way through to more important places who courtesy and decorum required should be entertained, and at these times Irene would don a better frock than her usual grey housedress and sit joylessly by Papa's side as he made desultory attempts at conversation.

Ernie and I were still in the schoolroom and our days, closely supervised by Nanny Orchard, followed a predictable pattern. We were awakened at 7am for a breakfast of porridge, baked apples and milk, and then we would be sent off to wash and dress. After that, promptly at 9am each day, we would meet with our tutors. Under normal circumstances, of course, Ernie would have been taught separately and I would have met with a governess and not teachers, but since there was just us, and since poor Papa remained bemired in straightened circumstances, I was allowed to share equally in Ernie's education.

This unusual arrangement gave me the benefit of a first class education and also allowed me to spend all my time, both at work and at play, with my darling brother, which was a great thing as Ernie was blessed with a sweet and lighthearted disposition that helped to leaven my more serious and contemplative one.

At least that is how I viewed myself. My dearest departed Mama had nicknamed me 'Sunny' when I was a baby for my happy nature, and the name stuck with me throughout my life, at least for those who were close to me; obviously I remained 'Your Highness' to the wider world. But that name 'Sunny,' at times it seemed a cruel joke to me. Had I ever been that wee innocent childy who could laugh so easily at the sight of a butterfly alighting on the roses in the garden? If so, where had that happy little girl gone? Had she followed Mama and Frittie and May into the other world?

I do not know. As is the case with everyone, I can only know the self I am aware of, and so the stories of me as a laughing child tended to irritate rather than charm me as I always felt there was a reproach in their telling. Even darling Grandmamma, whom I would see regularly as she would kindly send for Ernie and Irene and me twice a year, would tell me to smile more.

"Darling Alicky, show Grandmamma your sweet, happy smile."

It seemed an odd request, coming as it did from a woman who had been wearing black for my entire life and who indeed still slept with her dead husband's nightshirt, but I should not say such things. Dear

Grandmamma was always so kind to me and was, I'm sure, only trying to guide me.

Less helpful was my annoying cousin Alice who was often at Balmoral when I was there, Grandmamma being most devoted to all her grandchildren, no matter their worth, I suppose. Anyway, given the similarity in our ages, if not in our temperaments, Alice and I were often forced into each other's company in the garden if Grandmamma wanted peace and quiet, when she would raise her hand commandingly for no seeming reason and say, "Do go outside, children. Children should always be outside, I believe. A bit like wild animals, you creatures need to romp and run and shout, just not inside where you make Grandmamma quite nervous."

Really, it was unfair for her to group me with Alice and my other cousins in these proclamations. I was hardly the sort of young girl who "ran and shouted," but with Grandmamma there was no point protesting my marked differences to her more boisterous grandchildren, so out I would have to go.

I did not, however, hide my reactions to such unfairness and would often curl up on a bench and stare off sadly into the distance to make my resentment clear. Since oftentimes my only audience was the dreaded Cousin Alice, source of all the noise in the first place, I fear that my display was rather wasted on her. In fact, one afternoon in our fourteenth year, for no reason I can think of, she said to me, "You know, Alix, you always play at being such a tragic figure. I wonder what will become of you if anything terrible really does happen to you." As I stared at her, offended, she shrugged and added carelessly, "Well, who knows, maybe you'll like it. Right now you're just boring."

I burst into tears and ran immediately to Grandmamma to tell her what had happened. As I had awakened her from one of her three daily naps, she was hardly in a mood to listen and shooed me away peremptorily and unfeelingly to discuss the matter with Nanny Orchard, who proved scarcely more sympathetic. She just hugged me and told me that maybe my funny little cousin was right. "After all, you are indeed a very fortunate little girl and you have much more to be cheerful about than most."

Surrounded by people who thought that being an orphaned child from a small "unimportant" duchy, and never having many pretty clothes and no trips at all, except to see Grandmamma, and who kept telling me I should be delighted with my circumstances, did not help to make me so. A lack of compassion has always given me terrible headaches and made my legs ache besides, but I never – not once – "sulked," as I was always being accused of doing by everyone except darling Ernie who understood me perfectly.

So they went on, those quiet years, but even though it did not seem to me that things were changing, they were … or rather I was.

I had always been tall for my age and accustomed to hearing that I was really quite pretty from my own dear family, and of course from Grandmamma. Now, however, I began to notice that other people – people who shouldn't have, such as maids and footmen and shopkeepers – were beginning to comment on my appearance too, doing it in such a way that I found it hard to be as offended by their gross impertinence as I should have been. There were so many times when I would catch a long glance followed by a muttered apology. "Oh forgive me, Your Highness, I couldn't help staring. You're just so lovely."

Immodesty is the most unattractive trait that a young lady can possess, as I was always to remind my own daughters later, but I also despise disingenuousness and hypocrisy. Having said that, I can now freely admit I did not find my own image displeasing as I viewed it in my dressing table mirror. I had maintained the slender frame of childhood, while filling out here and there in the places best designed to make dresses – however mediocre – hang well. Additionally, I had – and even I can agree with this – rather glorious red-gold hair which, when loose, was long enough for me to sit upon, and I fancy that my features were not altogether distressing to the eye either.

However, my appearance seemed to drive poor Grandmamma into confused and conflicting states at times. One moment it was all, "Alicky my darling, you are a great beauty. Only the finest position in the world will do for you." Then, in the next breath she would admonish me with, "Alix, do straighten up. Alicky, why must you become so red and blotchy when you feel shy? Alicky, we really must hide those enormous hands and feet of yours."

It was, I am sure, Grandmamma's staunch criticisms that created my lifelong shyness that has plagued me ever since, but then I know too that she was merely trying to make a good modest girly of me, which is what every young lady must hope to be, while also plotting to make me the Queen of England.

When I turned sixteen, I was allowed to put my hair up and let my dresses down, and Ella and Sergei came over from Russia to attend the modest coming out ball that was all that Papa could afford. Indeed it was my dear Ella who trimmed my little white gown with orange blossoms since Papa could not afford real lace. I suppose Ella thought it would embarrass me if she and Sergei had presented me with a ball gown from Paris or even if she had given me one of her hundreds of castoffs. During her years in Russia as a Romanov Grand Duchess, she had become a terrible clotheshorse and rather hopelessly frivolous and vain, in my humble opinion.

She and Sergei had been married for four years by then, yet lacked children. Ella did not speak of this, and I didn't like to ask her about it, but I couldn't help noticing that she and Sergei didn't act at all like Vicky and Louis did. Of course, Vicky and Louis did have children, so maybe that was why, I didn't know. What I did see was that, while Ella had magnificent clothes and traveled with three maids even while in Darmstadt, and while, too, Sergei seemed to buy her jewelry every day, they didn't seem happy. In fact, they behaved very oddly together in that Ella would ask Sergei's opinions about everything, no matter how small or stupid the matter.

"Sergei Alexandrovich, does this dress please you? Sergei, do you like my hair this way? Dearest, do you think this is a proper book for me to read?"

Since I was unmarried and Mama had been dead for so long, I suppose I shouldn't have judged her, but I wasn't the only one who was obliged to hide giggles.

Nanny did too, and so did Vicky, and even Irene, who was by that time, at least so I thought, an old maid. Sergei, however, neither laughed nor simply ignored these inanities. Instead, to my surprise, he answered her dutifully and even chatted at length about Ella's clothes, hair, books and jewelry choices. Worse, he had taken to calling her "My child," and once at dinner was overheard telling her, "Hush, Ella, you sound ridiculous. No one here wants to hear your thoughts on anything."

I, of course, knew nothing of marriage and nor should I have at my tender age, and due to my Mama's early death had little to compare it with. Oh, there were Grandmamma's stories of her lost one, but they had been retold so many times, and each time she repeated them, Prince Albert became more heroic and perfect than during the last retelling, until finally he sounded less like a man made of flesh and blood and more like one of the saints I had begun to study, so there wasn't much there to dwell on in the way of how things should be in a marriage.

Irene and Louis, though, well if I dreamed of my future life as a bride – and what girl does not? – they weren't quite right either, for they seemed to be such good friends and so jokey and rather foolish with one another that I did not find them at all romantic. Still, if I had to choose, I would have preferred, I suppose, Louis's kindly tolerant love to Sergei's more disturbing ways with Ella, and yet … and yet Ella lived as though she were a princess. Of course, she was a princess, and a grand duchess, but I mean that she lived like one from my storybooks. There were the palaces and carriages and maids, and though Sergei treated her as though she were a somewhat annoying pet, no one else did. Ella was, in fact, treated with the sort of reverence that was second only to Grandmamma's and it made me wonder if Ella had not somehow disappointed Sergei. There were no children after all, and when he had courted her, he had been more than devoted and admiring, so then wasn't his changed nature somehow her fault? What if she had stood up to him more, demanded his respect, as I had long heard that Grandmamma had done with her lost love while he had lived?

Yes, I felt I had answered, or rather unlocked, the key to marital bliss, and done so at the young age of sixteen without any help. If a girl wanted a boy to worship her, then he must fear her just a little, just enough.

These bridal thoughts of mine were not based on idle musings, for after the long quiet years in Darmstadt, much was changing for me, and also, surprisingly, for Irene too. Poor Irene, who had long been regarded as yet another Hessian girl with "neither face nor fortune," had, somewhat out of the blue, received a proposal of marriage from our cousin Prince Heinrich of Prussia, our terribly annoying Cousin Willy's younger brother. Heinrich, who was very nice if not particularly remarkable, had often visited Darmstadt on family occasions. Poor Heinrich had always been considerably overshadowed by his awful brother, our Cousin Willy, and so I can't say that anyone had paid much attention to him, though obviously that was not true of Irene, who suddenly, a week following my presentation, announced rather carelessly that Heinrich had asked Papa for her hand and had been accepted, and that they were to be married right away at the end of May.

I heard in a letter from Grandmamma, which arrived almost upon the heels of this announcement, that she was most put out that Irene had not consulted her first before accepting Heinrich's suit, going on to say that she disapproved of first cousins marrying each other, but that "one must also embrace this proposal, as Irene is not pretty and can bring little to a marriage beyond her amiable nature." As a great pragmatist, Grandmamma then belatedly gave her blessing to the match and sent a fine silver service to the happy couple as a wedding present.

Irene and Heinrich's wedding ceremony was a nice, small family affair held at the new palace, and I was a full bridesmaid this time. Having just come out, it was noted by some that more admiring glances were cast my way than at the bride's, but I disagree. Irene simply shone with happiness, and happiness, as we all know, is a girl's greatest beautifier. And this time I was able to wave goodbye with a light heart as I was preparing to depart myself to pass the summer with Grandmamma at Windsor.

Sadly, I had no sooner arrived at Windsor than I received the sad news from Grandmamma that poor Emperor Frederick of Germany had died rather suddenly. All of Europe mourned this great man and looked askance at his successor, for it was none other than my terrible cousin Willy, who was now and forever to be addressed – as Grandmamma sternly reminded me – as his August Majesty Emperor Kaiser Wilhelm. I murmured assent to Grandmamma's directive, but in

73

private with Nanny Orchard I told her that, to me, he'd never be anything more than awful Cousin Willy, no matter how the rest of the world viewed him.

Grandmamma, possibly sensing this, did not take me with her when she traveled to Germany for her "darling grandson's" coronation. The 'darling' bit seemed rather sudden to me as I had always thought Grandmamma rather despised Willy who had been born with a deformed arm due to a forceps accident, and who in all cases seemed to have a deformed and bullying personality. But, there again, he was her grandson and the Emperor now, and Grandmamma was a strong upholder of birthrights and their prerogatives, as is natural for one in her own lofty situation.

While Grandmamma was in Germany, I was thrown much into the company of my English cousins. These were the children of the Prince of Wales, my Uncle Bertie, and his very beautiful wife Princess Alexandra, who was the sister of the Empress of Russia, but much taller, nicer and prettier. Uncle Bertie and Aunt Alix, as she was called, had five children. The oldest was Prince Albert, whom we called "Eddy," and then there was nice Georgie and the three girls, Louise, Victoria and Maud, not one of which poor girls resembled remotely their pretty mama, although they were very nice to me and used to fight amongst themselves over who would be allowed to brush my hair at night, their own being rather sparse. But as I say, they were just little girls then and I was already nearly a grown woman, so it was with Eddy and Georgie that I tended to spend most of my time.

We three would play bezique and other card games, and go for rides around Windsor Great Park, they on horseback and I in the pony and trap as I was already beginning to suffer from the condition of sciatica owing to my having grown so tall. My back hurt me dreadfully at times and that made my legs ache terribly, so, when I could venture out at all, I had to do so in the trap, though I had always liked horses and could ride quite nicely, I fancied.

I don't believe that there was ever a time when I thought of dear Eddy as anything more than my cousin, my older cousin, and one day heir to the English throne to be sure, which gave him a certain standing amongst our royal clique of children, but no, to me he never seemed like a boy, by which I mean not in the sense that Nicky was a boy whom I still thought of far away in the icy kingdom of Russia. But, if I did not think of poor dear Eddy that way, there were others who did, mostly Grandmamma who, unbeknownst to me, had long ago set her heart on a match between us. This was somewhat unexpected given that she had voiced such disapproval of Irene marrying Heinrich as first cousins, Eddy and Georgie also being my first cousins, Uncle Bertie having been my dear Mama's own brother.

But now it was different, and it was different because Grandmamma said so, and no one liked to disagree with Grandmamma as it tended to make her very angry and very ill, too. So, when she returned from Germany and summoned me to her, I was more shocked than happy when she held my hand and said, "Dearest, I have the most wonderful news to tell you."

I was quite excited because I thought she was going to tell me that she was going to take me to Italy with her, knowing that she was planning to travel there in September, so I leaned forward eagerly.

"Oh Grandmamma, what, whatever can it be?"

"Alicky, my precious darling, your dearest cousin, my most beloved grandson, his Highness the Duke of Clarence and Avondale –"

"You mean Eddy?" I interrupted somewhat impatiently, anxious for her to get on to speaking about our trip to Italy.

Grandmamma pursed her lips in irritation at my rudeness and I had to apologize once and then a second time before she would continue.

"Yes, Alix, I do mean Eddy, as you call your cousin Albert. It is indeed Eddy about whom I wish to speak to you, your Cousin Eddy, who is also, if you have perhaps forgotten, my heir after Bertie, and who will, one day, become the King of England and the Emperor of India in my place. The girl who wins his heart, Alix, will become the Queen of England, a small position, I suppose, but one which, by the grace of God, I have been rather proud to hold."

Oh dear, I thought, *somehow I have truly offended Grandmamma,* and since I did not know how or why, and since I was also feeling rather offended myself by then, I burst into tears. This was something that normally affected Grandmamma most deeply as she was quite sentimental and wont to cry easily herself, particularly when discussing her late husband, but this time my tears seemed to exacerbate rather than lessen her annoyance.

Seeing this, I quickly stopped crying and tried to pull myself together as much as possible.

Grandmamma sat in silence as I clutched my handkerchief to my face, and when I had given my last hopeful sniffle and still received no comfort, she deigned to continue our conversation.

"It pains me, my dear child, to see you in distress when I am merely trying to impart to you a matter of the greatest joy, but possibly your poor old Grandmamma seems to you nothing more than a foolish old woman and, moreover, maybe you are bored by this discussion."

I was not bored by the discussion, whatever it was supposed to be, but I was becoming angered by it. However, one cannot be angry at a queen, and so once again I was forced to apologize, although I could not see what it was that I had done to merit this most unfair attack. I said nothing of this of course.

"Dearest, oh very dearest Grandmamma, please don't be cross with me. How could you ever think I was bored? Why, Grandmamma, every moment with you is as heaven to me. Haven't you always been as a mother to me? And please, Grandmamma, know that my greatest joy is always in your company. If I seem fractious today, it must be because Madam Becker is coming to visit me soon."

'Madame Becker' is what all we girlies in my family called our womanly times and I knew that mentioning her would disarm Grandmamma as she was always most interested in both my health and my newly-hatched womanhood. And, indeed, my words did finally manage to reach her and to touch her most deeply, for her old eyes filled with sentimental tears and she stroked my face.

"Dearest Alicky, pretty, pretty darling Alicky, forgive me, my darling. Maybe Grandmamma has simply confused you. You are very young yet and cannot understand the ways of ... But no, let's begin again and Grandmamma will be more direct. Alix, my sweet little one, your cousin, your dear Eddy, has told Grandmamma that he has fallen completely in love with you and wishes you to become his bride. I am so pleased at this honor for you, my dearest, and while I know that earthly glory means little in the end, still old Grandmamma will be glad to depart this mortal plane one day, secure in the knowledge that her own little girly will occupy the greatest position there is."

I could only stare at her open-mouthed, but oddly this seemed to please her, for she struggled to her feet and clutched me to her perfumed bosom, appearing to be unaware that I was stiff with shock, rather than transported with delight, as I stood there in her arms.

When she sat back down, she gazed into my surely whitened face and smiled at me reassuringly.

"Oh I know, darling, I well understand how you must be feeling. I remember so well when I proposed to my dearest, my very dearest, Albert. He looked almost exactly as you do this minute. Ah how he would have loved you." She dabbed at her eyes, which had filled with tears as they always did at the mention of Prince Albert.

Shaking off her momentary melancholy, she continued on, filling the void left by my failure to respond.

"Alicky, you realize that there is more, so much more, that awaits you in this marriage to my dearest boy than earthly glory?"

I continued staring at her, aghast, until I realized a response was finally required of me and I managed to nod numbly.

"Well, yes, Grandmamma, I do, but I'm only sixteen and I hadn't thought –"

"Of course you haven't, darling. What girl, even my own wee granddaughter, could even let herself imagine such a future? No, no, your modesty is most becoming. I'm certain that my dear Albert finds it so as well. He loves you most ardently, my darling, and that is what Grandmamma means when she says that you will have all a girl could dream of. For what is a crown without a great love to make such a responsibility bearable?"

For the first time in our mad conversation I felt that Grandmamma might have been speaking sensibly. For indeed, what is a crown without love, and Eddy, my strange, long-necked cousin, could never manage to enunciate more than two words before either drooling or falling into unnerving giggles ... Eddy, with his odd collection of medical instruments and whose only enthusiasm, as near as I could tell, was for taxidermy. *Eddy?* No, it could not be and he couldn't possibly love me. He had never acted towards me any differently from anyone else, which is to say awkwardly and somewhat impossibly. Compared to Georgie, his handsome younger brother, he seemed a near-lunatic. Eddy could not even sit astride his horse correctly, and he cheated at cards and cried when he lost anyway.

I was appalled but knew that I must say something before I could escape this interview and run to Nanny.

I tried logic first.

"Grandmamma, I am too young for marriage."

Grandmamma's reply was steely. "You have come out, Alix, you have been schooled in the Lutheran faith, you are nearly seventeen, and I was a queen at eighteen, and a mother of a prince by nineteen."

"Well, yes of course, Grandmamma, but then I must ask Papa, as –"

"Your papa has already been consulted, Alix, and is naturally overcome with joy at this honor for you. It's an honor for him as well, it must be said."

I was just resolving either to faint or to attempt to throw myself out of the window to escape this awfulness when, thankfully, Grandmamma was interrupted by the arrival of one of her footmen to announce that luncheon was served.

How I got through that ghastly meal, I cannot to this day recall. There they all were: Uncle Bertie and Aunt Alix, who both smiled so tenderly at me; Eddy, who mercifully had to leave the table abruptly after he spilled his wine and then knocked his soup all over himself; Georgie with his cheeky grin, the little girls with their giggles; and, of course, Grandmamma with her serene smile. For them it was clearly all decided, without a word of consent from me or even a conversation between me and that idiot Eddy, a person who had transformed himself in my mind from a hapless soul and the object of pity to a creature of utter terror.

80

I should have known that a day so dreadful could only become more so, because instead of being able to escape to Nanny Orchard's comforting bosom, I was instead sent out to walk in the garden immediately following luncheon. The little girls, still giggling, asked their mama if they might accompany me, but Aunt Alix said, "No, darlings, not today. Your cousin Alicky needs to walk alone for a moment, although I do not expect her to remain alone for long." At this ominous pronouncement she shared a glance of complicity with Grandmamma that boded poorly for me.

I said, "Dearest grandmamma, Aunt Alicky, I find that I am rather tired and might instead just go up and –"

Grandmamma cut me off. "Certainly not, Alix. If one is tired, the very best thing for one to do is to take the air. Get along outside now and I'll see you again before dinner this evening."

At that moment, and only then, did I ever feel anger towards my grandmamma. *Take the air for tiredness,* indeed, this from a woman who would spend days in bed at the mere hint of a cough and who had always exhorted me to do the same. But not now … now I was to take the air. I knew what it meant and who it meant that I would be meeting outside, but there was no refusing Grandmamma, and so feeling the eyes of my gloating family upon my back and the weight of all the world's despair and fear upon my shoulders, I drew a deep breath and exited into the small walled garden that led off from the dining room.

As expected, within a minute or so Eddy arrived, wearing a fresh shirt to replace the one spoilt by his fumbling encounters with the soup and the wine. His valet should have insisted that he change his trousers too as they were badly stained with the remnants of the tomato consommé he had spilled over himself in a most unfortunate location. Horribly it was there that I cast my eyes while he spoke, to avoid looking into his sweating, earnest face.

He invited me to sit on the bench beside him.

I refused, which irritated him.

"Alicky, it's all very well acting the shy miss, but do try and be a good sport about all this, won't you?"

I did indeed sit down in shock as the realization of complete horror of the day tumbled down on me, but not in the girlish and anticipatory manner that Eddy was expecting from me. Rather, I crashed down gracelessly onto the bench and proceeded to bury my face in my hands.

Eddy harrumphed loudly and then stomped about, before finally settling down heavily beside me.

"So, you, you ... don't want to? I thought ... well, Grandmamma did say you would, and it doesn't seem too terrible, does it? I mean, I understand that it does seem terrible to you, or rather *I* do."

I raised my head and stared at him, my cousin, my old playmate. I supposed the latter was all finished now. As I thought that, I felt a deep sadness coming over me. Everything changes and I have never liked change. I've never found that it has brought better things; in fact quite the contrary.

I wanted to try and explain some of this to Eddy, if I could, so I laid my hand tentatively on his arm and he looked at me with oh so much hope that my eyes filled with tears.

He misunderstood the state of my emotions, and before I could get a word out he started speaking.

"Oh Alicky, you do care, then, don't you? Yes, well, of course you do. Grandmamma said so and the old girl's still as sharp as a pin really, isn't she? Well, come now, there's no need to look sad – quite the opposite!" He finished this embarrassing recitation by muttering, "Darling," and then abruptly leaned towards me to draw me to him, presumably either to hug me, or worse, kiss me.

I leaned away, which threw him off balance and we fell together onto the damp ground, with Eddy landing on top of me. Somehow he found this even more encouraging and leaned his anxious face in for a kiss.

I pushed him away with a strength I didn't know I possessed and we were both sprawling inelegantly on our backs when both Grandmamma and Uncle Bertie chose to join us, presumably in order to congratulate us.

Uncle Bertie cleared his throat and Grandmamma let out a little shriek. I hurriedly rose and began frantically trying to straighten my skirt.

This time I did manage to speak before anyone else could. "Oh don't … don't look at us like that. You've hardly interrupted an episode of passion."

"Alex, what has gotten into you?" Grandmamma demanded sternly.

"Eddy, what on earth?" blustered Uncle Bertie.

"Nothing, Grandmamma, nothing has gotten into me or into poor Eddy either. Uncle Bertie, please don't blame him. I pushed him off the bench and he was just … oh never mind. Look, I'm not marrying him, he's not marrying me, and I do not wish to hear another word on the subject … ever."

Then, mustering whatever dignity I could after this somewhat hysterical outburst, I removed myself from their presence without bothering to curtsy or to ask permission to leave, before dashing right past my other startled relatives and the servants, and not pausing until I was ensconced against Nanny Orchard's bosom where finally I let go the storm of weeping I had been holding in all day.

Chapter 6

It came as no surprise to me that, the very next morning, I discovered a note from Grandmamma on my breakfast tray. She did not mention the previous day's scenes, but she did say that she had decided to "repair to Balmoral for my nerves" that very day.

There was no invitation for me to join her.

I felt more than lost; I felt completely forsaken. Grandmamma, my own dearest one, and now this ... Worse, I knew this meant returning home to terribly boring Darmstadt for the whole summer, and due to Papa's financially precarious state there would be no trips or holiday sightseeing, and with Irene gone and Ernie visiting her and Heinrich for the summer in Germany, I would be left alone to consider my transgressions. This was no doubt exactly what Grandmamma wanted. I vowed not to give her the satisfaction of hearing that I was even in the slightest way upset by any of it.

When Nanny and I arrived back in Darmstadt, it was even worse than I had anticipated because poor Papa insisted on spending an inordinate amount of time staring reproachfully at me and sighing over my lost opportunity, rarely missing a single opportunity for several weeks to say longingly that, but for my "childish whims," I could one day have become the Queen of England.

I suffered these assaults in silence and merely waited for ... well, I don't know quite what I was waiting for, but never had I been more certain that events were changing around me, or would do so, but the how of it still eluded me.

That summer passed in this manner and then Ernie was home finally from Germany and filled with great admiration for our Cousin Willy's "grand armies and pageantry." I observed to him with some humor that I found his fondness for the "Kaiser," as he now called the terrible Willy, somewhat "novel" since he had been the first to poke fun at him in the past. But even my darling Ernie was changing and he seemed to find my referring to his former attitudes childish. He also found my refusal of Eddy disappointing and I caught him and Papa whispering in corners on more than one occasion as the summer deepened into autumn.

I was resentful of their judgment of me and somewhat at a loose end altogether. These feelings must have been apparent to my sisters in my letters, for at the beginning of October I received an invitation from Ella and Sergei for all three of us to visit them in St. Petersburg for the whole of the winter season at their palace there, the Belosselsky Belozersky Palace.

Papa was reluctant to do so owing to the costs that would be incurred, disguising this genuine, if embarrassing, concern by insisting it would be irresponsible for him to be absent from his duties in Darmstadt for so long, but Ernie and my recent coldness towards one another was completely healed by the invitation and we were as one in urging Papa that we should go, otherwise we would be seen to snub Sergei and Ella's generosity, although in truth we simply very much wanted to winter at their fabulous home and, in

Ernie's case, to partake of the fabled delights of a St. Petersburg season.

I, who was never comfortable amid large, glittering gatherings, was driven less by my desire to attend an endless round of balls and entertainments, and more by ... well, I suppose, curiosity. It had been five years since Ella's wedding and five years since I had met Nicky, Nicholas, the heir, the Tsarevich, the lovely-looking boy who had treated me with such kindness and attention, the boy who had made me feel things that I fancied few twelve year old girls had ever felt.

What would it be like, I wondered, to see him now that I was utterly changed from a wee girly to a young woman? Would he like me still? Would he like me more? Would I find him terribly changed too? But then I thought not. Boys are much different from girls, and Nicky was the same age as my own darling brother, and being twenty-one hadn't changed Ernie a bit. Oh, he wore whiskers and waistcoats now, but he was still the same dear child at heart – and mostly in his habits – that he had always been.

I remained lost in these private musings as we prepared for our trip, and it was these thoughts and questions that occupied my mind as we traveled by train for three days and three nights across what seemed to be more sea than land. I had only been to Russia once before and it had been summer then. But I was learning, and would learn more deeply, that Russia is not a land of summer. In fact, all the other seasons that touch other lands – spring, summer, autumn – they are not real to Russia or to its peoples; only winter is real to Russia.

And such winters! They begin almost in August, that sleepy time of late summer when those in other countries are just beginning to appreciate a coolness to the breeze, to anticipate the autumn colors, and maybe even to speak longingly of the prospect of snow. But it is different for the Russian peoples: Winter is a living thing to them, a nearly endless season that dominates all of their lives from the grandest ducal palace to the flimsy huts of the peasants, or *muzhiks* as they are called in Russia. These people live and die in tiny townships that are stretched so thinly across the Russian vastness that at times a whole day can go by before a traveler in a train will see the barest sign of civilization. Whether they be countesses or *muzhiks* does not matter, for they are alike in this one thing: the knowledge that either winter is coming, or its having arrived, that they cannot truly know when spring will reappear.

Autumn is not a gentle thing in that country. It comes, as I have said, in August. All the snow geese suddenly gather and fly off. A few days later, a deep frost strikes. This knowledge, this knowing of winter, lies deep in the souls of Russians and the *muzhiks* respond with yet more haste to gather their crops before they are spoiled, and in the great palaces the ladies sigh and shiver too. Darkness comes with the winters, a night that begins at noon and ends at ten the following morning. The snow blankets their world and silence beds itself across the land, broken only by the lonely howling of the wind and of the wolves who roam the endless white expanse of this far northern place.

In St. Petersburg, the nobles try frantically to shield themselves from winter by pretending that beyond their brightly lit palaces the nearly seven million square miles of frozen suspended darkness does not exist. They hold their season as the champagne flows, and the gowns and jewels and bright jackets of the nobility and of the Cossacks speak of brighter times. But they know that it is all illusory; that when the cold, endless nights are upon the land, Russia is impervious to the fragile human lives carved out upon it; that Russia is winter and darkness, and that it might be that, if the music were ever to stop or the bells on their troikas were to cease ringing, they would be as the others are, the *muzhiks*, cold, huddled, hungry, and living with the ever-present knowledge that this winter might be *the* winter, the one that lasts far too long for them to survive it, to see summer once again.

But, you see, you must see, that was not what I noticed, not my first winter, the magical fairytale winter of 1889, the winter that Nicky and my love was kindled. My train journey through the whiteness did not seem ominous to me, no indeed. The snow, clean and covering all the world, seemed a blessing, a purity if you will, and the cars of the train as they struggled through it seemed to beat out a song.

> *You are going to see Nicky.*
> *You are going to see Nicky.*
> *Almost there now.*
> *Almost there now.*

I suppose in my deepest heart of hearts I had imagined, or at least hoped, that Nicky would come to the station in St. Petersburg to meet our little party, but of course that was a very foolish thing to think, as Ella sternly informed me when she was helping me to settle into my room at her palace that night.

"You must understand, Alicky," she chided me while looking through my limited wardrobe and shaking her head simultaneously, "that Nicky, as I am permitted to call him, being a member of the imperial family, and of course as his dearest aunt and friend –"

"Oh Ella, surely you don't really think of yourself as his aunt, do you? You're only four years older than he is. It's a bit much."

Seeing her wounded look, and knowing Ella as I did, I realized that if I didn't apologize immediately in some way, she'd become silent and sulky for the rest of the evening, and then I'd never get to talk about Nicky, so I leaned over and kissed her cool cheek.

"I'm sorry, dearest. I only meant that you are simply far too young and far too beautiful to be any grown man's aunt. Why, you look as young as I do. Even younger," I quickly added when her face didn't immediately smooth.

It did finally at those words, and she smiled forgivingly at me and patted my hand.

"Oh how silly! I'm ancient, although I do try my best and maybe my little potions are helping somewhat."

Curious in spite of myself, I had to ask, "Potions? Ella darling, are you a witch now? What does Sergei think?"

I laughed as I asked her these questions, but so typically of Ella, who always made everything about herself and who could choose to be either offended or delighted according to her mood, she chose to be offended yet again, rising from the side of my bed and frowning down at me.

"A *witch*, Alix?" There was no mirth in her peel of laughter. "Oh hardly. I'm just a married lady, a very happily married lady, who tries to keep up her appearances as best she can. Appearances are so terribly important to Sergei, you know. And by potions I simply meant that I make some little creams and unguents to try and keep my face and hands smooth for him. Hardly the province of witches, would you say, Alix?" Then, not giving me the time to answer, she leaned forward and pressed her cold lips briefly to my forehead. "You need to rest and I need to see to Papa and Ernie before I myself can retire, so I'll leave you now. Goodnight, dear. I'm so glad that you've come to visit us. We'll speak of Nicky another time, shall we?"

There was no point in trying to raise the subject of Nicky again, I saw that clearly, and so I gave her an equally cool kiss in return and waited until I heard the door of my chamber clicking behind her before rising from my bed.

I was in a strange mood. I was glad to be alone in this magnificent chamber. I hadn't seen anything like it since my last visit to Russia, or maybe Windsor, but at Windsor I, as one of Grandmamma's many little granddaughters, was never allotted state rooms, obviously. No, at Windsor I usually shared a room with a cousin or two in the nursery wing. Here in Sergei and Ella's palace in St. Petersburg it was far different and I wanted to absorb everything without Nanny or anyone else about me.

The Belosselsky Belozersky Palace was new to me. I had driven by it during Sergei and Ella's wedding celebrations but I hadn't fully absorbed it. It had been Tsar Alexander III's wedding gift to Sergei and Ella. He was obviously a very kind and generous brother to Sergei because the Belosselsky Belozersky was quite magnificent. It had been so, even before it became Sergei and Ella's, with its five hundred rooms, each one grander than the next, stretching along the River Neva with its own private jetty. But Sergei had enriched and enlarged it even more, installing a private library larger than that in the Winter Palace, adding an astounding private Slavic Chapel, and, as a final touch, having it painted bright red so that it could be seen from Siberia, I suppose.

My own room was as large as any of the public rooms in the New Palace at Darmstadt, but much more lavish. The floor was inlaid with rose marble and the walls were hung with a deep green moiré silk that nicely complemented the dark green marble fireplace and deep velvet curtain hangings. My bed was the largest and most ornate I had ever seen and required steps to climb upon it. Best of all, it had its own pink marble bathroom and dressing room, and it was this chamber I dreamily walked into.

At home we did not yet have indoor plumbing, and so it was a great novelty to me merely to be able to turn on taps and watch the large silver bath fill with warm water. As it did so, I dreamily unfastened my dress and my undergarments and let my hair down. My hair was still long enough to sit on when let down, and at that time a bright red-gold.

When I was as naked as the day I was born, I scandalously walked in that vulnerable state into the nearby dressing room. One of Ella's numberless and nameless servants must have slipped in and silently lit the surrounding candles, and it was only in their light that I wished to indulge in this ethereal mood – or possible ritual – of mine.

I turned down the gas lights, leaving the room illuminated only by the golden candles, and then I sat down in front of the rose and lace silk dressing table in whose mirror, for the first time in my life, I saw myself, all of myself, and I was glad, for the girl I saw in the glass was no longer a girl. I was a woman, and a woman of surpassing beauty.

I felt a power run through me such as I had never felt. I could, I knew then, achieve anything, gain any favor, ascend to any place …

Then I shivered and rose quickly and pulled my robe about me.

What did I mean? What was it I thought I wanted? What place? I had spurned Eddy, and by so doing I had relinquished once and forever the greatest place there was. Grandmamma had said so, and she was right, for what higher earthly honors were there, what was more important, than to be the Queen of England?

Well, there was one greater place, a place so high that only God was above one, and here on earth that meant no higher place. The wealth, the size, the power of the tsars' empire vibrated in every inch of this land, a land more magnificent, richer and more colorful than any imagination could conjure up. The Tsar and his Empress, they were not mere beloved figureheads, as, for all her pride, was darling Grandmamma. They were divine, chosen by God alone, and to God alone they answered. One day, the sweet blue-eyed boy who had looked at me with such affection would be the Tsar-Emperor of all of this and the woman beside him would be divine as well.

It was hard to imagine dear Nicky as the mighty Tsar, the Tsar of legend, but oddly I could see myself beside him as Tsarina. *Or wait*, I thought … *is it immodest of me to even be considering this or have these reflections been sent to me by God?* For hasn't it always been known that God could, and did, choose to impart special knowledge upon certain exalted ones, ones he loved and trusted to see to his kingdoms on earth? Yes, it could be, but, no, I was a girl, a nobody, the youngest living daughter of a mere grand duke and too insignificant to be thinking such things.

I prayed that night harder than I had in years. I prayed to increase my faith and never to ask for what was not freely given to me, but still a tiny spark remained, the knowledge that the woman I had seen in the mirror might indeed be granted everything she could ever wish for.

Whatever grandiose imaginings I might have had the night before were certainly dissolved in the freezing reality of my first full day in St. Petersburg.

Ella had barely let me finish my morning chocolate when she began fussily nagging me to get dressed as people would be calling to see her family to pay their respects and I should certainly not keep them waiting. So, as I am not of an athletic disposition, and nor am I used to rising at dawn, I was rather out of sorts when I descended to Ella's morning room shortly before 11am that first day.

Nor was my mood improved by realizing that her Imperial Majesty the Empress Minnie was amongst the ladies gathered there. She did not look up at my rushed entrance as the other ladies did, but merely glanced at the diamond-encrusted watch upon her bosom and slid a look towards Ella, accompanied by a raised eyebrow. I thought it was really unkind of Ella not to have told me that she would be there, but when I looked her way she gazed at me in helpless horror, so I could see that she too had been caught unawares by the Empress's visit.

I had entered the room as quietly as I could, which was rather difficult as it was so crowded with ladies and their skirts, and in attempting to make my way over to the Empress to curtsy, while simultaneously trying not to brush up against any of these judgmental strangers, I accidentally knocked against a small, unstable whatnot table with an enormous samovar on top of it and sent it crashing to the ground, where it seemed to explode with a huge crash, sending hot tea spilling everywhere.

As I stood there frozen with humiliation and confusion, I heard *that word* for the first time ever. It rippled throughout Ella's overcrowded, over-scented drawing room in whispers, but ones I could hear with such strange clarity in those moments. "*Maladroit*" – "clumsy" – followed by titters and averted glances. Even Ella took nearly forever, or so it seemed to me, before coming towards me with an embarrassed little laugh.

"Oh Alicky, don't look so stricken, darling, it's only tea. Here, ladies, let us all go and inspect Sergei's new orchids. He's been working on them forever and I think the results are quite astounding."

So saying, she gathered up all the overfed, overdressed women of the court, the mighty Empress included, and gracefully herded them from the room.

I didn't move and Ella shot me an exasperated glance. "Alix, aren't you coming to see Sergei's orchids?"

Numbly, dumbly I shook my head, a head now aching with the onset of a terrible migraine.

I stared at her beseechingly, wanting her to help me, but she only pursed her lips and said, "No, I see. Well, maybe it's for the best ... You must go and rest and change, and later –"

"Change, Ella?" I interrupted her, for I have always been of the belief that one should be honest at all times.

She stared at me long and searchingly before shaking her head and resuming the superficial social smile that came so easily to her.

"I meant only your dress, darling. What else could I have meant?"

I knew at that moment that Ella was so greatly changed that all intimacy between us was at an end. She was not in the least upset about the unkindness her guests had displayed towards me, her small, orphaned sister. She cared only for appearances.

As this truth came to me, I knew that I would not show her my pain and embarrassment, not then, not ever again if I could help it.

I smiled brilliantly right back into her deceitful eyes.

"Of course that's what you meant, darling Ella. I need to change my dress. I'm all tea-stained, aren't I?

Yes, I'll go and do just that, and I hope I can be quick enough still to have time to view Sergei's orchids. Don't worry about me in the least. After all, you mustn't keep the Empress waiting, must you?"

That was the moment when Ella could have chosen once more to be my dearest sister, but instead she preferred to act the part of the empty-headed society creature she was becoming by nodding silently and rushing after her cherished guests.

I drew a deep breath and nodded to myself. Yes, this was the way things were going to be during my stay, at least in front of Ella and the ladies of St. Petersburg, the mighty Empress included. This is how they would be, but I wondered if that would also be true of the once shy, adoring boy who had looked at me so longingly all those many years ago.

Chapter 7

I had been in St. Petersburg for a fortnight, but it might as well have been a decade, so utterly changed was my life. Everything I thought I had understood about people and situations was different now,

For, you see, I was loved … was loved and did love.

Nicky, Nicky, Nicky, Nicky, who was now, and forever would be, "Pelly Two" to me, and I, I was no longer simply Alix, I was "Pelly One."

"Pelly One" was what Nicky called me and it meant I was special in a way I had never been before, and special to the only person for whom I would, or could, care, and that was absolute, that was forever.

It's so very odd, too, one's heart, for at our first meeting, or rather I should say our first time re-meeting, I didn't know that I would love him so completely. In fact, and I blush to recount this, at first I wondered if my own dearly cherished memories of a divinely handsome boy dancing with a wee girly in a little ballroom had been simply illusions I had held.

My first thought upon seeing Nicky, oh Nicky, oh Pelly, the sunshine of my heart, was 'He's very small.' And then my next traitorous, mad thought was, 'He looks exactly like my Cousin Georgie, only his teeth aren't as good.'

These silly ideas were, of course, brought on by initial nerves and I understand that now, because Nicky is not at all too small – it's just that I've always been unusually tall for a girl – and he doesn't look a thing like Georgie really. And since I mentioned his teeth to him just once, he's always smiled with his mouth closed and he looks divine when he does so. That his smiles are mostly directed at me only makes them yet more perfect.

Our new and most lovely love began somewhat insouciantly upon my third day in St. Petersburg. Sergei, who I had decided was an angel of kindness, could see, as Ella either could not or preferred not to see, that I was unhappy.

Indeed, I was unhappy. Ella had not done a single thing to make my stay enjoyable. In fact, it appeared at times as though her every action was undertaken expressly to make it less so or maybe I am being as uncharitable and as unsisterly as she was seeming to be to me. Possibly it was simply that Ella's very existence, an existence, I must add, that she made not the slightest adjustment to despite the presence of her own family, was one that offended my very deepest self.

I do not wish to be unkind, and my faith cautions me that to judge another at all is wrong, but truly Ella's life seemed to me an unremitting round of empty and, yes, terribly boring, activities. To my eyes, she had virtually nothing with which to occupy herself and so had made a career of occupying herself with nothing. And despite having invited her small sister to visit her, she refused to change a single moment of her empty, if not to say empty-headed, schedule.

She rose at 8am and insisted that the maid she had provided me with should also rouse me at the same hour, something that, of course, I would not have protested, for I do believe that one must remain active at all times, except that I appeared to be awakened for no reason at all that I could ascertain, other than to attend, or should I say act as a witness, to Ella's silly days.

They began, as I said, with our rising at 8am, but the rising merely meant that Ella rose and moved over to her terribly elaborate dressing table, where she would take her morning cup of chocolate and drink it with excruciating slowness while staring blankly into her mirror. By this time I would have joined her at this stupid exercise, and if I dared to speak, for example to say something as inappropriate as "Good morning," she would glance, not at me, but at my reflection besides hers in her looking glass, and imperceptibly shake her head as though offended by my mere attendance at this sacred ritual, one in which she had insisted I participate. Then, slowly, ever so slowly, she would drop her gaze from the mirror and begin to sort through the hundred or so bottles and jars littering the top of her dressing table.

After what seemed like hours, she would seemingly then find what it was she needed and begin to apply a layer of one sort of cream to her eyes and another to her forehead, and after that she would call to one of her silently waiting maids and have yet another cream rubbed into the front and back of her neck. This fascinating procedure appeared to satisfy her long enough to allow her to address me and ask the ever-important question of what I planned to wear that day to breakfast with her and Sergei and Papa and Ernie.

Heaven forbid that I should shrug away the question as being pointless and frivolous. Oh no, that would not suffice, and she would inquire with all seriousness, "But Alicky, if you do not know what you are wearing in the morning, I shudder to imagine what you will wear this afternoon, for today we are calling upon Aunty Miechen and, you know, the Empress might be there."

To see the Empress, which as near as I could tell she did nearly every day, seemed to be the sole point of Ella's existence, or at least the highlight of it. Given her constant sightings of the Tsarina, I could only gather that the latter's days were as empty as those of my own sister.

The whole procedure left me to ponder, in the hours between seeing Ella at her morning toilette and then at breakfast, and then again two hours later when she had disappeared to change her dress for luncheon, what the purpose of all this was. These joyless activities were followed by a third change of clothing before the commencement of afternoon calls and I did, naturally, begin to wonder whether any of these women had ever accomplished a single thing other than to manage to avoid being caught twice in the same gown, and if so why they cared, since they seemed only to see and do the exact same repetitious activities day after day, these to be followed by a rest, another bath, dinner, and then either a ball, or worse, a reception, by which I mean the receptions, unlike the balls, involved seeing the same people you had just seen hours before during afternoon calls and being forced desperately to come up with another inane conversational topic to discuss with them, when you had nearly been driven to distraction earlier trying to find one.

Of course, our time there had been different for Ernie and Papa. Papa, I could see, was quite happy to spend his days relaxing and being pampered by the attentions of Ella and her rather enormous staff of servants. Indeed, freed from his heavy cares of state in Darmstadt and the oppressive atmosphere that had lain there since his disgraceful marriage, he seemed more contented than I could remember him being. I was, of course, happy for him in this regard.

As for Ernie, he was in truth only a boy, a mere child, and his twenty-one years sat lightly upon him, and in Russia he seemed to feel free to be himself. Sergei was most especially kind to Ernie and let him accompany him in all of his officer-based duties.

Ernie occasionally appeared a bit worse for wear in the mornings, but was all enthusiasm as he eagerly recounted his adventures of the night before. There was one game in particular that seemed to enchant him. It was called "to the wolves," and involved all the officers and their guests removing their clothing and running out into the snow to leap around a bonfire whilst drinking yards of brandy. Then the dear things would howl like wolves. I found it an amusing activity and wondered why Sergei, so kind in every other way, would continually tell Ernie to hush when he told of these romps.

But, for me, a mere girlie, there were no games or days of quiet rest; no, Ella was seeing to my "improvement in society," as she termed it, and by Day Three I was becoming somewhat desperate.

Then he came.

I would so much like to credit my dear sister for having arranged the wonderful surprise that met my eyes when I came down to luncheon that day, but I must remain true to my own history. It was Sergei who had sent Nicky a note of invitation, having recognized my increasingly drawn appearance and having, all spontaneously, organized an afternoon skating party on the hard-frozen Neva for a "few, dear young people." He therefore approached Nicky and his darling little sisters, Xenia and Olga, and some young officers whom Ernie had particularly befriended, and arranged it all without saying a word to Ella!

Naturally she pretended to be delighted, but I later saw her thin lips compress in annoyance after her first effusive welcoming of the heir to the Russian throne. To Nicky it would be all, "Oh darling, what a delightful surprise. How clever of my dearest, dearest Sergei to think of an impromptu afternoon of skating," but while I stood at the doorway to the drawing room watching Nicky, who had not yet seen me, my heart in my throat, I was well placed to hear Ella whispering to her lady in waiting, "Run, hurry, send notes and cancel all my afternoon calls. Oh, stop gaping at me you, fool! Oh, and if you can pull yourself together, tell my idiot wardrobe mistress to try and find my new skating costume. Good heavens, this is a disaster."

Ella, it seemed was not the sort of hostess given to having spontaneous changes to her schedule imposed on her. In fact, her entire life was so terribly scripted and false that it was obvious to me that it left scant room for family joy and intimacy, let alone for the slightest chance of true fun. But Sergei, warm-hearted and filled with *joie de vivre*, was different, and he had gone behind her back and arranged this,

And there was Nicky, and there I was, and then Ella seemed to jolt to this awareness suddenly and, turning on me, whispered harshly, "Well, go on then, Alix, there he is. You've got what you wanted. All your sulking has paid off, thanks to Sergei. Go on, go ahead, this is what you came for, isn't it?"

Her accusation was so utterly unfair that I could neither move nor speak, and at that moment my only desire was to turn and flee to Nanny, and then run much farther and keep going until I found my way home to Darmstadt, where I could be left alone and not be so uncharitably judged. My eyes filled with tears, and before I could move one way or another without being spotted, I saw a tiny smile cross Ella's face as she advanced towards Nicky, hands held out in welcome.

"Darling Nicky, this really is such a treat for us, especially for my little sister. Why, I think she's been bored to tears being stuck inside with her old sister, your aging auntie."

This was such a terribly obvious bid to fish for a compliment that, despite my anger at Ella, I felt embarrassed for her. It's funny, too, because as I was to learn, Nicky is always so exquisitely attuned towards the feelings of others, even to a fault, yet on this occasion he barely glanced at her.

As soon as he heard the words "Little sister," his head jerked in my direction and once again my eyes were met by the blazing blue of his own.

They fell away then, the years I hadn't seen him, the thousands of miles ... and something else vanished when our eyes met – my girlhood. In that second of time I became a young woman, and it was as a woman that I returned the gaze of the utterly devastatingly handsome man that the sweet boy of my memories had become. I did briefly register with some dismay that he had grown no taller and that he truly did look almost exactly like Cousin Georgie, but then I realized that, despite being short, he had a manfully powerful build and that, unlike poor Georgie, his own glorious blue eyes did not protrude, and that never, ever could I have seen, or wished to have seen, in Georgie's eyes the expression of wonder I saw in Nicky's as he looked at me.

He rushed over to me, ignoring the startled glances of those gathered around him.

"I say, Alix is it? Why, I think I would have recognized you anywhere ... but then no ... possibly I wouldn't. I mean to say, you do look like Ella so much now ... but well, not like her ... I mean to say ... oh, dash it, I'm making a confounded fool of myself, aren't I? All I meant to say ... am trying to say, that is, and making a terrible hash of it as usual, is that you've grown even prettier, but I don't see how you could have, because when I think of you ... I mean to say –"

Here he stopped in confusion, turned an adorable crimson, and dropped his head to stare at his feet. This made me feel, for possibly the first time in my life, that for once I knew the right thing to say.

I waited a moment until he had finally gathered his nerve to look at me again and I smiled gently at him.

"When you think of me ...?" I said in a teasing tone.

He blushed even more brightly but smiled back, delighted.

"Well, of course I think of you. After all, we're cousins by marriage, aren't we?"

The way he faltered on the word "marriage" made me blush in turn.

This seemed to renew his confidence. "Do you ever think of marriage, Alix?"

It seemed such a sudden, even awkward, question, considering that we had only just met up again, and yet it wasn't.

I decided to banish all my shyness and just speak to him as I would a friend. That, in and of itself, was odd for me since I didn't really have any friends, if you didn't count Ernie and Nanny, but somehow I knew I had one in Nicky.

"Well, I've rather been obliged to think of marriage recently. Your grandmamma, that is Her Majesty Queen Victoria, thought that I might want to marry Cousin Eddy, and it seems he liked the idea too, so he –"

"I know. I mean, I heard," Nicky said quietly as he searched my eyes.

It took all my strength to hold his gaze, but I did, and then I said, "Whatever you heard, as you can see I'm here and I didn't."

"I know and I'm so glad. You see, I ... well, I ... I mean to say that I've always rather hoped –"

Sergei chose that minute, of all times, to walk over to us and drop an avuncular hand on Nicky's shoulder. Then, beaming at the both of us, he said, "Well met, you two, I see. So nice for us all to be together again. Now, much as I'm one to encourage conversation between such fine young people, it seems to me that if we don't all get out onto the ice soon, the little ones will be most upset." He gestured towards Xenia and little Olga who seemed less anxious about having lunch and getting onto their skates than they were curious about Nicky and me, and when we glanced their way, both girls blushed, elbowed each other, and started to giggle.

Nicky giggled too in response, a rather high-pitched, girlish giggle, I thought, but then I immediately changed my mind and decided that Nicky, like my own Ernie, was simply filled with boyish spirits and that, underneath the handsome prince, there was still an impish little boy.

I felt my heart nearly turn over in my chest with tenderness.

That was the day I learned that Nicky called his younger sister Xenia by the pet name of "Chicken," and by the end of our delightful skating adventures I was calling her that too and she was calling me "Pell Mell" in honor of my somewhat determined skating which, for me, involved gritting my teeth, being launched forward by either Sergei or Nicky, and struggling to remain upright and in a forward position.

The next day, when Nicky, Xenia, Sergei, Ernie, Olga and I met again to go sledding on an ice hill that Sergei, angel that he was, had ordered his soldiers to construct for us the night before, Xenia started calling both Nicky and me "Pell Mell" for our dual misadventures on the sled, several of which ended, I blush to admit, with Nicky sprawled on top of me at the bottom of the hill.

Each time this happened he rose a fraction less hurriedly and then held out his gloved hand to assist me to my feet.

I allowed my hand to linger in his appreciably longer than necessary, too. It was all so sudden, this knowing, and yet it wasn't sudden at all. It had all begun years ago, when Russia, that land of dramatic seasons, had been in full summer, when a wee girlie met a boy on the cusp of manhood and all was known with a glance.

We were in love and all those around us could see it.

During those halcyon days, those winter days of adventure that were made summer by the growing warmth of our love, Nicky taught me about Russia. Over hot chocolate, and while stamping our feet outside by the fires to keep warm, I asked him if all the Russian peoples liked to skate and sled during the winter months, or were these activities confined to St. Petersburg?

He laughed and looked at me tenderly. "Sweet little Alix, of course such activities are for those of us who have to live in the cities. It's a way of amusing ourselves and getting some much-needed fresh air at the same time."

"But don't the people who live outside the cities like fresh air?" I said, gesturing at the laughing pair of Nicky's little sisters playing the fool on the ice. "Surely the children must enjoy the same activities in the winter, don't they?"

Nicky frowned, whether because he was uncertain of the answer or because he didn't like my question, I don't know. In any case, Sergei, who was standing nearby, answered for him.

"Alix, it is inevitably hard for a foreigner to understand the mentality of the Russian peasants, but they are not as we are. Their children prefer work to play, and in any case, they receive almost too much fresh air during the summer reaping season, so during the winter –"

Nicky interrupted him eagerly. "Yes, that's right, Alicky. It is as Sergei says, the peasants, you see, are almost always outside, while those of us stuck here are often forced to spend whole days inside, even in the summer. Poor Papa can almost never get away from his desk and we children are detained by our duties from dawn until dusk. So they don't really need to skate and things. Also, they don't have any skates!"

He and Sergei laughed spontaneously at this comment, which left me yet more confused. Nicky, seeing this, reached out as if to touch me, and realizing that we were not alone, pulled his hand back, reddening and glancing nervously at Sergei to see if his indiscretion had been observed.

If Sergei had noticed, he chose to ignore it. Instead he put a friendly hand on both my and Nicky's shoulders to draw us all together in one intimate circle, then smiled kindly at me, and said, "What Nicky is trying to tell you, Alix dear, is that the peasants are not as we are, and while they may not have skates, it's because they don't need them. Their feet, you see ..."

"Their feet ...?" I asked, more puzzled than ever.

Nicky laughed. "Yes, their feet. Their feet are structured utterly differently from ours. You see, they won't even wear shoes, and who knows, maybe they skate on their bare feet up and down their frozen rivers all winter long, while pitying us poor creatures in our confining skates here in town."

I wasn't too well versed in girl and boy exchanges, except with Ernie, but I knew enough about men and their ways from Papa to know when not to continue with a line of conversation. So I laughed, too, and said that, unlike those of peasants apparently, my own feet were quite unused to the cold and I was longing to have the relief of warming them up again.

So the subject was closed for the time-being. Oddly, it was Nicky who raised it again two days later when he and Xenia called upon me unexpectedly and asked if they might take me for a sleigh ride.

Naturally we were not alone, though we were as nearly alone as we'd ever been, since only small Olga was with us, because darling Xenia had a cold and Ella, who would have leapt at the chance to spend time with Nicky, had been caught all unawares and was tied up with company.

She looked terribly annoyed to be missing out and I'll guiltily admit that I found her resentment gratifying. I knew she wished that she could say that our ride "wasn't on," that we were insufficiently chaperoned to satisfy society's sense of decency, but should that have been agreed upon, not one but two imperial children would have had their treat called off and in the end she had no option but to acquiesce.

Thus it was that I found myself in a very small, brightly-painted sled drawn by two black horses and a red-jacketed Cossack. The sled had only been designed to accommodate two people, and there were three of us, including Olga, so I had no alternative but to press up against Nicky in a way that would have been utterly scandalous were it not for the presence of the excited little girl seated to my left. As it was we still drew a great deal of attention as we rode swiftly down St. Petersburg's own Vanity Fair, the Nevsky Prospekt, our bells jangling merrily.

Nicky, born as the heir to all of Russia, seemed hardly to notice the swiveled heads and nudges of the occupants of the other sleighs, and Olga proved equally unselfconscious, making us even more conspicuous by waving gaily and exclaiming happily at every familiar face that passed us. I felt myself to be on show, however, and I blushed horribly to be the object of such attention and, no doubt, gossip.

But I was with Nicky, and the sun was shining on the golden filigree of the palaces that lined the Neva, and so, despite my anxiety at the unwonted attentions of strangers, I was happy to be there, and he was too, and unlike me, he was also relaxed. I think that is what made him decide to reveal, nay to entrust me, with such a personal revelation.

Before he began to speak, he glanced at Olga to make sure that she was otherwise distracted, and once he was reassured of this, he twisted on the bench to gaze into my eyes. Our faces were so close that our breaths, visible in the frosty air, mingled and became one.

This intimacy caused my blush to deepen, but if Nicky noticed this, he did not say that he did, and in an uncharacteristically solemn voice he said, "Alix, Pelly, I … I want to tell you something, something I think you should know about me, about my family. You see, I …" He trailed off and the pained look on his face nearly broke my heart.

I feared that he was about to tell me that he had become engaged, so in a colder voice than I had ever employed with him before, I said, "Oh Nicky, it really isn't necessary. What possible business of mine could the private affairs of your family be?" At this remark he

112

looked so wounded that I gasped and said quickly, "Oh no, don't look like that. I didn't mean ... I mean, I only thought ..." At his continued look of pained confusion, I looked down and finished in a whisper, "I only thought that ... well, that you wished to tell me that your parents had found a worthy bride for you and that—"

His face changed in an instant and became as bright as the golden spire above Peter and Paul's Cathedral, glistening against the early afternoon sunshine.

Boldly, he reached out to me and tilted my face to his, and smiling into my by then tear-filled eyes, said, "A worthy bride, Alicky?" When I didn't answer, he seemed to grow in stature and breadth, and with more confidence than I had ever heard from him, continued, "You ... you thought I wanted to tell you that I was going to marry someone ... I mean anyone, anyone in the world besides ... Oh Sunny!"

We were both too moved by the subsequent realization to look at each other or speak, and when I finally did work up the courage to look at him again, I saw tears in his eyes.

Throwing all caution to the wind, I timidly reached out my gloved hands towards his. He was quite startled by my boldness, I could tell, but nevertheless he eagerly grasped my hands in both of his, and holding onto them tightly, collected himself enough to respond.

"Oh Sunny, Alicky, my own ... no, I daren't call you that, dare I? But one day ... well, I mean of course Papa and Mama ... and oh, I'm making such a muddle of this. I always do when I try to say something important. It happens every time. Why, Papa thinks I'm not very bright, and it's all because I think and feel things so

113

deeply, and then, when I try to say them out loud, all the words come out wrong, and then ..."

He broke off in midsentence, which made me feel that I had acquired the maturity of a woman twice my years, which was very endearing.

I smiled. Nicky's sweetness could always do that to me. Right from the beginning, his angelic and hesitant ways would raise my own confidence and give us a sense of solidarity.

"Nicky, Pelly Two, forgive me, I don't ... well, I'm not so very good at always remembering to think first before I speak. My emotions rule my tongue at times, and of course your papa is very wise, but maybe this time he is not right, for I think that nothing you say comes out wrong. Please will you, can you, impart to me now what it was that you wished to tell me?"

Holding onto my hands so tightly that it was painful for me – although I did not let him see that he was hurting me – he told me this remorseful little tale.

"Alicky, I'll never be able to thank you enough or to show you what your faith in me means, not if I live to be a hundred, but you see that's what I wanted, no needed, to tell you. You see, we Romanovs don't generally live to be a hundred, or even forty, sometimes."

I smiled at him in what I hoped was both a tender and a teasing way. "Well, Nicky, only God can know how long or short our lives will be, and we cannot ask him such questions. Anyway, forty years seems a very great age to me."

He smiled sadly. "Oh Sunny, I agree, of course we must at all times resign ourselves to God's will, and I

114

maybe more than others, as, you see, I was born on the day of Job, but that isn't really what I meant. I mean, yes, God decides these things, but sometimes in Russia so do the anarchists. We can never imagine that God wishes any soul to come to him by means of violence, but in my family ..."

"In your family ...?" I prompted him gently.

"Yes, well, you see ... in my family ... often ... we, I mean the Tsar ... I mean my very own dearest grandpapa ... was blown to pieces almost right in front of me by anarchists. I saw him die, Alix, I saw him die in agony, and surely that was not God's will, but the will of the anarchists who hunt my family, hunt us like animals. Papa says so. It's why we have to live as we do, almost as prisoners, and I want ... I want ..."

"You want ...?"

All in a rush and speaking so loudly that even Olga's attention was caught, he said, "I want you to be my wife, Alix of Hesse. I want to marry you and to live with you, and to ... oh, forgive me, I can't speak of any of this until I request permission from Papa and Mama, and of course you might not want to ... and that's why I had to tell you about Grandpapa, because even if .... Oh, if my dearest heart's desire were to come true and you did want to, then dare I ask you for your hand because it might not even be safe for you, and I could never bear a single thing to happen to you? I mean, even if you did want to ... and you probably don't ..."

He was almost panting, a state that provoked Olga to gape at him comically and say, "Nicky, have you gone mad? You can't just ask her like that, and in a sleigh, too. What's wrong with you? Poor Alicky, she must be so embarrassed. Just ignore him, will you, Alicky?"

I smiled at her, somewhat glad of the distraction.

Nicky, however, scowled.

"Olga, you must never interrupt grownups and you must never, ever listen in on adult conversations. I have half a mind to report your behavior to Mama."

Whereupon she stuck out her tongue and said, "Go ahead and tell her, see if I care. I've a whole mind to tell Papa what you just said. I bet he won't scold me for interrupting grownup talk, not that you are a grownup anyway, so there!"

I took this opportunity to gather my wits, retrieve my hands from Nicky's, grin at Olga, tell her how naughty she was, and tickle her until she admitted that yes, yes, Nicky and I were the most grown up grownups she'd ever known, then, while she was laughing too loudly to hear me, I whispered to Nicky, "I do want to."

Oh, the look in his eyes, in fact the look of the whole world, for at that moment no place had ever been as beautiful, nay as perfect, as St. Petersburg was at that hour on that day.

Nicky ordered the sleigh on the instant to turn back towards Ella's house, whispering to me under Olga's protests that he must return to the Anichkov Palace, where his parents were staying, without delay in order to consult his papa and mama on this issue as early as possible, professing that he wished he could make the sled fly so as to make it travel faster. Then, naughty boy that he was, he grinned and suggested that maybe that was not the solution: perhaps we should rather continue sweeping through the world in our little sled forever.

Oh the joy of that ride! Oh the terrible suspense of the next few days! For, you see, I could not disclose what had transpired between us to anyone alive except Nanny, at least not until he did, or not until his parents gave their consent and made an announcement.

For three days following our ride, nothing was said at all – not a word came from the palace, and worse, not a word came from Nicky either.

Ella was all sympathy.

"Poor Alicky, you don't look well. Do you think perhaps ...?"

"I don't know what you are referring to, Ella dearest, and I'm sure I look quite well. I certainly feel quite well."

"Oh, do you, darling? I am mistaken then. I thought perhaps you had caught a chill during your ride. So many people who chanced to see you that day have mentioned to me that you looked terribly flushed."

"I suppose one might look somewhat flushed, Ella, when outside in an open sleigh, but, no, I assure you that I've never felt better. Thank you for worrying about me, dearest, but it's quite unnecessary."

"Oh well, then. Delightful. In that case you won't mind accompanying your poor old sister on some calls, then, will you? I'm terribly behind and people will think me the rudest thing. And then, too, of course, they so enjoy spending time with you, darling, or would do if only you weren't so terribly shy. But no matter. Shall we go now?"

And go we did, to Aunty Miechen – or as the world knew her, Grand Duchess Maria Pavlovna – and seemingly to every grand duchess and countess ... countesses who were only that and not at all grand. At last, after an eternity seemed to pass, on the third day Ella took us to call upon "dearest Minnie," the Empress, and it was there that I believed I finally understood Nicky's absence.

The Empress's drawing room was, as usual, overcrowded with her ladies, the innumerable simpering members of her family – my sister included – and the rest of the court. It was overcrowded, over-heated and over-bejeweled, and in addition the cloud of so many heavy perfumes mingling all in one room – some, I fear, from the gentlemen gathered there – made me feel quite giddy, my nerves and apprehension having already been stretched as far as they could possibly go.

Worse, the Empress, who usually either ignored my presence or pretended to have forgotten my name when she did see me – "Alice, is it?" – seemed that day to be staring directly at me. She even grandly ordered two princesses of her court to vacate their seats so that "darling Ella and little oh ... yes, little Alix ... that's it!" might join her.

Ella was, of course, delighted and practically dragged me across that scrimmage of a drawing room, nearly feverish at the opportunity to sit beside the mighty Empress and discuss such weighty subjects as who had worn what the day before during calls, and wasn't the weather quite nice for December, and "Oh Minnie, dearest, your hairstyle is particularly becoming today. I do so like that ..."

For her part, the Empress chose to ignore Ella's inane chatter, electing to address me instead with a seeming *non sequitur*.

"Do you dance, my dear?"

I thought I detected a conspiratorial spark of mischief in her brown eyes and I suspected that she was trying to imply something or to ask questions to test me, but that since we were surrounded by others, she was reduced to speaking in some sort of code.

I didn't like to dance at all, as it happened, for it made my legs ache and I always felt terribly conspicuous. I wanted to say as much to the Empress, to "Minnie" as she had asked me to call her, but I didn't because I had a sudden intuition that the word 'dance' was standing in for something else, something more like, 'Do you think you'd like to dance with Nicky and to continue to do so for the rest of your life?'

My understanding of this encouraged me to assure her that, yes, I adored dancing and boldly I pressed her small hand confidingly in order to emphasize my whole-hearted feelings for Nicky.

The Empress drew back and glanced over at Ella inquiringly.

Ella, who was not in on the secret of what had passed between Nicky and me, tortured me on the ride home by asking in a most irritating way, "Alicky, what in the name of heaven got into you back there? You *adore* dancing? Since when? Why, even poor Papa – and you know he is such an angel about everything – has spoken to me of his despair at the reports of your dancing master, and Ernie says he dreads having to dance with you because you are terribly likely to cripple him by stepping on his feet. And worst of all, did I see you press Minnie's hand? Good Lord, Alix, what is wrong with you? Have you taken leave of your senses this morning?"

I didn't rise to her bait; I felt no need to. I knew something that she didn't know and indeed would not, if I had my way for once, until the rest of the world did, but as always with Ella, she had managed to wrest my small moment of triumph from me.

"It was really embarrassing for me, Alix. I mean, didn't you see ... couldn't you tell ... that the Empress was simply trying to be polite and to make you feel at ease?"

Annoyed beyond endurance at her obtuseness, I snapped back. "No, Ella darling, I really couldn't see that, since I don't recollect the Empress – or Minnie, as she has asked me to call her too – inquiring of any other lady in her entourage as to whether or not she is partial to dancing. In fact –"

"Yes, well, there you see, Alix, *in fact* exactly. That simply shows how kind Her Majesty was being to you because she probably realized that you were the only girl there who did not already know that their highnesses are having a ball tomorrow night and she wished to include you in the conversation, which simply shows her facility for society, because it must by now be obvious, even to one of her elevated nature, that making small talk with you is something of a struggle."

I was thrown into confusion again. *A ball? Tomorrow night?* Nicky hadn't even sent me a note and everyone else knew about it already? Shouldn't I have been informed about a ball to announce my engagement before the rest of St. Petersburg heard about it, and moreover, what was Ella talking about when she referred to my lack of conversational *finesse*?

I stared at Ella in puzzled hurt and, as sometimes happens when I feel that I haven't understood something, my head began to pound.

When she saw me wince and put my hand to my head, her own expression changed to one of sympathy and she reached out and patted my knee lightly.

"Oh, Alicky, are you having another one of your headaches, darling? I'm so sorry. I shouldn't have spoken so frankly to you. Sometimes I forget how very young you are. It's just, you see, dearest, the Empress's approval of everything is so important to the Tsar. Tsar Sasha can be a bit difficult, even with his own family, his own brothers. And Sergei, he does so rely on me to maintain good relations with Minnie because that means Sasha is happy too. And, well, you know, Sergei might be chosen as the next Governor-General of Moscow soon, and while I suppose that nothing a silly girl like me does can have any significant impact either way, I feel that I should at least try to please their majesties, and so when my own younger sister acts inappropriately in the Empress's presence, I worry. But forgive me all the same. None of this can possibly concern you, darling. Here, let's talk about what we'll wear tomorrow night, shall we?"

I didn't want to talk about that with her; I wanted to ask her – no, I wanted to confide in her – because suddenly I was desperate to tell Ella what had happened between Nicky and me, and what he was planning to do about it. Only, maybe I had misunderstood it all, but if that were true, then ... No, I couldn't bear to tell her after all, but I did still want to know what she meant when she said it was a struggle to have to converse with me.

That is what I wanted to discuss with her, but what actually came out was, "Why don't you have any children, Ella? Why is it only you and Sergei after all this time? Is it you? Is something wrong with you?"

Oh the horror of that moment, the look on her face.

"Ella, Ella, no, don't look at me like that. I didn't mean to ask you that. I don't know why I did. My headache ... I ..."

I proceeded to burst into noisy sobs but she did not reach out to comfort me; indeed she didn't utter a word. She looked like a woman fashioned from ice and snow, and her terrible, cold, silent anger froze me even more than the winter weather outside ever could have.

The ride from the imperial family's winter palace, Anichkov, to Ella's own Belosselsky Belozersky Palace could not have been more than two miles, but by the time we arrived back I was as chilled and as stiff as if I had staggered there all the way from Siberia. Despite my frantic apologies, Ella did not address another word to me, not in the carriage, not when the footman helped us out, and not when we entered the foyer as she swept upstairs without a single backwards glance, leaving me shivering and alone in the entrance to her vast palace.

It was, oddly, Sergei, an hour later, who helped me. I was realizing more and more, despite Sergei's aloof appearance and the persistent rumors of his propensity to be harsh with people, that he really was quite sensitive to the suffering of others, possibly because he himself suffered a great deal. He was always good to me, but although I felt we became very close, I never did learn what it was that lay beneath his pride and caused such anger and torment to rise up inside him and flash into his eyes.

But that day, as I nervously entered the drawing room for tea, anticipating I did not know what from Ella, he was there alone and his blue eyes shone only with kindness

I glanced around, surprised.

"Sergei, forgive me, am I early or late? Did Ella decide to serve tea upstairs? Where is everybody?"

He smiled at me. "It's just you and me today, dear Alicky. Your papa and Ernie have been invited to tea at Anichkov with Sasha and Minnie, and the children and Ella … Well, Ella is feeling somewhat unwell and is resting. You may see her later at dinner, or not. It depends, I suppose."

"On whether she's feeling better?" I inquired somewhat disingenuously, for once again I was filled with too many questions and emotions to be able to sort them out quickly. Why had Papa and Ernie been invited to tea with Nicky and his family and not me? I had just been over there too and not a word had been mentioned about my own family having tea with the Empress later. Was this a good thing? Did the Tsar – "Sasha" – wish to speak to Papa?

More immediately, though, I was concerned about the imposition of this strange *tête-à-tête* with Sergei. He

123

and I had never been alone together before. Had Ella told him what I had said in the carriage?

Sergei obviously understood what I was thinking, for he gestured to the two chairs drawn up before the small tea table. "Here, come sit with me. I'm parched myself. I was out all morning with my regiment and a fellow does grow anxious for his tea. You must be ready for yours, too, aren't you, Alicky dear?"

I did as he asked, for in truth I was both terribly hungry and terribly thirsty. I let Sergei pour for us both, something he did with a wonderful delicacy that is unusual for a man, and after he had filled his own cup and eaten a biscuit, he smiled gently at me.

"I imagine you know why I asked to be alone with you this afternoon, Alix."

As there were a few different reasons why he might have chosen to do so, I was not being dishonest when I simply shook my head, indicating that I had no idea why we were here alone together.

He sighed and looked at me with what might have been disappointment, or maybe not, one could never really guess what Sergei thought on any subject. Unlike my dearest, my most darling Nicky, Sergei was an opaque man at the best of times.

"I see. Well, Ella spoke to me ..." At the look on my face he quickly continued. "Oh no, you mustn't think that she wished to tell me about what happened, Alix. It is only that my wife is so open and innocent, and of course we are the most united of couples, so I could see at once that something had upset her badly. I had to work quite hard to prise it out of her."

I was entirely unruffled by this statement. In fact, I found that the thought of Ella being the one who was upset for a change made me feel rather good about myself. After all, wasn't she forever prodding and poking at me, and endlessly, endlessly, "advising me for my own good"?

I nodded at Sergei, helped myself to a second biscuit, and after swallowing it, said, "Oh yes, I'm delighted that you two are so close. My, these biscuits are awfully good, aren't they? I know I'm simply terrible but may I have a third one? Aren't you eating anymore, Sergei dear?"

"Alix," he began reproachfully, "Alix my dear child, you must be aware that your question could only have been terribly upsetting to Ella and that –"

"Oh well, Sergei, I wouldn't worry too much about that, if I were you. Sisters can fight. We do it very well, in fact. Why, if I ate a biscuit for every time that one of Ella's questions upset me, I'd be the size of an elephant. It would be better to overlook our little exchange by considering it a storm in a teacup, as it were."

I finished my statement by raising my teacup to him and smiling quite cheerfully into his surprised face. I was feeling rather triumphant and grown up at that moment, and proud of myself for boldly taking the initiative, but Sergei was obviously considerably dismayed at my lack of remorse and said as much.

"I don't understand you, Alix. Are you unhappy here with Ella and me? We thought that you would enjoy your visit with us. In fact it was Ella's idea. She was so concerned about you after hearing how disappointed dear Queen Victoria was with you when you rejected Eddy's proposal, and she thought that –"

Detecting a not-so-veiled threat in Sergei's words, I interjected quickly, "Sergei, dear Sergei, please don't say such things. Of course I'm happy here and I adore Ella, and when I see her later I'll apologize again. I'm sorry if I've distressed either of you. It was quite silly of me."

His eyes narrowed and he gazed back at me in what I can only describe as a calculating manner. My appetite vanished, and despite my mouth suddenly becoming dry, I set my cup down rather shakily.

"I see. Just a silly little girl's mistake, then. All very well, Alix, but you aren't a little girl anymore, are you? No, you're quite a young lady now and a very beautiful one. I'm certain that you're aware that I'm not the only member of my family who has noticed this."

"I don't quite understand what you mean, Sergei."

"Don't you? Why, I thought that even in your innocence you might have gathered that our Nicky was somewhat ... oh, dare I say 'enchanted' ... with you, as are we all, Alix, as are we all."

I felt myself reddening and I looked down, away from his assessing eyes. He made me feel almost sullied with his expression. Otherwise I remained silent, afraid of what either of us might say. At that moment it seemed as though anything could be said and that none of it would end well.

He spoke first.

"Forgive me, Alicky dear, I thought that since you chose to question my wife regarding matters matrimonial, matters that I might have considered previously to be of no interest to a young unmarried girl, that you did so because you had begun possibly to think of your own future and were seeking sisterly guidance from my Ella. If I'm wrong and you meant merely to pry into our personal life out of some sort of prurient curiosity, then do forgive me for any misunderstanding on my part."

"Sergei, please," I raised my hand in defense, "I ... your words ... questions ... I feel I am being placed under attack, and no, I did not mean to be, as you unkindly say, prurient. I'll admit, if I may, that Ella sometimes angers me, with or without cause. As to my own matrimonial prospects, well I have none, so possibly we should draw a line under all of it and you and Ella can merely view me as the queer spinster relative whom you've kindly invited for a visit."

By the end of my little speech I felt hot tears of anger and humiliation running down my face. I swiped at them angrily and began to rise. I would retreat to Papa's room and wait for him, and when he returned I would insist that he take me home to Darmstadt that instant.

Sergei rose with me and then did the oddest thing. He bowed to me.

I could only stare at him aghast, torn between my desire to flee the overheated room, the palace, the whole mad hatter's tea party of a country – no matter whom I had to leave behind – and curiosity.

The latter stayed my flight for a moment and it was long enough.

"Don't go Alix, beautiful Alix, queen of all you survey, or you should be. Don't you know that Ella's a fool and Sasha's a fool and Minnie's a fool and a virago, and I, who am not a fool, suffer for all of it. You're not a fool either. Don't let an accident of birth make you one."

It's so odd how clearly that scene comes back to me now. If I close my eyes I can hear the fire crackling in the porcelain stove and smell the stewed tea in the samovar. I can see Sergei's handsome face, full of strained ambition and anger, staring at me. I do not know if I have ever before or since experienced such a moment of perfect understanding with another human being.

I knew him then, and he, Grand Duke Sergei, the younger brother of the Tsar, the handsome one, the brilliant one, allowed me to glimpse for an instant his whole thwarted, wasted existence, but there was no true way to return such a confidence and I could only show my understanding and acceptance by sitting down again and doing what has never come easily to me.

"Fools, Sergei?"

He sat down too and poured us each a cup of scorched tea. It tasted perfect in that setting.

"Yes, fools. Your sister, in case you haven't noticed, though I rather assume you have, is an empty-headed, self-absorbed creature who hasn't a single thought inside that pretty head of hers beyond how best to display herself and to gain acceptance and admiration from those she looks up to. And she only looks up to those who are more powerful than her. Everyone else is valueless. If we were to have children, I'm sure they'd be treated badly, children being abysmal impediments to the gaining of social approbation."

"Oh you're awful, Sergei. And your brother?"

We smiled at each other delightedly.

"Sasha would have made an excellent bear. He even looks the part, don't you think?"

I looked around nervously to make certain that neither Ella nor a servant had surreptitiously entered the room, and then seeing no one else, nodded and grinned at my newly dear brother-in-law.

Encouraged by my admiration, Sergei stood up, extended his arms, and made growling noises as he lumbered about the drawing room, going so far as to swipe bear-like at one of Ella's hideous wax flower arrangements.

At my giggles he returned to his seat and spoke seriously. "Yes, Sasha, our mighty autocrat, his Imperial Majesty Tsar Alexander III, wasn't meant to be the Tsar, you know. Did you hear about my oldest brother, Nicholas?"

I nodded. Everyone knew the tragic story of the young and handsome Tsarevich Nicholas who had died so tragically before attaining manhood.

"Then you know that Minnie, our mighty mouse of an Empress, was once Nicholas's fiancée, and yet now, of course, she loves only Sasha, the man who is Emperor. Why, it is as though Nicholas never existed. Funny the stature a crown gives a man, isn't it, Alicky?"

"Not every man needs a crown to have stature in a girl's eyes, Sergei." I said, blushing furiously.

He laughed.

"I know you are not referring to me, young one, for I have plenty of stature," he indicated his great height, "but no crown. No, I think our little Alicky is referring to a younger, shorter fellow. So tell me, for it is time for you to speak frankly as well, do you love him?"

It was too hard. I had never said it aloud, not even to Nicky, but I wanted to. I was desperate to tell someone, and here he was, my newest friend, maybe the only friend I had ever had, so I replied simply, "Yes, yes, I do love him. I love him quite terribly."

Sergei was unmoved.

"Is it him you love, Alix, or the crown he'll someday wear, the crown he could give you to wear?"

"What a terrible question. How dare you? And I thought … I thought you wished us to be friends and to be kind to me."

"Oh, I do, and maybe you don't know, can't know, the answer to that question yourself. It is probably unknowable in any case. Who can say? For all I know, maybe Minnie truly believes she loves Sasha."

"Is that why you think she is a virago, Sergei, because you think she only believes she loves her husband?"

"No, wise little owl Alicky, I think Minnie is a virago because she is one, as you will see for yourself. She doesn't like you and she doesn't want you. She would prefer someone like her own daughters who can't even stand up or sit down without asking permission from their mama first. Actually, your own beloved is not so far different, or is that why you love him and not the crown?"

I chose not to take offense. "I don't think so. I think he is simply the dearest person I've ever met. But how can one separate such things anyway? If Nicky weren't the Tsarevich, he would be different and not Nicky at all. So, in the end, what does it matter? As for the Empress, why do say she doesn't like me?"

"She sees power in you, Alix. You are self-willed and won't be led, but you could lead. Two such women cannot occupy only one throne."

"Well, we wouldn't occupy only one thrown, would we? I mean, of course I hope the Emperor lives forever, but if he doesn't, there would only be one Empress, the one married to Nicky."

Just then Ella appeared. She looked terribly pale, and when she saw Sergei and me alone together, her lips compressed thinly.

I started at her nervously but Sergei merely smiled sardonically.

"Ah, welcome, my dear. I didn't expect to see you so soon. Your headache is better, then?"

Ella looked at us coldly and poured herself a cup of tea from the samovar. Raising it to her lips, she sniffed at it suspiciously.

"Why, this is burned. It's horrid. Why didn't you call for some fresh tea, Sergei. You know I can't bear it when it is spoiled."

"I apologize, my dear, but I was not expecting you and I suppose I didn't notice. Alix and I have been having such a delightful conversation."

"What sort of delightful conversation?"

Sergei yawned, stretched, then rose to his feet.

"Oh, Alix was telling me about her dress for tomorrow evening. You know how I enjoy a good recitation on fashion, darling. But here, I return to you your sister, and I'm sure you will have a great deal to add regarding hairstyles and furbelows, and I find I really must attend to some papers, so I'll leave you two delightful girls to your plans."

I rose too.

"Oh, Ella dear, do forgive me, but I'm a little tired and I've drunk so much tea I couldn't face another drop. I'd adore talking more about my dress for tomorrow night, but your darling Sergei has been such a help that I've decided after all to wear my funny old white gown, the one I came out in. After all, I can't possibly hope to compare with you or any of the other magnificent St. Petersburg ladies, so I might as well appear as my own self, the country mouse. I'll see you at dinner, then, shall I? Oh, and Sergei, thank you so for keeping me company."

With that, before Ella could gather herself and before I could burst into laughter at the surreptitious wink that Sergei threw me, I swept as grandly as I could from the room. It occurred to me that, after all, I might not find life in Russian society as challenging as it appeared to be. All one needed was the good fortune to have one's true bosom friend at one's side, and for the rest, the trick was clearly never to say anything of any consequence at all.

Chapter 8

It's really terribly difficult to explain one's actions when they do not turn out well. Human nature is supposed to protect us from our missteps, and so to the inevitable question of *'What were you thinking?'* the only answer that can be given to end such miserable interrogations is to say, 'I don't know' or 'I don't remember.'

That is, of course, what I said to Ella the morning after the ball when she confronted me, but it's not true: I do remember that evening – it is etched inside of me, for good and ill, because in so many ways that night was to define Nicky and my story altogether.

We should have, well *he* should have ... it wasn't me, not then, not ever, who created problems for us, or, as I should better say, who let others create problems for us. No, that was Nicky, always Nicky. If only he had defended me that first important evening, the night they began to hate and judge me, it could have all ended so differently.

I remember clearly walking, nearly on air it seemed, down the staircase at the Belosselsky Belozersky Palace to meet Sergei's outstretched arm and to smile inwardly at Ella's disapproving expression.

They spoke simultaneously.

Sergei said, "Alix, you look like an angel."

Ella said, "Oh good heavens, Alicky, I can't believe that you are really wearing that dress. Why didn't you ask to borrow something of mine?"

I thanked Sergei and smiled sweetly at Ella.

"Ella darling, I can't remember you offering me a gown for tonight, and anyway, I distinctly remember you telling me you simply loved this dress when you came for my coming out ball."

Sergei sighed, already impatient with our exchange.

"My dears, fascinating as this discourse is, we cannot arrive after the Emperor and Empress, and so I'm afraid, all sartorial matters aside, we must leave now."

Ella and I followed him silently to the carriage. I, for my part, was determined not to enter into an exchange with my sister that would dampen all our spirits, but Ella was not of like mind, and as soon as we were seated, she resumed her criticism of my attire.

"Alix, dearest, I certainly did not mean to imply that you aren't utterly charming in your little dress, one that is wholly appropriate for a small dance in Darmstadt, but you must at some point begin to see that here life is different. St. Petersburg society holds to certain standards, and while your simplicity and innocence are, of course, too sweet for words, I feel that, as your sister, I should point out to you that others, and by 'others' I refer to Minnie in particular ... well, they might feel somewhat slighted by your lack of effort, you see?"

I looked down and fingered my little white muslin gown which had, an hour ago, seemed so right for me – so young and, yes, even bridal in nature – and fought back tears.

Once again Sergei, who I now felt I had always misjudged, came to my rescue.

"Ella, you are behaving perfectly atrociously. Alix looks exquisite. I fear, my dear, you are more concerned with how stiff, and might I say even matronly and

overdone, you and the other ladies will look beside her."
He yawned elaborately, ignoring Ella's look of horror
and her own incipient tears. "I've always found
something rather sad in a woman who, staring into the
abyss of approaching middle-age, attempts to cover it all
in jewelry and velvet as if painting over cracks. It never
really works, don't you agree, Alicky?" Before I could
answer, he continued his soliloquy. "Oh, forgive me, my
little Alicky. What a ridiculous question to ask someone
so young and fresh. You couldn't have the least idea of
that of which I am speaking. What do you think, my
dear?"

He turned solicitously to Ella, and ignoring her tears,
waited for her to answer with an attentive expression.

It was most odd because, until Sergei said that, I had
been inwardly admiring, and possibly envying just a bit,
Ella's magnificent dark-red velvet gown, set off by the
resplendent rubies she was positively dripping in. But
seeing her through Sergei's eyes, as I did then, I had to
agree that she was looking every day of her twenty-nine
years and that the color she had selected made her look
somewhat drawn.

Ella's eyes sharply met mine and I caught malice in
her expression. Towards Sergei, however, she merely
ducked her head and delicately dabbed at her eyes,
speaking brokenly.

"I ... I apologize, Alix, I meant no harm, and Sergei
darling, I'm shocked that you would assume otherwise."

Sergei smiled and reached over and patted her knee.

"Yes, of course, my dear, you meant no harm, but
then one might wonder at your eleventh-hour concern
for young Alicky here since you didn't apparently offer

her any alternative attire. Ah well, no matter. It appears that we are here. Shall we, ladies …?"

The coachman opened the door, Sergei alighted and held out an arm each for Ella and me, and the evening moved forward.

The Winter Palace was ablaze with light from a thousand windows and countless chandeliers. The lights were so bright that they lit up the ice-darkened Neva to create a defiantly festive atmosphere.

I absentmindedly noticed the hundreds of scarf-shrouded peasants milling around, hoping, I imagine, to enjoy the sight of all the grand carriages and beautifully dressed guests, and if they should be so lucky, to observe some of the dancing as well from their distant vantage points. It was terribly cold but Sergei, repeating Nicky's words to me of a few days previously, assured me that they did not feel the cold the same way as I did, and that, later, leftovers from the ball would be distributed amongst them, as the Emperor insisted upon the practice under the guise of being "the father of his people."

Once inside it was as though winter had been banished by royal decree. The lights blazed and the air was perfumed with the scent of a thousand roses, and I noted, to my delight, that dozens of live orange trees in ceramic pots had been placed around the ballroom to create the illusion of a summer garden. Champagne flowed from crystal fountains and gorgeously clad footmen clustered around us to take our wraps, to offer us canapés and refreshments, and to bow ceaselessly, the music emanating from the orchestra making even their movements seem like dancing.

I breathed in the sweet warm air and cast a covert glance over Ella's shoulder to see where Nicky was. I was expecting him to have been watching for our arrival, for I knew what this ball was, but Nicky was not amongst those who came to greet us, or to greet Sergei and Ella, and those who did so barely spoke to me. I attracted a few nods and raised eyebrows, but no one addressed me directly.

I felt the confidence that Sergei's words in the carriage had given me drain away and I shivered in spite of the heat.

Then we were moving through a series of grand white and gold rooms where the gold was matched with lapis and jade, and I paid attention to none of it because I was waiting for Nicky as my eyes became blinded with tears yet again.

He didn't come, and he didn't come, and I had to walk through all of those endless rooms filled with cold-eyed, terrible people, the men smiling faintly at me, the women not at all. And the Empress, who was leading the dance with her husband's prime minister, swept by me in a quadrille and threw me the same disdainful look as did all the others.

Suddenly I could see myself through their eyes. My legs became sore, sweat broke out on my forehead, and I had to struggle for breath. I felt as though I might die. Never before had such a terrible feeling come over me. Then it was as though I had left my poor struggling body and was floating up against the high painted ceiling and looking down on myself.

There I was, a tall, awkward girl in a cheap white dress, standing stiffly out in that blazing, opulent room like a tacky potted palm imported from a middle-class home to adorn a state banquet. The stunning gowns and jewels of the women and the braided gold of the men did not make them look aged and overdone: it made them look as though they belonged there. Everyone in that crowded room belonged there, except me. I would have been better off outside amongst the frozen, waiting peasants, where I might have been complimented for being pretty. I was nothing more than a sad, rather peculiar object of pity and scorn.

And then ...

"You are here! I've been looking everywhere for you. Oh Alix, oh my Sunny, you look so beautiful. How could I not have seen you right away?"

Nicky!

I came out of my fevered dream and all my strength returned to me when I saw his glowing blue eyes and ecstatic smile. What a fool I was, what fools everyone was. Now all would see us together and they would never look at me critically again.

Nicky was speaking excitedly. "I spoke to Mama and Papa right after we talked, and they –"

"What did they say?"

Nicky laughed. "Well, they didn't say anything at all, they never do about important things. Not when they are asked, of course, and –"

"What do you mean, Nicky? Why didn't they say anything? Didn't you ask them again?"

Why wouldn't they discuss it? I did not understand. Wasn't Nicky the heir? Wasn't this the only subject that could possibly be of any importance to them?

Nicky looked a bit abashed and his face fell into sulky lines.

"Well, Alix, that is how it has always been about everything. We children find a good time to mention something to Mama and Papa, or sometimes just to Mama if Papa's too busy, and then we wait. They don't like to have a thing brought up again." His face cleared and he laughed. "In fact, when I wanted a new horseless carriage – it's really the most cunning thing, it's called a Cugnot and I saw one at the exposition, it was a corker, you should have seen it – anyway I asked Mama and Papa and they didn't say a word to me. So I waited, you know, as a lad does, but didn't hear anything. So I couldn't bear it any longer and I brought it up again, and they got quite annoyed with me and said that since I'd pushed for it, I wouldn't be able to have it at all. I was deuced upset. Another time, when Xenia wanted, oh I forget what, some gewgaw –"

I cut him off rather angrily, I fear.

"Nicky, I really can't see how our engagement compares to a car or a gewgaw, or anything else at all! You're the Tsarevich, the heir, you can't just let them treat you like a child asking for a treat. I would never let my own papa treat me so and I'm no one of importance at all."

I must have become very flushed as Nicky smiled lovingly at me. "Of course you're important. You're the most important person in the world, you must know that. Now let's not quarrel about silly things. I want to dance with you and make all the other fellows jealous."

With that, and without addressing a word of what I had said, he swept me off into a brisk polonaise which

139

immediately made my legs feel crampy and caused my feet to swell uncomfortably in my shoes. I would have been able to overcome these afflictions and simply lose myself in being with Nicky, but I was upset that my questions had been dismissed so lightly. Nor had I liked him calling himself a child. He was, after all, twenty-one and that seemed quite grown up to me at seventeen.

Sadly, I should have relished it, because a moment later the imperial couple swept out onto the floor and approached us. Empress Minnie was glittering in dark-blue satin and diamonds and sapphires, while the Emperor appeared to be wearing a stained nightshirt that he had clumsily tucked into a pair of patched trousers.

Nicky's mother smiled at me briefly but her face was dazzling with love when she addressed her son.

"There you are, my darling boy. Your old mama has been looking everywhere for you. I was hoping that we might have one teeny dance before the night ends, and look, Papa can dance with your little friend."

Nicky was so obviously delighted at this maternal attention that he relinquished me to his father without a word and swept off with his mother in a lively quadrille that the orchestra switched to at a glance from the Empress. The poor Emperor, whom I noted seemed as miserable as I, wordlessly nodded at me and held out his enormous, not very clean hand. I curtsied and took it.

The dance ended abruptly when his gigantic boot came down heavily upon my own skippered foot, crushing it so painfully that I was unable to prevent myself from crying out in pain.

He merely grunted and said gruffly, "My apologies. I don't like these silly evenings of Minnie's. You'll be all right."

With that he left me horribly alone in the middle of the floor, watched by amused expressions as I limped painfully across the room to find Ella. Nicky, who must have seen it all happening, declined to leave his mother and come to my aid.

That evening still spins in my head. If I close my eyes now, I can feel the terrific heat of all those bodies pressed under the lights, swirling, staring, and as I later found out, tearing, tearing at my fragile hopes, as an animal will tear at the flesh of its prey.

"Too stiff."
"Too wooden."
"Cold eyes."
"Badly dressed."
"Can't speak French."
"Can't speak Russian."
"Strange, jerky motions when she bows her head."
"There's something wrong with her legs."
"There's something wrong with her face."
"She's wrong, wrong, wrong, wrong."

Ella passed on all these criticisms of me the following day, even as she assured me lovingly that these were the kinder things that had been said about me, because doubtless she had been shielded from the worst of the gossip, as, "How would they dare to say really unkind things to me about my own darling little sister?"

How indeed?

Nicky never came by again, merely sending me one cursory note, a note he had obviously scrawled in a hurry on his way to somewhere ... somewhere I wasn't.

Darling Alicky,

Mama and Papa have decided they absolutely must go to Livadia for Lent.

I have to go to. I'll write quite soon.

Best love,

Your Nicky.

I kept that piece of paper for years, I can't say why really, but I suppose I did so because I had to wonder whether this was really his 'best love' and whether he was indeed 'my Nicky.'

How could he have let it all happen, and by 'all' I mean nothing.

After the ball I was a mere hour counter: how many hours until we could go home to Darmstadt?

Papa and Ernie mercifully seemed as anxious to get home as I was but for their own reasons. Ernie complained ceaselessly that none of the fellows he had met were good fun at all, whatever that meant. Papa simply despised Russia. He didn't like the weather and considered the social climate to be dangerous. Papa was a most kind man and he always found the milling peasants on the Neva an uncomfortable sight. When

Sergei would tell him that they did not feel the cold and that they enjoyed nothing better than watching their betters at play, Papa would not argue, for that was not his way, but he simply became even quieter.

So it was no great struggle to convince both of them that it was best to return to Darmstadt before the Russian Orthodox season of Lent began. Dear Papa always did enjoy his food and I think that, more than my own obvious distress, precipitated our departure two days after that ill-fated night.

Chapter 9

And they all lived happily ever after...

If anyone should ever read this, they might think that I am being humorous. They might think, 'Oh she's trying to put her best face on things after her humiliations and rejections in Russia.' However, this would be to make assumptions, and making assumptions has never served anyone well.

In truth, I had long known that I was never really meant to marry. This is not to say that I had not fallen truly, deeply – even madly – in love with my poor darling Nicky, for I had, but it wasn't my right self, my truest self that did so. If that marriage had occurred, I would have been forced to bend and twist myself to fit into a life of grand, cold palaces filled with people who thought their own interests and accomplishments were the only ones worthy of attention and judged everyone else accordingly.

I like to think that each person can be of value in their own small way and I had been primarily raised, since the death of poor dear Mama, by darling Grandmamma who taught me the value of a well-run home, and it was in this arena that I like to believe I might have shone a little.

I did grieve, I did, for what might have been between Nicky and me, for a life unlived, for one that I had imagined on and off during the years of my girlhood – what young girl has not held such waking dreams? – yet, and this has been cruelly misrepresented by persons of ill-will towards me, I never loved Nicholas Romanov,

Tsar-Emperor of all the Russias, for his crown and for the subsequent glory it might bring, for hadn't I turned down Prince Eddy without a second thought, and if a crown had been my goal, then becoming the Queen of England would have neatly satisfied all the ambitions any young lady could imagine.

I had no such ambitions. What I had always wanted, I suppose, was to find in a mate the same level of love and comfort that I had in my dearest Papa and my brother Ernie, and I thought for a wee moment that I had found such a thing in Nicky, but it was all so obvious that to Nicky I would never be first, as I was with Papa, as I was with Ernie, so upon arriving back in Darmstadt I decided firmly to settle for enjoying my life with these two dear men who so loved me and, yes, who needed me too.

In fact I considered myself to have been terribly selfish in not having tried harder to become a better companion to poor Papa following the twin grief of losing Irene and then that disreputable woman he momentarily married, as I had come to realize that Papa had married that creature for no better reason than that he suffered terribly from the absence of amiable companionship, and who amongst us does not?

With Ernie that had never been an issue. We two had always been as different sides of the same coin, and if our every interest was not precisely the same, we understood each other so perfectly that it never mattered. We simply adored every moment we spent together, whatever the reason.

I usually rose later than Ernie and would have my maid Gretchen Von Fabrice bring me my coffee and chocolate, for I liked to drink both in the morning. And then, usually before I could even put on my wrapper, there would be my darling Ernie, peeping mischievously around the door.

"Oh thanks be to heaven you are finally awake, Alicky. I've the most marvelous thing to show you!"

It was almost always a picture he had discovered in a magazine of some sort of Art Nouveau room, or even just a piece of furniture he found fascinating. Ernie was so very creative and he was transported by all things Art Nouveau and dreamed of one day being able to recreate an Art Nouveau wonderland in the New Palace. Of course, Papa forbade even the contemplation of this for reasons of both economy and esthetics, as he, in contrast to Ernie, considered this sort of building and décor the very height of bad taste. I fear they often disagreed on this issue over dinner when I would find myself being torn between these two men I so loved.

Since Papa would not endorse Ernie's Art Nouveau visions, the poor boy was reduced to merely covering the walls of his rooms with pictures he had cut out of magazines. Wanting to please him, and enjoying painting in watercolors, I would often make up, in paper, little miniature cozy corners with the rounded sofas and chairs he loved so much, and then we would both hurry to his room and paste them on the walls. We always had such fun doing that.

In his turn, Ernie would sit or sleep for hours beside me in the music room while I played the piano, but of course I knew that none of this was lessening Papa's loneliness and so I resolved to become more attentive to his interests. It was a bit of a struggle at first as Papa had

147

by that time become so withdrawn that it was hard to know just what his interests were. Because I did not breakfast downstairs and Papa always took lunch elsewhere, either in his own rooms or in the company of old generals he had once soldiered with, I had to work quite hard to engage him.

Before I began my campaign to cheer up poor Papa, our dinners, I'll admit, were rather quiet affairs between just the three of us, and if any conversation should actually take place at all, it was usually of a somewhat unpleasant and strained nature. Papa liked to read his newspaper at dinner and often Ernie, in an attempt to engage him, would either try to show him one of the paper miniatures I had made him that day, or sometimes, to be amusing, he would come to dinner wearing one of dear Mama's old dresses, complete with curled wig, to make me laugh.

Poor Papa thoroughly disapproved of Ernie's antics and made his opinions known to us by periodically rattling his newspaper while otherwise remaining silent. Determined to change all this after our trip to Russia, I simply begged Papa to read his newspaper out loud to us during dinnertime. He brightened immediately, taking to doing so with much enthusiasm, and this became our nightly dinner ritual. This so pleased him, in fact, that he took to joining Ernie and me regularly for luncheon, when he would read out loud to us the British newspapers he so enjoyed. This in turn immediately generated new responsibilities for me because I had to begin ordering up new menus for luncheon, as before this development Ernie and I were content with letting cook serve us anything she liked, while Papa, of course, expected to be offered both a meat and a pudding course at luncheon. This led Papa to wish to invite some of his old generals to dinner, which meant that I had to oversee the seating and menus for these occasions as well, and before I knew it I was the busy hostess of a fair-sized ducal home.

It's true that I am, and always have been, shy, but I'm not at all reserved around those I know well and never around my own dear family, so I fancy that I rather held my own in conversations when we had the generals for company, making Papa visibly most proud of my accomplishments.

In every change, though, there are growing pains, and it must be admitted that my darling Ernie did not truly enjoy these luncheons and dinners, feeling, I think, somewhat constrained as, like Papa, none of these old soldiers knew, or wished to know, a thing about the Art Nouveau movement. Nor could Ernie wear Mama's gowns to amuse me, as he had previously.

Still, for my own part, I felt as though I was renewed and the days began to fly by as I was always terribly busy and in demand. If I wasn't helping Ernie with the decoration of his walls, I was consulting Mrs. Canon, our cook, over the luncheon and dinner menus, and I was always trying to find a minute to improve my rather limited wardrobe by sewing, as I was now required to dress each evening for dinner. And then Papa, who had, I must modestly say, never looked so well, began to accompany me to church each Sunday, which caused such delight as one can only imagine amongst the parishioners, given that he had been rather reclusive until that time.

I had nearly forgotten Nicky by the time spring came and brought with it a thick letter accompanied by yet another invitation from Ella and Sergei for us to visit them in Russia, an invitation Papa announced to us in a somewhat offhand manner over luncheon that rainy day in the April of 1990.

"I have had an interesting letter from your sister Ella. It seems that she and Sergei are preparing to decamp to their estate of Illinskoe in June and have asked all of us to summer there with them. For my own part I think I shall be obliged to decline their generous offer, but you children might like to go."

While I was astonished, Ernie was disdainful. "*Illinskoe?* I think not. Isn't that in the very middle of nowhere, Siberia possibly. What should I do there? Ella must be mad to think I should want to go. I don't hunt, for heaven's sake. I suppose she wants someone there to keep Sergei company while he goes out and kills things. Well, it won't be me, I can tell you that!"

He rounded off his declamation with a dismissive sniff.

Papa regarded him for a short while and then nodded somewhat sadly. "No, I don't suppose you would enjoy yourself much at Illinskoe, Ernest. For the record, I do not believe your brother-in-law Sergei does hunt, but then again I'm certain that whatever pursuits he does indulge in to amuse himself during the summer are not those you would wish to participate in yourself. Without having a map to hand, I somewhat doubt that Illinskoe is in Siberia, but all of that land looks the same to me anyway, so I really wouldn't know."

I was thrown into great confusion. I had no idea what Papa was implying about Sergei's pursuits and I was quite dismayed to have the trip brought up and then dismissed before I could even decide whether I wanted to go or not, although of course I was quite certain that I should not have wanted to go even if Papa and Ernie had been interested in doing so.

Then, to my surprise, Papa dabbed his lips with his napkin and said, "Alix my dear, if you have a moment I'd like to speak to you privately in my study."

I glanced at Ernie who looked as puzzled as I felt. Papa had never asked either of us to his study, nor did we ever speak of anything that required privacy at all, but since I was both curious and unable to refuse, I gave Ernie a shrug and followed Papa into his inner sanctum.

Once inside this rather gloomy room, Papa gestured me to a chair next to his, then leaned forward and stared into my eyes in a most disconcerting, pointed way.

"Alix my dear, as you know I am not in the habit of interfering in the private lives of my children. I like to think –"

"Papa, have I done something to displease you?"

He looked at me, startled. "No, of course not, my dear. Why do you ask me that?"

Now I felt as confused as he looked. "Well, because you never ask me to come in here and because –"

"Oh well yes, I see. I only asked you in here as I thought that this might be a matter you would prefer to discuss with me in private, but if it makes you uncomfortable, we needn't. As I say, I prefer not to interfere in any of your lives. You can certainly take your leave, my dear, and continue on with your day."

With that, Papa looked down at his desk and began rummaging around it. I remained seated, anticipating that he was intending to pass something to me, possibly Ella's letter, which I assumed had brought about this strained *tête-à-tête*, but I was mistaken. He was apparently merely looking for a magazine he wanted, and when he found it, he picked it up and commenced reading it.

I gaped at him in disbelief, which was pointless as he continued reading it for some minutes until, driven to desperation, I burst out, "Papa!"

He started visibly at my impulsive exclamation and dropped his magazine.

"Good heavens, Alix, are you still here? What is it, my dear?"

I could not allow myself to show any signs of temper with poor Papa as I knew they would only make him go quiet and not speak for days, so I inhaled deeply and counted to three, something that my sister Irene had once taught me to do when I was at risk of losing control of my feelings.

"Papa darling, forgive me, but I find I am most curious as to what it was you wanted to speak to me about. Forgive me if I am importuning you, but I would so like to hear what you were going to say."

He gazed at me puzzled but uttered not a word.

I prompted him, "Could it have been something in the letter you received from Ella?"

His face cleared and he smiled gratefully at me.

"Oh yes, yes, that was it exactly." He removed his spectacles and rubbed his forehead. "Alix, my dear, as you know I am not in the habit of interfering in the private lives of my children. I like to think …"

"You like to think …?" I prompted gently.

He looked at me and nodded. "Yes, I do. I've always enjoyed thinking."

I prayed to God for the grace of patience.

"I know you do, Papa, you are a great thinker, and I've always known it. So were you thinking of what Ella said in her letter that you wanted to tell me about?"

He shook his head and then his eyes cleared and his gaze was direct.

"No, my dear, I did not wish to tell you about it, I wished to *ask* you about it, and that's a rather different thing, isn't it?" His voice had hardened and then I rather wished that I had left while I had the opportunity to do so.

"Ask me about what, Papa?"

"Alix, your sister informs me that you may have come to a secret understanding with the Tsar's son. Is this true? Did you make a promise that you should wed without either of you considering the need to consult me on the matter?" Before I could stammer out an answer he raised his hand for silence. I had never seen him look so fierce. "You need not trouble yourself to honor me with an answer. I can see from your expression that what your sister has related to me is entirely true. Well, my dear, I wish you luck. You'll certainly need it."

I wanted to beg his forgiveness. I wanted to tell him that it had all come to nothing. I wanted to fling myself against his dear old chest and cry out all the humiliation and pain I had suffered in so much silence.

Moreover, I wanted to know what he meant.

"Papa, I am sorry and it came to nothing anyway. It was just a silly boy and an even sillier girl dreaming, but it was very wrong of us, and please forgive me, please do. As I say, it didn't come to anything at all and it never shall, but I must know why you say I should need luck."

He sighed and turned away from me to stare out of the window, but I sensed that he wasn't looking at the square below but rather into a distant, unhappy time. His words confirmed this.

"Alix, when I met your mother, Princess Alice as she was then, I too was just a silly boy in love with a less silly girl. But then maybe that is wrong, maybe she was even sillier than I was. After all, she was always much, much wiser than I, and so she should have known, don't you think, she should have known …"

"Known what, Papa?"

"Known that love is the very least of the ingredients required for a happy marriage, my dear."

I flushed and felt tears start in my eyes. "That's not true, Papa, it isn't, and you and Mama were happy, you were terribly happy, everyone says so. Grandmamma told me …" I choked on the lump in my throat.

Papa turned his gaze back towards mine, waving his hand dismissively at the mention of Grandmamma.

He smiled thinly. "Your esteemed grandmother has too sentimental an attachment to the memory of our flawed union as either a great love story, or if the mood strikes her, as the story of a noble princess from the world's greatest dynasty who died far too young because she married so poorly. I tend to agree with her on the latter assessment, if not much else." Then, remarking my distress, he softened his tone. "Never mind, my dear, it is all long past, and poor Alice is either in heaven and over her sorrows or still wandering these halls as unhappy a ghost as she was a woman. It is your happiness I am more concerned with now."

"You shouldn't be, Papa. I told you –"

He waved away my objection.

"Alix, whether I should be or not will only be revealed in time. The young man has obviously developed an affection for you, an affection, as I understand it, that his parents do not as yet share. In and of itself that is not unusual. Our little duchy is often the court of last resort when the greater houses are seeking a mate for one or other of their children. Nevertheless, it often comes to pass that we enter into consideration, however belatedly, and you happen to be very beautiful, my dear, and, even more pertinently, a granddaughter of the great Queen-Empress Victoria. As regards the situation at hand, we humble Hessians have never fared well in our grand marriages and it is for that reason that I say you will need all the luck providence may be so munificent as to provide you with. Do you love this boy, my Alix?"

I was too moved by his honesty to prevaricate and merely nodded.

"I do, Papa, but I wish I didn't, and he … he has been weak and untrue, and –"

"Yes, my darling, I imagine he has. The present Empress is a woman of iron will who has dominated her children, and will, I fear, continue to do so, much like your own grandmother and the late Dowager Empress of Austria who, as you may or may not know, made your cousin of a sort, Sissi's, life a great misery for many years. Her husband, the Emperor Franz Joseph, is not a weak man, but he has always deferred to his mother's intentions in private matters. Young Nicholas, in my opinion, is not a strong man and any woman could and will dominate him. His mother, who does indeed dominate him, is fully cognizant of this and perceives a threat in you. A young bride such as yourself might initiate a shift in power between them, particularly a young, beautiful bride with a strong will of her own, and you are in possession of each of those virtues."

"Thank you, Papa, but as I said –"

"Yes, that's right, my dear, you have already predicted that this informal understanding will come to nothing and I thank you for the honor of your disclosing your private feelings to me, but I fear I have an appointment in town and must leave you momentarily, so I will end this discussion by asking if you would like me to accept your sister's invitation to Illinskoe on your behalf."

"But you and Ernie have already indicated you do not wish to go and –"

"No, we don't, and nor shall we. There is precious little to interest either of us in Russia. However, yours may be a different case, and so I ask you again, would you wish to go?"

There were so many things I wanted to ask him and to tell him, but I could see that he was done speaking and, in the end, the truth is all that ever matters.

"Yes, Papa, I would like you to accept the invitation on my behalf. Thank you."

Chapter 10

Illinskoe was Ella and Sergei's version of the Hameau Marie-Antoinette had built at Versailles. They referred to it charmingly, or so they thought, as their tiny Russian peasant farmhouse, but since, before that summer, I had never seen any of those fabled Russian peasants or their homes, I was in no position to make the comparison. However, I did know that I simply adored Illinskoe on sight and that it would forever thereafter influence my love of simple Russian life, something that, of course, I was never truly able to recreate from the lofty position in which God eventually chose to seat me.

Illinskoye's beauty lay not so much in the house itself, which was a long, low-lying two-story bleached house of fifty rooms or so, decorated by balconies and fretwork, and surrounded by enormous terraces that Ella had simply ruined by giving in to her passion for ivy. She had ordered this invasive creeper to be planted all over the base of the house, so it had grown up the sides and then slipped over onto the balconies and choked off the views from the windows and terraces, and, as if one wasn't sick unto death enough of all the dank-smelling, dark, green stuff, she had stupidly scattered large Grecian urns around the tiled terraces and filled them with yet more ivy plants. It made for a bizarre scene and created a never-ending problem with vermin.

The inside of it might have been very pretty, as Ella had done up what she called *her* rooms – the dining room, main parlors, music room and sitting room – in dark pink and lavender, and Sergei had chosen dark blue

157

for *his* rooms – the library, billiard rooms, smoking room and his study – but the cursed ivy had made them all so dark that they had to have electric lights on all day long to prevent the occupants crashing into the furniture and to enable the staff to serve tea and me to differentiate between the keys of the pianoforte.

The poor servants spent an inordinate amount of time being lectured by Ella on their lack of proper dusting, but how could they have been expected to see any dust under such dim lighting? Worse, rats predictably nested in the ivy and were in the habit of skittering into corners, so I quickly had to become adept at throwing my shoes at the loathsome creatures to drive them off when I entered my bedchamber at night.

Yet none of this truly mattered because, despite Ella's pretensions and her ubiquitous ivy, Illinskoe was an enchanted paradise for which I must give Sergei most of the credit.

Illinskoe was only an hour's train ride from Moscow, and yet one would think one were in the very middle of a vast unpopulated land, as Sergei had cleverly bought up several thousand more acres of land and let them go to grass so that his herd of darling, bright Jersey cows might graze there. His peasants kept these animals wonderfully clean and they all sported jaunty ribbons around their necks and were so tame that one could pet them.

The peasants of Illinskoe only added to the place's overall enchantment. They were very happy, as it seems peasants tend to be by nature. They would wave and bow at Sergei and Ella and me as we rode by in one of Sergei's antique charabancs and were always so happy to see us that at times it seemed they could barely restrain themselves from breaking into dance. Their love of Sergei was in fact so great that they would bow down and kiss his shadow as he passed by.

The church that Sergei had built at Illinskoe was an exact miniature replica of one in Moscow and he allowed the peasants to attend it on Sundays so that they could pray in the same space as he did. Afterwards there was almost always a little craft fair outside the church where the brightly-scarfed women and their cheerful babies sold their humble wares.

I must say that while I had quickly come to love the dear peasants out waving in the fields, and that while I found their little fairs very sweet, I was hard pressed to find something to buy from them, so I decided to raise the issue with Sergei one evening at dinner, for, unlike Ella, he seemed to actually have a fondness for his peasants and a tendency to mingle with them during the craft fairs. Ella, to her credit, did send her lady's maid to their little booths to buy their primitive objects but, unlike Sergei, she did not spend time asking them questions and patting the heads of their children.

So, based on his seeming interest in his people, I grew sufficiently bold to make some suggestions.

"Sergei, would it be all right if I asked you about the peasants?" I ventured timidly.

He turned his head from the man with whom he had been discussing a new form of gold braid and looked at me, surprised, as apparently everyone was, for conversation around me stilled and I felt Ella and her ladies' eyes lingering upon me.

I flushed but Sergei smiled and said, "Ask away, my dear little Alicky. Your interest in my peasants is charming. I only wish my wife would take more interest in them, but then, of course, Ella is not Russian and seems to have very little interest in becoming so."

Ella's eyes filled with tears and I felt bad for her, for while I did enjoy Sergei's kindness, even favoritism, towards me, I did wish that he didn't feel the need to seize nearly every opportunity to humiliate Ella and demonstrate to the entire world what an obvious failure their marriage was. Their union seemed to me less like a wedding of two souls, as marriage should be, and more like a constant war of attrition, one Ella was ill-equipped to fight.

In this spirit of charity I looked at her apologetically, but her ice-cold eyes froze my soul. I understood then that I was wrong to pity her; she had brought Sergei's disapproval upon herself. She was as cold and as disinterested and judging of him as she always had been of me, and I saw no further reason to comfort her in her distress, so I smiled sweetly back at Sergei.

"Thank you for saying that, Sergei dear, truly. I, of course, know nothing of Russia or its peoples but I am indeed most interested in both, so I was wondering specifically about their crafts."

"Their crafts, Alicky? Surely you aren't complaining of the fit and comfort of a pair of birch bark shoes, are you? They're the very latest in demimonde fashion."

He waited a beat for the laughter of his guests to subside and smiled at me amused.

I laughed obediently as well.

"No, Sergei dear, I'm not complaining about anything, though they are a tad scratchy and I fear that they might dissolve at the least hint of dampness."

Ella espying, or so she hoped, an opportunity to embarrass me, joined in the conversation with her usual lack of humor.

"Good heavens, Alix, have you been wearing those things? I hope no one saw you in them."

Sergei sighed and shook his head. "Our Alix was making a joke, Ella. You know, it's one of those things people say to be amusing. Or no, I suppose you wouldn't know, would you?"

Fearing that if I didn't say something, the evening would quickly dissolve and I would never be able to get my ideas across, I hastily interjected, "Sergei, it is a very funny idea actually wearing them, and of course I would never do so, but that's the thing … who could? And it's the very same thing with those scarves they sell. The fabric is just stained with berry juice and not dye, so it all comes off on your hands, or –"

Ella, seemingly determined to ruin the conversation, jumped in with with, "Or on one's upholstery. I hadn't wanted to mention it, Alicky, but that pile of so-called clothing you bought yesterday and left in my carriage has simply ruined the silk on the seats, and I –"

Sergei cut her off. "Yes, dear, clearly Alicky's thoughtlessness has destroyed your upholstery and now you'll have to order a new set," he gestured dramatically, "but then every cloud has a silver lining, doesn't it?" He drained his wine. "Now you'll have something to do tomorrow besides figuring out which ribbon to wear in your hair. That should be entertaining for you."

161

Ella paled and swayed in her chair. She then rose shakily, made a choked apology to the guests about something to do with a headache, and hurriedly left the room.

The table fell into yet another uncomfortable silence. Possibly I should have given up on my line of inquiry, but I did want to get my point out and I felt that if I let Ella's hysterics dominate the evening, I would appear as sulky and un-Russian as Sergei, and no doubt his guests, found her to be.

I waited a moment, cleared my throat and smiled in what I hoped was a delightful way before continuing to to speak to Sergei while addressing everyone in general.

"I am sorry about the upholstery. I was careless and I should have realized what would happen from the fact that my own hands were dyed quite a bright red from the scarves I bought."

A lady in waiting of Ella's, whose name I did not know, raised her eyebrows and in horribly accented English asked, "But if these peasant items are so awful, why would you buy them, Your Highness? I never have. I just drop a few coins out of the carriage window as we pass and it keeps them from coming any closer and is much less difficult than having actually to address them. And besides, what *does* one do with those things if one does actually purchase them? Surely these are not gifts you are planning to take home to Darmstadt, are they?"

Sergei's friend General Isolveven intervened. "Oh, Countess, I'm sure that the pretty little princess isn't buying those dreadful things to give to anyone. She simply means to be kind, don't you, Princess?"

I began to nod but then shook my head in frustration.

"Thank you, General, for your kind words and, yes, I do want to be kind to the poor peasants, but the reason I introduced this topic in the first place is because I was wondering if there might not be something we could do to help them –"

This time it was Sergei who interrupted me. "*Help them?* How would you help them, Alix, and why? They're perfectly content as they are, I assure you. You see, Alix, I'm Russian and I know my people."

At this point in this ridiculous conversation everything had strayed so far from the small idea I had originally had I could barely remember why I had started it in the first place. I felt simply exhausted and was beginning to envy Ella's abrupt departure. Still, I had begun and what one begins one must finish.

I drew in a deep breath, smiled apologetically at Sergei and company, and tried to finish.

"Of course you are right, Sergei, I'm not a bit Russian, but I do love your country and the peasants seem so sweet and simple, and I just thought that if they could make things that people might actually wish to possess, then it would improve their circumstances a bit, that's all."

I was nearly breathless with triumph at finally having been able to air my idea.

"What sorts of things do you think the peasants might make that people, such as ourselves, might wish to possess, as you say, Alix? And before you reply, I must tell you, my dear, that your mildly offensive implication that the peasants' circumstances require any sort of improvement at all is somewhat off the mark. My family has always cared for them, and as you may or may not

163

be aware, as a German, my own beloved Papa was the tsar who freed all of them from serfdom. It's astounding to me that you, as a foreigner who have now seen the peasants – what twice? – have come to the precipitous conclusion that they need anything more from us than whatever we Romanovs have already given them."

I felt faint. "Sergei, I didn't mean –"

"No, I'm sure you didn't, my dear. It's just the sort of thing that all foreigners think about us and our people."

"No, no, I didn't mean that at all. I just thought that they might like to make a little more money, I don't know, for…" I trailed off, my body soaked in sweat and my throat filling with incipient sobs.

"For …?"

"Oh, I don't know. Please. I'm so sorry I said anything. I must have had too much sun today and I feel quite tired suddenly. Please forgive me. I think I had better take my leave and bid everyone goodnight, and –"

"Yes, I can see that you are tired, Alix. In fact you look quite diminished. You should go up now, my dear, but before you do so, might I inquire, for I'm all agog to hear, as are my guests, what you think the peasants might sell instead to, as you say, improve their terrible lives under our repressive rule."

I stood up on shaking, aching legs. "Sergei, I did not say anything of the sort. I only wanted to help and I thought –"

"Yes, of course, my dear. Germans have always only wanted to help us poor backward Russians."

Our fellow guests laughed as the room began to swirl around me, but Sergei was merciless.

"No, truly, Alicky, do tell us what the peasants should sell, something you and other German ladies, such as your sister, might like. What would it be – rubies, diamonds? Do tell. I really must hear this."

"Vases!" I ended up shouting out in frustrated rage. "I only thought they might be able to sell painted vases and maybe picture frames, and that people would like the things they painted and the peasants might like having something to sell that wasn't utter rubbish, like this whole stupid conversation. Now, if you will forgive me, I'm shall retire to my room."

With that, I stumbled out of that somber dining room, knocking over a table of Ella's ugly whatnots on the way. I heard them laughing as I passed all the way through the hallways and up the stairs and I heard Sergei exclaim, "Vases! Perfect! Well, she certainly breaks enough of them to create a cottage industry enough to keep any number of artisans occupied. I'll have to ask her in the morning if she suggests we establish a series of porcelain factories for the peasants to produce such necessary items."

So went my days and my nights. I would spend as much time as I could outdoors wandering the fields, and as much time as I could inside avoiding company.

It wasn't as difficult as one might think, for I had begun to suffer from daily headaches and neuralgia pain in my face and teeth. I did not ask to see a physician because I had no interest in spending any more time than necessary receiving advice from Ella or Sergei, which would have been inevitable if a doctor had been summoned. And while I suffered, I waited, I waited for word from him, I waited for the sight of him, and I waited for a resolve that I knew I would need both then and for the rest of my life.

However, Nicky did not come, and he did not write, and slowly, painfully I became aware that I was going to have to embark on a future without him, and that once I did so, I must never, ever look back in either regret or hope, for those are the things that will kill one's future as surely as the thwarting of dreams can destroy one's youth.

It's odd, but I knew even then that one day Nicky would find in himself the courage to demand my hand, to stand up to his parents and begin to end his protracted boyhood. Oh, it's not that I saw his love as indestructible, or at that point even sincere, and it's not that I viewed myself as the magical fairy princess of his or anyone's dreams. It was more that he did, or had at least for a moment, fancied himself in love with me, a sentiment that would be revived one day when even his mighty parents came to feel that it was time for him to be married. He would remember me then, maybe not for myself but because there was a terrible dearth of suitable princesses available to him in Europe for the purposes of marriage; ones that would please him, anyway.

His mother, the frightening Empress who so obviously disliked me, would surely have preferred to set him up with a Danish princess, but there was none this side of seventy years of age. So then who else was there? My cousins Ducky or Missy were out of the question as the Russian Orthodox Church forbade marriage between first cousins and their mother was Nicky's paternal aunt. Thereafter, the Empress might

166

turn in her quest towards Germany, despite her notorious hatred for that country, and cast her eye on Cousin Willy's sister, Mossy, so nicknamed for the fact that hair was rumored to cover her entire face like a fine layer of moss, and should it ever be removed successfully, a man might in any case die in instant shock at the hideous aspect that lay beneath. That left just me as a suitable potential bride of royal stock, or possibly, given the recent Russian-Franco alliance, there was the beautiful Princess Hélène of France, the daughter of the French Pretender, but she was not of the Orthodox faith and was extremely unlikely ever to deign to become so.

Which left me, and I wouldn't have it: He would not turn at last to me as the princess of last resort, and his parents would not be given the opportunity to decide that, whereas they considered me completely hopeless, it was still better to have a hopeless daughter-in-law than none at all and, more convincingly, thus no heir to their darling son. Nicky would not be allowed to treat me in this casual and discourteous manner and then blithely declare his renewed sense of devotion to me when his mama should whimsically decide that it was now all right for him to consider marrying such a girl as myself, no matter how clumsy, poor, unworthy, stiff, and all of the other horrible things she had doubtlessly attributed to my person, I might be. No, I would not have it.

Pride may be the very coldest sort of comfort but it is at least a form of comfort, and I knew that if I didn't find some comfort somewhere and stiffen my spine with it, while I might still end up the Empress of Russia one day, I would do so as an object of pity and disdain to the world, but worse to myself.

167

There was a way ahead. To some it might have seemed a narrow and lonely path but the more that I considered the great happiness and peace I had recently been blessed with in living both with and for Ernie and Papa, the more I realized that this was how I wished always to live, and all I had to do was to close, once and forever, my heart to Nicky, and proceed to consecrate myself to Papa's faith, the Lutheran Church, and keep my vows to it. This would end any possibility of a future for Nicky and me as I take my faith most seriously. While, to some, faith may be like a garment one can put on one day and discard the next, to me it is inviolable. I would go home to Darmstadt, I would go through the rite of confirmation, and then I would marry myself to a very different future.

Now, here is the strangest part of my story, and I suppose I will die before I fully understand what it meant, but as soon as I decided this, all the days that followed, through my goodbyes to Ella and Sergei, and during the nearly endless return train ride home into Papa and Ernie's embraces, and while I stood and was anointed with the holy oils that brought me into the faith of my people, and for many months afterward, I was happier than I can ever remember being.

It is certainly true that everyone's memories of youth can at times be tinted by a golden haze of nostalgia, but I don't think it is that simple. I was happy, I felt well, my headaches vanished, my legs were strong again, my stride was firm as I bustled about the new palace arranging flowers and ordering up menus and entertainments for Papa and Ernie, and I wasn't stiff or shy or clumsy; I was simply a woman in the very center of the place and of the people she belonged with.

If the greater world was beginning to see me as an object of pity, the Grand Duke's beautiful, but odd, spinster daughter, that was not what I saw in my own bright countenance as it reflected back to me in my looking glass. Nor was it what I saw reflected in the proud and loving eyes of my dearest Papa and Ernie. No, it was all true … and then it all ended.

On the coldest, grayest day in October, my Papa fell ill, and before I could even allow myself to become greatly concerned by the state of his health, he was dead, and Ernie and I were alone, orphaned and alone, and once again the darkness descended over the new palace and the ghosts returned to outnumber the living.

If it hadn't been for Ernie's constant love and support, I would have gladly joined my dear lost family in paradise.

Chapter 11

It was then, in my darkest hour, when there seemed to be no possible future for us, that Nicky at last wrote me a letter, albeit a banal letter of sympathy for the irreparable loss that Ernie and I had suffered, but he signed it 'Love, Nicky.'

I didn't reply, although I imagine Ernie did so, on both our behalfs; for even if I had cared to do so, I couldn't have, not then. I wasn't replying, I wasn't talking, I was barely breathing, and the many people who descended upon us in Hesse-Darmstadt following my father's death were unable to coax me out of my bed of tears, or as Ella unkindly put it, out of my "fits of hysteria."

They had all come: Irene and Henry from nearby Prussia, Louis and Vicky from England, and Ella and Sergei, of course, from Russia. Regarding the latter, Ernie was driven caustically to observe, "Those two seem to have a lot of time on their hands. They probably sit in amber until someone either dies or gets married, and then they wind themselves up like clocks and move forward, worst luck for us."

Ernie, my dearest, my darling, my brother, my friend, in those bleakest of days he tried his hardest to be Papa to me too. He was the sole consolation in my despair, for in my brother I had the other half of my soul, but even his efforts were insufficient to draw me out of my slough of despond. I responded to no one and could not eat. I could not stop crying and even my short walks to the water closet became agony as my legs throbbed and ached, as did my head.

My family huddled around me in despair and below me in many conferences. What to do with poor Alicky? Ernie, Irene and Vicky feared for my life, and Ella feared for my sanity, but they were all in agreement that only Grandmamma could save me and an urgent letter was sent to her at Windsor.

She responded speedily and wisely, as she always did to any crisis afflicting those she loved, and somehow my dearest brother and my sisters managed to transport my enfeebled little self, and my sad newly-dyed black dresses, off to Grandmamma, who had decided to meet me at Balmoral where "the best air in the world would soon restore poor little Alicky to full health, though of course she'll never be the same."

I had never exactly shared dearest Grandmamma's passion for Balmoral, which is set deep into the Scottish Highlands. The land and the castle were gifts to Grandmamma from her adored husband, Prince Albert, and so retained the highest place in her heart, and she did, I know, feel that it was a place of magical beauty. In truth, it was somewhat desolate and the wind was so fierce and continuous that only the hardiest of trees could survive there. The sun rarely shone, and if it did, the castle itself still remained dark, lying as it did in the shadow of the mountain of Lochnagar.

It was August when I arrived and so the weather was at its balmiest, reaching possibly several degrees above freezing on any given day.

As if all of this wasn't distressing enough, Grandmamma, who did indeed love Balmoral and its countryside, feared that since her family and servants tended to huddle inside around the badly smoking fires, they were not receiving the benefit of the "best air in the world." To remedy this, she insisted that nearly every window in the castle be thrown open to the elements at all times. The wind was hard on all of us, but particularly on the servants, as it whistled and sometimes screamed through the castle, blowing over bibelots and bringing in great piles of dirt, although possibly their tireless labor created warmth for them as they remained pretty nearly always on the move.

We, her family, were not so fortunate.

Grandmamma, who besides being a mighty queen was also made of sterner stuff than the rest of us, would sit happily by the open windows, her small lace head-covering flapping madly in the wind-filled rooms, exhorting us all to breathe deeply. We tended rather to breathe shallowly, for the ever-present fear of pleurisy and pneumonia lurked. I was already unwell upon arrival and the terrible cold and darkness didn't do a thing for my health and spirits, and soon even Grandmamma was forced to acknowledge that after all I might be so ill that even Balmoral's bracing climate was not going to restore my mental or physical equilibrium on its own.

Accompanied by Nanny, I was packed off to my bedchamber to await hot water bottles that were usually cold by the time they arrived and things became much the same for me as they had been in Darmstadt, save that there I had Ernie and heated rooms. Grandmamma, however, was no woman to concede defeat, informing me lovingly, if briskly, that she had suffered and endured much greater pain and loss than I had, and declaring that what I really required to pull up my spirits was congenial company.

To that end she summoned a group of my English relatives, apparently feeling that they were the liveliest of people and that I would respond accordingly and rise phoenix-like from the ashes of my grief. The guest list was nothing if not surprising, as it included Duchess Marie and her daughters. Duchess Marie was the wife of Grandmamma's second son, my Uncle Alfred, and was the sister of my own lost Nicky's papa, Tsar Alexander III, and therefore a Russian Grand Duchess in her own right. But since she was somewhat fat and ugly, and terribly mean, the only match that had been offered her was Grandmamma's second son, which made her a regular English Duchess besides.

Being a Duchess in England carries with it considerable status, but it seems that Duchess Marie never quite recovered from what she saw as her demotion from Grand Duchess in Russia to plain Duchess in England, for plain she was indeed.

Grandmamma tended to make snap judgments on people. They were either nearly perfect – and I say 'nearly,' recognizing that the word 'perfect' is otherwise universally considered an absolute – as only my late, lost Grandpapa Albert was entirely perfect in her eyes, or they were terrible and beneath contempt. As she was very wise and as she was the Queen, her judgments were never questioned. In the case of her daughter-in-law the former Grand Duchess, she detested her on sight and that dislike had never wavered. Grandmamma, who was rather stout herself, hated stoutness in others and used to

174

say of Duchess Marie that the only grand thing about her was her girth.

This seemed a somewhat unkind observation, but really she was the most terribly overbearing of women and her marriage to poor Uncle Alfred was considered a disaster as she had managed to make him as unhappy in his own country as she was at being there. Worse, she produced only one son and four daughters, and it was three of these daughters who were the first to be given the responsibility of cheering me up, or so I thought at the time, but I came to understand later that Grandmamma had been trying to prepare me for something else altogether and had hoped that by my spending time with Duchess Marie's second daughter, my cousin Ducky, what she had in store for me would come as less of a blow.

As I have said, Duchess Marie had four daughters, and her oldest one, Marie – known as 'Missy – was one of the prettiest girls anyone had ever seen and, all too aware of her charms, delighted in telling stories about what people had said when they encountered her, such as, "Oh, yesterday I saw Princess Marie in a new hat and I nearly fell over in amazement. Never have I seen such a fetching girl. If she weren't a princess, she would be featured in magazines." Funnily, she really was so utterly charming and adorable and beautiful, and somehow innocent, that instead of finding her vain and tedious I was totally taken by her, as apparently everyone else was, because when she wasn't describing her latest overheard compliment, she was happily agonizing over which prince to marry. Both my Cousin Georgie, Prince Bertie's second son and third in line to the British throne, and Crown Prince Ferdinand, the heir to the throne of Romania, were rumored to be desperately in love with her. I found her fine, if frivolous, company and greatly enjoyed her visits to my room.

Her youngest sister, Princess Beatrice – known as 'Baby Bea' in the family – was merely a little girl of not yet ten years old, a sweet if somewhat vacuous child who immediately became my little slave and annoyed her adored oldest sister, the pretty Marie, by musing aloud whether "Cousin Alicky isn't even more beautiful than you are, Missy dear."

In between these two lovely girlies was the second daughter, my dreaded Cousin Ducky. I had met Ducky – who was actually Princess Victoria Melita, but known as 'Ducky' because that is what her ghastly mother called her – a few times before, but our enforced togetherness at Balmoral was our first opportunity to spend any real time together, and for my part I found her as inclement as the weather.

She wasn't nearly as pretty as Marie – in fact I thought her quite ugly with her lidded eyes and somewhat heavy jawline – but almost everyone else called her pretty, an adjective they tend to ascribe to any princess, even if she were to resemble a two-headed stag. It was this, and her mother's obvious favoritism towards her, I think, that had turned her personality into the humorless, self-absorbed, domineering character that she manifested all too clearly that summer at Balmoral when I was a grieving girl of twenty and she a spoiled madam of fifteen.

If I had been feeling better, I could have avoided her, but she, while bored and miserable at Balmoral, tended to follow her sisters petulantly into my sad little bedchamber on each of their visits. Plopping herself down gracelessly, she would perch on the edge of my bed and either listen whilst rolling her eyes at Missy's darling stories or dominate the conversation with her own woes, which were myriad.

She was in love with her first cousin, who was also Nicky's first cousin, the Grand Duke Cyril, and maybe because of my connection to the Russian imperial family through Ella, or because she had heard the gossip about Nicky and me through her odious mother, she had marked me out as her best audience and victim. Yes, I say 'victim,' for that is the sort of girl Ducky was even then when she was very young.

I need to speak here of the tangled family relationship that existed between us. Her mother, Duchess Marie, was born one of eight children to the ill-fated union of Nicky's grandpapa, Tsar Alexander II, and my own grandmother, Marie of Hesse. My poor grandmamma on Papa's side – thus my paternal grandmother – gave the Tsar eight children, two girls and six sons. The first girl, who was hailed as a very pretty child, died young and then there came sons, then sons, then sons. Nicky's own papa, Alexander, was a second son who became Tsarevich after his older, and I understand much more promising, brother Nicholas died.

Alexander also inherited Minnie, who was engaged to him, as I once heard, on Nicholas's deathbed according to his brother's dying request. I always found that story illustrative of the sort of woman Minnie was:

177

highly ambitious and intent on becoming Empress of Russia, whichever Romanov she would have to marry to get there – all quite sad, I think. She subsequently produced six children for Tsar Alexander III, including my own Nicky, his brother George, the girls Xenia and Olga, and Nicky's little brother, Michael.

The next brother in Tsar Alexander II's family, after Nicholas and Alexander, was Nicky's Uncle Vladimir, who had married another Marie who became the second lady in the land, after Empress Minnie, upon Tsar Alexander III's accession to the imperial throne. This Marie was known as 'Miechen' to differentiate her from Minnie and was a terribly proud, unpleasant woman who, according to Ella, had led the whispering campaign in St. Petersburg against me during that ill-fated winter when Nicky and I had become secretly engaged, by describing me as stiff and clumsy.

She and Vladimir had three living sons, of which the oldest was Cyril, the object of Ducky's infatuation, this despite her own mother being Vladimir's younger sister and therefore her aunt. Cyril, as Vladimir's oldest surviving son, was in line for the throne only if Nicky, George, and Michael were to predecease him without issue – a somewhat extreme possibility – but I still think somehow Ducky dreamed of that very thing coming to pass and envisaged herself as a future Empress of Russia, if only … if only everyone died and if she could stiffen the spine of her love object Cyril sufficiently for him to defy the canon laws of the Orthodox Church that forbade marriage between first cousins, and quite rightly so. Then, even if the Orthodox Church should allow a marriage to take place between them, Cyril's place in the line of succession to the Russian throne would thereby be forfeit unless the previous Tsar formally forgave him.

From everything I had seen and heard about Tsar Alexander III, that seemed most unlikely, so Ducky had gotten herself into this silly affair that had no hope whatsoever of turning out the way she wanted it to and then had the utter temerity to compare her own failed hopes to mine.

Flinging herself face down next to me, she pounded my bedding. "I'm going to be a spinster, a strange old maid, and everyone will gossip about me as they do about you, Alix."

I gasped in horror, as did Marie and Bea, while sweet Marie tried clumsily to defend me.

"Ducky, you are horrible, horrible. I'm going to tell Mama what you said to poor Alicky. She'll be so angry, and besides, Alicky is so pretty that even if she is old, I'm certain someone will still want to marry her."

Little Bea climbed up next to me and nestled into my side. "I'll marry you, Cousin Alicky!"

In that moment of complete humiliation I wished either for the ability to swoon at will or for the facility with witty and cutting words that would annihilate the ghastly Ducky. Then I thought of them.

"I can hardly be considered a spinster, Ducky dear, for if you will but recollect, not one but two heirs to great thrones have asked for my hand already. It is not I who have been obliged to resort to trying to marry one of my own first cousins, which, if you ask me, is rather akin to marrying one's brother, but then you don't have any brothers, do you, Ducky? In point of fact, instead of wasting your time pitying me, you should rather pity your poor mother, for how she'll ever find enough husbands for all of you is beyond me. At least in the case of Marie, Alex and little Bea's there is hope, but for you …?"

Unfortunately Marie held an unreasonable affection for her horrible sister, so flushed and appalled, she immediately berated me.

"Why, Alix, how unkind of you, and after I said such nice things about you, why –"

Ducky cut her off. "Oh, don't worry about me, Missy darling. Nothing Alix can say can upset me. After all, everyone knows that old maids are always odd … odd and bitter."

She shrugged and arose from my bed. Marie and little Bea got up too, although they at least had the good grace to appear shamefaced at Ducky's behavior. At the doorway Ducky stopped so abruptly that both girls ran into her. There was a brief giggle and then Ducky turned to gaze at me with her ugly, shaded eyes.

"Anyway, it is not true what you said, is it, Alicky darling."

Completely enraged, I sat up and glared at her, my anger making me overheated for the first time since arriving at Balmoral.

"What isn't true, you rude girl?"

Ducky threw back her head, laughed, and nudged her sisters.

"Oh my, just look at the poor old thing. She's so upset she has almost drummed up enough energy to get out of bed, and God knows none of us wants that to happen. She'd probably stagger all the way down the stairs to tea and accidentally knock over all of our plates while telling Grandmamma that someone finally told her to her face what everyone already says behind her back."

I crumpled back onto my pillows and felt my legs and head begin to ache terribly, and then held up a hand to stop her words, but she didn't stop.

"Oh, don't try to look like you're dying or something, Alix. You just don't like the truth very much, do you. Marry my cousin, you say? That's like marrying a brother, you say? Well, everyone says you would marry your own brother if you could, Alicky, that is if he even likes girls. And as for all the heirs who want to marry you, you must be deranged. Everyone knows that Grandmamma pushed poor Cousin Eddy into asking for your hand and that he was so relieved when you said no because he has always been in love with Princess Hélène of France, although she might not say yes either because I hear Uncle Sasha and Aunt Minnie want her for Nicky, who didn't try very hard to marry you either, did he? So don't you judge me, Alix of Hesse-Darmstadt. You wait and see, I'll marry Cyril, you see if I don't, and you can kneel down and kiss my hand if I can ever persuade Ella and Sergei to feel sorry enough for you to invite you back to Russia one day!"

I was moaning by then and reached frantically for the bell pull to summon Nanny, but as I did so I knocked over my bedside table and sent my medicines and water carafe crashing to the ground.

Missy exclaimed in horror and started towards me.

"Oh no, poor Alicky. Look what you have done, Ducky. Here, Alicky, let me help you, I –"

Even Ducky looked taken aback as she pulled Missy towards the doorway.

"No, don't bother her, we should go. Listen, Alix, I … Well, I'm sorry. I've been upset about Cyril, and maybe you are right that I will never get to marry him after all and we will end up two funny old spinsters attending Missy's wedding to some handsome prince or other. I'm sorry I said all of that. Please, can we forget it?"

Little Bea, who was sobbing, looked back and forth between the two of us in horror and I, unable to bear a single instant more of any of them, flung myself onto my stomach and pounded at my pillows, all the while wailing incoherently and beyond choking out a single word.

The next few days at Balmoral, following this tumultuous scene, were a comedy of strained manners. Grandmamma was appalled by the unseemly discord between her spoiled and badly raised young granddaughters, and it was in vain that I tried to appeal to her while we were alone, pointing out that I had done nothing wrong and had been attacked, for no reason, by the ghastly Ducky. Meanwhile the latter complained in exactly the same way about me, which caused Grandmamma to decide that we were both in the wrong and must apologize to both her and Duchess Marie.

Grandmamma, who hated any sort of family discord, would, I fear, have been much sterner if she had not become somewhat exercised at the sight of Aunt Marie's entrance into the room, covered from head to toe in furs.

"Girls. Good. Now you stand here in front of me and apologize nicely to me, and then do so again to your mother and your aunt, and … Oh, good God, Marie, what are you wearing? You look as though you have dressed in preparation for an expedition to the Arctic wastelands. Or is it that you are planning a visit home to Russia and have failed to mention the fact to me?"

Duchess Marie grimaced and shivered theatrically.

"Really, dearest mother darling, how amusing you are. No, I am not planning any trips. I fear, though, I have been somewhat compelled to encase myself in as much warmth as I can find simply to endure the rigors of coming to see you in here. Why, this room is a veritable Siberian icebox."

Grandmamma scowled fiercely and drew herself up as high as she could in her chair, all head-coverings and shawls aflutter. Ducky, to my surprise, reached out for my wrist and began to tug me towards the door. Too taken by surprise to resist, I allowed her to guide me into the outer corridor and all the way down the hallway before she released me to bend over, gasping with laughter.

"Oh Alix, wasn't that too delicious. Grandmamma looked just like an angry little lap dog and Mama resembled nothing so much as an oversized angry bear in her furs. I suspect they will be snapping back and forth all day, but I had to get us out of there before I started to laugh. Can you imagine the level of disgrace I'd be in then?"

I couldn't believe it: Here was Ducky, my newest and worst enemy, confiding in me and, worse, doing so in such a playful fashion that I could not help but grin back at her all-too-correct description of poor darling Grandmamma and Aunt Marie.

When Ducky saw my warm response, she reached over and hugged me impulsively. "Let's be friends, Alix. I know I'm an awful girl at times and I know that loving Cyril and not being able to marry him has made me a sour old cow. I'll be as dreadful as Mama if I continue in this fashion. I don't really think you are old or a spinster, or anything like that. I think Baby Bea is right and you are the prettiest girl in the whole family, and I think old Cousin Nicky is a perfect muttonhead if he doesn't insist on being allowed to marry you. Who knows, maybe if he does, you can tell him to let Cyril marry me. What do you think?"

I was disarmed by her frank friendliness and smiled and hugged her back, feeling the need to unburden my own leaden heart. I hadn't really ever had a girlfriend before.

"Well, I don't know that you will ever have occasion to be grateful to me in that regard, but all the same I thank you for saying so. Nicky doesn't really want to marry to me. I'm not sure he wants to marry anyone. He is not very grown up really, and –"

"Oh, that is just exactly my problem with Cyril. These Romanov boys are all tied to their mamas' skirts, if you want my opinion. I don't know, Alicky, maybe we would be better off waiting until their mamas die, don't you think?" Before I could give her a shocked reply, she went blithely on. "Oh, don't mind me, I have shameful thoughts, everyone knows it, and anyway, Aunty Empress Minnie and fearsome Aunty Miechen may be gorgons but they're not very old and they'll probably stick around for another thousand years or so. I know Mama will, and she will terrorize me every day that she lives until I marry someone, anyone – anyone suitable, that is. Otherwise I will end up like poor Cousin Vicky. Can you imagine? 'Yes, Mama darling. No, Mama darling. Three bags full, Mama darling!' "

Our poor Cousin Vicky, whom Ducky was deriding somewhat cruelly, was the middle daughter of Uncle Bertie and Princess Alexandra, the Prince and Princess of Wales. I had always found Aunt Alix, Vicky's mother, to be kind and dear, a much nicer, and it must be said more beautiful, version of her sister, my *bête noire*, Nicky's mother, the Empress of Russia, however what Ducky was saying was unfortunately and confusingly true. Aunt Alix had made a regular dogsbody out of poor Cousin Vicky. She never let her out of her sight and she had a habit of barking orders at her in a way that she would never think of doing even with her lowest scullery maid, whom, of course, she would never have directly addressed at all. This treatment had turned poor Vicky into an early, and desperately unattractive, near-caricature of a spinster, making her seem so dull-witted and whiny with her constant refrains of "Mama says this and Mama thinks that," that one could barely spend ten minutes in her company without being sorely tempted either to laugh out loud or throw tea in her face.

So when Ducky spoke of herself as one day becoming like poor Cousin Vicky, I had to laugh, as the thought was so preposterous, and I told her so. This seemed to please her and she linked her arm companionably through mine, saying cheerfully, "Well good, then that's settled. If we do end up old maids, let us make a vow to become old maids of the terribly difficult sort who are so fearsome that no one in the family will ever dare to ask us to do a single thing, and especially nothing involving embroidery. I despise embroidery and crewel work, don't you, Alix?"

I didn't, as it happened, but since by that juncture I was somewhat seeking Ducky's approval, I simply nodded.

The following day found us four cousins mixing in perfect amicability, but the same could not be said for Grandmamma and Aunt Marie, who seemed to have entered into a long drawn out conflict that was both amusing and inconvenient for us girls, as Aunt Marie's insistence on wearing piles of furs and having a brazier ostentatiously carried around behind her by a footman was offset by Grandmamma's equal determination that her own footman should follow her around opening every door and window that Balmoral possessed.

Meanwhile, Grandmamma had decided, or at least claimed to have decided, that the entire unpleasant atmosphere in the house was due to there being too high a proportion of females gathered in the same place, and so she accordingly sent for Ernie to come and, as an invitation from Grandmamma was the same as a summons, he arrived two days later. Ducky was then forced to realize that her silly remark about Ernie not liking girls was quite untrue, as his presence immediately lightened the atmosphere, and within an hour he and Ducky and Marie and Baby Bea were indulging in a lively game of hide and seek. I would have joined them, but Ernie had brought with him a packet of letters that had arrived for me in Darmstadt, two of them from Nicky.

186

My dearest Alix,

I hesitate to write to you as you did not reply to my letter of condolence over your dear Papa's passing, so then I must ask myself, and now you, dear Alix, are you angry at your old Nicky? If so, please relate to me all the reasons and I shall endeavor to fix whatever it is you feel I have done to wrong you.

I do so care for you, Alix, more deeply than I think you know and I did very much want to come to see you at Illinskoe when you were there last summer. I suffered a great deal at your being in my own country and at my being there too, but of course I was in St. Petersburg and unable to visit you.

Did you think, dearest Alix, and oh I must call you that, for that is who and what you are to me, my dearest, that I would ever choose not to see you? No, no, you couldn't believe such a thing of your old Nicky. You know that I am devoted to you and have been so for many years now, since I first encountered your sweet face at Sergei and Ella's wedding.

If you do think that I would ever choose not to see you, you are being terribly unfair to me and I consider myself wholly within my rights to say so. You cannot think that, if left to my own choices and wishes, I would ever choose to be other than by your side. Sadly, Alix, God has chosen to place me elsewhere.

As my Papa's first son, I am also his first subject. God, who controls all things, I pray will allow my Papa to remain Tsar for decades to come, but one day, one terribly dark day, which I hope will remain far in the future, my papa will move on to join God, and I will become the Tsar. I do not wish for this, in fact I dread it, all and apart from the great grief which will come to me upon losing my papa, a grief that I know, my dearest, you are experiencing all too painfully yourself at this testing time in your life.

Oh, forgive me, Alix, forgive me. I know I have spoken too frankly and maybe only increased your grief, but truly your silence towards me leaves me muddled and confused, and I did think, given your great, good heart, that you would not mind too much if I wrote and asked why you are so silent.

Your Old Nicky.

Before I could even begin to address the feelings that such a letter had aroused in me, there was another one to read, and when I examined the date it had been written, I realized that it had been sent a mere three days after his first letter to me.

Dearest Alix,

I see I mustn't call you dearest, must I? Your continued coldness towards me has assured me of this.

Alix, do you see what you are doing to me? All my hopes and dreams are tied up in the memory of one matchlessly beautiful face. Yes, it is your face I dream of, Alix, but no, Nicky may not see his beloved's face and now finds that even a word is too much to hope for. You are too cruel to me, Alix.

Last night I was driven to such longing and despair that I went to see Sergei and Ella. They tried to comfort me but it was to no avail, for in Ella there is such a resemblance to my own longed-for one that it could not but hurt me more to see her, she who is not and cannot be Alix!

There is nothing more I can think of to say. You have chosen to punish me for things I cannot help and I suppose this leaves me with little to do but to live out a shadowy existence, always wondering if Alix could have cared for Nicky, the boy, if he had not been so terribly unlucky as to be the heir to a throne.

Ever your always loving Old Nicky

I, of course, was unsure as to what a girl in my position should feel and I could not confer with my cousins as this was all far too private a matter, so I allowed myself to write back to him with what I myself felt, and I fear I entertained many unkind thoughts in so doing, although absolute honesty should never be deemed cruelty.

Dear Nicky,

You write to me as though it were I who have wronged you. Have I run mad, Nicky? Did you not ask me to be your own wee wify three years ago, a time in which all things seemed possible to me, when my darling papa was still alive, when hope was still alive. Did you not? Did I but dream it all?

And then did I dream of the cruel rejection, of the gossip and the averted eyes of St. Petersburg when nothing happened ... nothing but my banishment. Did you not utterly desert me and without as much as a word, breaking forever my trust in you and my young girl's heart?

Was I not promised all the bounty that a girly can dream of, to be a bride and to be the bride of her one true love, the longed-for one?

Oh I was, I was indeed, and then you vanished as if into the icy mists of your country's lost land of Siberia, while freezing my heart at the same time. I have had to mourn you and then mourn my dearest Papa. And, no, I denounce your reference to your being the heir of your own still living and protective dear papa, may God keep him so. That was not what I loved, Nicky, not the throne, nothing but the man, and yet he does not exist, does he?

No, what I loved was a chimera, a prince who was no prince at all but merely a frightened little boy, a wee child, who could only jump up and down in obedience to what his mama told him to do.

How dare you write me now, and so importuningly, to say such things? Well, I will say these things in return and I will tell you this too.

Despite the summer weather at dear Illinskoe, I froze yet again from your absence, and when I left Russia, I did so never to return. I went home to my darling Papa and Ernie, and I took the vows of my father's church, the Lutheran Church, and I did so with a truly believing, if still broken, heart. I am beyond your tentative, pusillanimous reach now, little boysy. For, even if I could ever bring myself to forgive your betrayal and your cowardice, I cannot, and will not, change my religion. Yes, do go and look at Ella, go and look because she is the nearest you shall ever have to my countenance, whether it be beautiful, as you say, or otherwise.

Forget me now, Nicky, as I have forgotten and forgiven you.

Alix.

Of course I did not send this letter. Instead I sent a coldly polite little note, thanking him for his letters, ignoring his impassioned cries, and merely stating that my mourning of Papa and the obedience I owed to Grandmamma in carrying out such duties as she demanded of me had made a poor correspondent out of me. Furthermore, I held out no hope of future correspondence between us.

Then it was time for me to leave drafty Balmoral and my Grandmamma, and my silly but delightful cousins, whom I knew I would miss, and Ducky whom strangely I might miss most of all. I hugged the latter goodbye the hardest and whispered into her ear a prayer for luck in all that she desired as we departed.

Buoyed up by my own courage and by the presence of my dearest Ernie, who chattered so gaily on the train about all his plans for our future, I felt as though I might, after all, find both meaning and purpose in my life, even with Papa gone and Nicky now relegated to a closet of my heart, which I was determined should henceforth remain forever locked and best forgotten.

Chapter 12

Once Ernie and I arrived back home in Darmstadt, he began almost immediately to realize his long-held dreams of living surrounded by the Art Nouveau rooms and furniture that had, until then, been confined solely to pictures and the paper furniture I had made for him.

I think, or I like to think, that I understood his need to put his own stamp on the new palace; after all, as the Grand Duke, it was now all his, and I adored all things Art Nouveau as well. It was simply that, as the workmen came in and all the old furniture and ornaments were packed away into the attics, I felt Papa vanishing from each corner too, charmingly rounded and accented as those corners were.

Still, I am sure Ernie was right to undertake the renovation as soon as he did, for in no time at all the palace was filled with potted palms and bright chintzes, and cozy lowered ceilings with pastel walls, and as he said confidingly, "I know Papa wouldn't have liked the way things look, but oh Alicky, it is just our little home now, isn't it, where we can be so happy together and do whatever we like all the time, and it will be like this forever now for you and me, won't it?"

The comfort and security of these words and the true heartfelt emotion behind them is impossible to describe, but you must see it. Everyone, all my life, had always left me behind, either through death or marriage or false promises, everyone but my dearest Ernie, my darling brother, my lovely more lighthearted other half, and it was with this feeling of surety and rightness that I finally allowed myself to let Papa go, and put away my black dresses to settle into mauve, which is half-mourning and, by a small stroke of good fortune, also my favorite color.

I began, too, to act as Ernie's hostess. He had, of course, always been well known to the generals and burghers of Hesse-Darmstadt but as Papa's dear son. It is quite a different thing to be the Grand Duke and titular leader of the state, and I fancy that my small luncheons and dinners were in no small part the reason that he was so quickly accepted as such.

There was also a quite new aspect to life at the "new, new palace," as Ernie playfully called it. Ernie, unbeknownst to Papa and even to me, had, it seemed, long cultivated a group of the liveliest young men – local artists and artisans – whom I had never met before but who now seemed to congregate almost daily in the palace, although Ernie rather inexplicably did not invite them to my little luncheon and dinner parties with the generals and burghers, despite my urging him to do so as I felt they might add a much-needed touch of liveliness to these pleasant but somewhat dull affairs.

In this delightful way we passed the second year after Papa's death. The only dark notes, if I may be so bold as to play upon words, was the nearly ceaseless stream of letters that had begun to come from Nicky. I think it is a feature of young men that the unobtainable, even if the unobtainable were once quite obtainable, becomes desirable, or maybe I wrong him; maybe he had just grown up a great deal and realized now, too late, that we would have made something close to a perfect couple.

In this approach he was now aided by Ella, who was relaying messages to him about my secret longings for his love, and that this was in no way true did not deter her. While I did not believe then, or ever, that Ella cared a whit about Nicky and my happiness, nor do I think she wanted me to become the wife of the heir, I do think she relished the drama of the thing, having not much else to occupy her, and moreover her part in this conspiracy of dunces made her necessary to Nicky, who I'm sure she wished had viewed her, and not my reluctant self, as the object of his admiration.

As if Nicky's importuning letters of love and Ella's dramatics were not enough, one of the two of them had even persuaded sweet little Xenia to write to me. The letters themselves were the dear, innocent outpourings of a young girl confiding the details of her activities and of her growing love for her cousin Sandro. I enjoyed them and answered each one, but inevitably, tacked on as though in afterthought, or more probably at Nicky's urging, there would be a plaintive little post script:

> *Alicky dear, don't you like Nicky anymore? He says you're terribly cruel to him.*

Or:

> *Oh Alicky, my dear old hen, Nicky is so out of sorts these days. He's like an old bear. Won't you please write to him?*

I did not blame dear little Xenia for these notes: She was a very young girl feeling the first stirrings of untainted love and Nicky was her adored older brother, whom I am as sure she loved as deeply as I did my own

197

Ernie, but I felt beset all the same, from Nicky and Xenia's letters and from Ella's ridiculous games, and I think I might have become quite nervous and ill again if it hadn't been for Ernie's laughing dismissal of all of them.

"Oh posh, Alicky, who gives a fig? It is just Russians being mad, for really what else can one be in that dreadful climate? It's always night there, isn't it? That would drive even a cheerful fellow like me off his head."

So saying, he would shiver theatrically and roll his eyes until he had reduced me to gales of laughter, whereupon he would grin mischievously.

"There, that's all right, then. Say, why don't we go down to the square and torment old Peter?"

Poor "Old Peter," as Ernie affectionately referred to him, was actually a very young, handsome Peter who worked in his father's blacksmiths shop. For some reason that I couldn't fathom, Ernie enjoyed nothing more than to pop in and out of there at will and tease young Peter by calling him "old fellow" and making him blush, but that was Ernie all over. He was always up for a gay time and a jest, and could turn anything at all into an adventure, and he wanted me with him at all times. So, thanks to Ernie, my dearest one, I was never allowed to become too broody about what Nicky's letters meant to me, if they meant anything at all.

> *Alix, darling, may I call you that? No, I may*
> *not. Alix does not love Nicky. Alix says that I*
> *am too late, but then that isn't true, is it, my*
> *Alicky? It can never be too late when one*
> *loves as I do. Can't you see it, my darling?*

Don't you know that you are the only girl in the world for me? When I close my eyes I see your sweet face, and when I open them too, because Ella has given me a lovely picture of my longed-for one that I have hidden under my pillow lest Mama come to my room to visit me unexpectedly.

Sometimes, though, they were just a delight to read and filled with fun tales of his family, but even then there was a longing. After Princess Hélène, the French Pretender's daughter, had refused poor Cousin Eddy because she would not convert from Catholicism to Anglicanism, Eddy had become engaged to poor Mary of Teck, and then promptly died. Then poor Cousin Georgie, his brother, had been forced by Grandmamma to propose to her instead of continuing his pursuit of Cousin Marie, pretty Missy. This, in turn, made Marie decide, doubtless based on a narrowing in the field of royals heirs to marry, to get engaged to Crown Prince Ferdinand.

Nicky's letter about all this was quite funny.

Poor old Hélène has now turned down Eddy and lost her chance to be a Dowager Princess of England, which I'm sure is much better than being a permanent old maid of France, because, despite Mama's urging, I'm certainly not going to marry her, and besides, as I very reasonably pointed out to Mama, if Hélène won't give up her Catholicism for England, when it was widely

199

reported that she was quite in love with poor dead Eddy – at least while he was alive – then why would she adopt the Orthodox faith for a boy she has never met at all and who is, as the whole world knows, quite in love with one Princess Alix of Hesse?

Speaking of changing religions, my darling one, did Ella write and tell you yet that she is going to become Orthodox? As you know, she didn't need to, since Sergei is so far from the throne, but she wants to. Now, if that doesn't tell a wee girlie something of the beauty of our religion, I don't suppose I can say any more on the subject, at least not in this letter!

Say, would you think of coming to England next month for Georgie and Mary of Teck's wedding? It should be awfully good fun, though I hope both of them remember whose name to say at the wedding, as it wasn't very long ago that poor Mary, or May as all call her, was about to marry Eddy. And as for Georgie, Mama says that her sister, Aunt Alix, told her in the strictest confidence that he still carries a miniature of Cousin Missy upon his chest. Poor old May: two English princes and neither one much wanted her, but I suppose it will all come out all right later on, though don't you think, Alicky, that it must be better all round just to marry the

right person, the one who has loved and
wanted only you, right from the beginning?

Yes, I did think of him, and not just when his or Xenia's letters came, and despite my having to write a very harshly worded letter to Ella after I received the following idiocy from her.

Darling Alicky, you'll be so pleased to know
that I told Nicky to write to you addressing
you as 'Pelly I' and sign them as 'Pelly II,'
this in case they should fall into the wrong
hands!

I could not believe her ... code names? I think that even our good Lord in his heaven must have occasionally sighed at the utter stupidity of Ella, and I told her as much by return post.

To his credit, Nicky, never once addressed me either in a letter or in person as Pelly anything, although years later at Illinskoe, we would erupt into giggles at the memory of it all, while Ella blushed in embarrassed annoyance ... but that was later, of course.

Then, oh then ... what did I feel then?

I felt so many things that even now I find them nearly impossible to articulate, but I must try. Did I still love him? Yes, because in my sadness I could not seem to *not* love him. Oh, by then I knew his faults: He was weak and subsumed utterly to the will of his mama, and he was afraid of the destiny to which God and birth had consigned him, and I, who was never afraid, hated his cowardice, but strangely it never lessened my love for

201

him. I could be a harsh judge, of both myself and others, I knew that. It is a sin which I have never managed to overcome.

So why then did his failings never lessen my love for him? I do not know. I can only speculate that, as the Bible has promised, there is one person whom God alone, in his infinite wisdom, has chosen for each one of us, and for me that was Nicky. Rather than change him, I merely wanted to protect him, but none of this meant that I was willing to change my religion and marry him.

Why did I cling so fiercely to my Lutheran vows, and to my brother, and to our modest palace, and to my four dresses, and to my small life? Because I knew them, because I was safe in and with them, and because I was afraid, the emotion I never admit to having and always deny if confronted with it. In fact, despite great moments of discomfort while in company owing to my physical weaknesses – my sore legs, my headaches and my terrible shyness – I would always push my courage to the sticking point and do what I knew I should.

Yes, I missed him and thought of him, and imagined him, and imagined us, and I never truly planned to become a silly old spinster, and my heart had long ago forgiven him his weakness at the time we first acknowledged our love. All of these things were true, as was my fear. That vague, free-floating but very real dread was also true: something awaited me if I were to give him his heart's desire; something dark and terrible would come upon me.

The ghosts of the new palace whispered to me, "Stay here where you are safe. There are things, Alix ..." but I could not hear what. Maybe even the dead did not know themselves what they were but the dead do know darkness and that it awaited me, whereas if I could only continue to deny him and my own longings, then I could be safe. If it was a lonelier life than I had once wished for, I still had my home, my church, and my darling brother; and for me, I regret, the comfort of the known has always outweighed any other choice, even if that choice promised much.

I was twenty, then twenty-one years of age, a birthday Ernie and I celebrated quietly at home, just the two of us, and as he toasted my health I felt that I was right to remain where I was and how I was.

I believed this until the very moment when Grandmamma, my dearest Grandmamma, my true mother, chose to take it all away from me.

Chapter 13

Grandmamma decided, how and why I will never know, to arrange for my Ernie, my one-and-all in this world, to become engaged to Ducky.

Ducky!

I received Grandmamma's letter a week after she had written to Ernie proposing this arrangement, something he had told me nothing about, so my shock was incalculable.

> *Dearest Alicky,*
>
> *By now Ernie will have shared with you his happy news, but I wanted to write to you personally to tell you why this is much the best course of action for all involved.*
>
> *As I write this, my dear, I don't know that you will not find old Grandmamma's idea a silly one, even an upsetting one, although I know how well you got along with little Ducky when you stayed with me at Balmoral not long after your dear papa passed from this world of cares.*
>
> *My own life, my dear child, has been one of almost ceaseless sorrow and responsibility, and, as you know, I have found meaning only in caring for my dear ones since the*

*senseless and tragic death of my dearest
love.*

*It is because of this care – no, due to this
care – that I have arranged the coming
marriage of my two beloved grandchildren.
It was simply the only solution for both of
these dear children, as you too must see,
Alicky my darling child.*

*Poor little Ducky had set her heart on a
match with her Cousin Cyril, and it could
not be! The imperial family does not
approve of marriage between first cousins
and such a marriage would necessarily
remove Cyril from the line of succession.
Naturally, Cyril's mama does not wish this
for him, as he is fourth in line to the throne.
Little Ducky has now realized the
impossibility of her choice and was all too
ready to listen to Grandmamma. She has
therefore agreed, with great good grace, to
marry Ernie, of whom she is very fond.*

*I know you will say, my child, but what of
Ernie? I know, my dear Alicky, that Ernie is
your dearest brother and your companion –
you may even say your one-and-all since
your dear papa has gone – but you must
realize, child, that he is also the Grand Duke
of Hesse-Darmstadt and you must have
always known that one day he would have to*

marry and produce heirs for the comfort of his people. This is the first duty of all of us who have been set over others by God.

I do know, child, that you will feel somewhat displaced, but in all truth, Alicky, that was only your place until you chose to marry, which is every woman's duty, whether she be royal or not, and I cannot help you with your future decisions now, my dear. You might discuss them with dear Ernie, who will, I am sure, continue to offer you a home with him and Ducky, as it is his duty to do.

In the meantime, you are welcome to come and stay with old Grandmamma after the wedding for a few weeks to give the young couple privacy as they get to know one another and embark upon their lives.

I remain your devoted old Grandmamma

Victoria R.

I put down Grandmamma's letter with shaking hands and stared blankly out of the window of the morning room where I had been reading it. Suddenly the perfectly ordinary view of the gardens and the town square beyond it seemed unusually precious and I could hear my heart pounding out a rhythm accompanied by the words 'not yours, not yours, no longer yours.'

I then opened my latest letter from Nicky, one I had received a week earlier in response to my own letter in which I had begged him to abandon all hope of our being together.

Things had changed over the last year within the calculations of the Russian imperial family. Nicky's suit for Princess Hélène's hand, one pressed on his behalf by his mother, had failed, just as he had predicted it would. She would not even consider changing her religion. Nicky's parents had then tried to persuade him to marry Mossy, our Cousin Willy's sister, but Nicky forcefully declared to his parents that he would rather become a monk than marry her. That left only me, clumsy, stiff, graceless, old me, and since even I was preferable to his having no wife at all, they had at last agreed to his asking me formally for my hand.

He did so immediately and in writing. I refused his offer on the grounds of religion, knowing that any other excuse would sound baseless. This resulted in a renewed spate of interference from Ella and more of Xenia's letters, who was herself engaged to her own Sandro.

Nicky did not give up. It was strange that he was so stubbornly determined to have me now when he had run so quickly away five years ago at a mere shake from his mama's head, but he was indeed determined and continued writing letters that became ever more demanding in their intent, obliging me to become ever clearer in my own.

Never, ever, will I change my religion, so stop torturing yourself and me, as what you wish for cannot, and will not, ever come to pass, was the gist of what I attempted to impress upon him, but in response he wrote yet again, this being the letter I was now contemplating amid much changed circumstances.

Alicky,

Please forgive me for taking so long to respond to your last letter, but when I read your words, your terribly damning words, I could not bring myself to respond to them.

Yes, my darling, I do say damning and I will not ask for your forgiveness for my impetuous language, for that is what you will do to me if you do not marry me, Alix – you will damn my life.

Do not say no so directly, my darling. Do not ruin our lives, my own and yours, for I know, as maybe you do not, that we are all for each other and that neither of us will have a moment's happiness in this world or the next if we do not tread the path of this life together, whether that path should prove to be smooth or rock-strewn.

Please, my darling, if you do not know, if you have fears, let me put them aside, for I do know: I know that this is right, that it is what must be, that we are what must be.

Forever, Nicky.

I refolded the letter and sighed. It was all up for me now and maybe he did know. God alone knew that I was no longer sure of anything.

I composed myself and went to Ernie. I kissed him in congratulation and soothed his fears, assuring him that that, yes, it would all be fine with Ducky, and more than fine, and thanking him for his offer that I should always have a home with him.

Then I thought and I thought, all that day and the next, and then on the train to Coburg with Ernie for his wedding, until my mind became quite feverish.

Nicky was there to meet us at the train station. He looked so dear, and so small, and so vulnerable. He began pressing his suit the next morning, everyone did, all the countless aunts and cousins who had gathered there in that lovely spring, lavender-drenched week to watch my dearest Ernie marry Ducky. It was "right." It was "destiny."

Ella put it another way. "Do you really want to be a burden to your family forever, Alix? I mean, of course you can visit Sergei and me sometimes, and I imagine Irene and Louis will –"

I held up my hand to cut her off, to cut all of them off. "This talk is all unnecessary. I agree to marry Nicky."

Then I told him yes, too. He was transported with joy, all the family was, and suddenly strange, spinster Alix was the most desirable and important girl in the world, and in his love and joy, and in my family's beaming approval, I put away my fears and hesitations. I was going to marry Nicky and one day I was going to be the Empress of Russia, and we would all be so terribly happy and there would be a time when I would laugh at my own stupid concerns.

I was going to marry Nicky and live like every princess would wish to live, happily ever after.

It is most strange, but from the moment I agreed to become Nicky's own wifey, I became so terribly important that it made me realize how abjectly insignificant I had been up until that day.

I hadn't really been mindful of this. After all, I had always been dear Grandmamma's much-favored granddaughter and she was the most powerful woman in the world; I was closely related to the Emperor of Germany and had narrowly avoided having the ever-annoying Willy as my brother-in-law; I was considered by many to be the prettiest princess in Europe, or at least one of them, alongside Missy, and my beauty was often compared with that of Empress Sissy of Austria.

I suppose that if I had thought about my place in the world at all, which I hadn't, I would have said, at least to myself, that I was someone of some import. Clearly I would have been mistaken.

This I understood within a day of becoming the future bride of the future Emperor of all the Russias. Immediately there was not a single member of my enormous extended family, a family known affectionately to ourselves as the "royal mob," who did not seek me out. Nicky's love had apparently given me the wisdom of Solomon, the beauty of Helen of Troy, and the holiness of the saints. I do not exaggerate this, because at every turn I was either being asked my

211

opinion on nearly every matter under the sun or being lavishly complimented for my seemingly unending virtues.

> *From Ducky, whom I found I once again disliked: "Now we're truly sisters, Alix darling."*

> *From Sergei: "Little sister, now little cousin, so tell me, dear Alicky, are you not glad that your future father-in-law has passed the Pale of Settlement Act so that no filthy Jews will cross your pretty path?"*

> *From Georgie: "Dearest Cousin Alicky, I say, I am so fond of my dear old May, but I do hope you'll help her pick out a hat exactly like the one you're wearing today. You look simply enchanting."*

> *From Willy: "Alix, it appears it is not Sergei I should envy, but that dearest boy Nicky, for hasn't he obtained the treasure of the world."*

Even Grandmamma, someone I had always considered to have been most fond of me, was much fonder of me now. Instead of her previous offer that I could stay with her for a few weeks until Ernie and Ducky had settled into married life, she was now insisting that I remain with her right up until our wedding, which Nicky predicted would be no later than the following spring, a mere year away.

All of them wanted me to visit them: Uncle Bertie and Aunt Alix, even Missy and Ducky's formidable mama, Aunt Marie. I was simply overtaken by invitations.

Did I say that I also appeared to have become, on the instant, as rich as Midas. No? Well, so it was. Every jeweler in England flocked *en masse* to Coburg to show me, or rather to show Nicky, their very best wares. Nor were they disappointed, for Nicky did not deny any of them as they gave him an opportunity to present me with a fabulous new piece of jewelry on the hour. In addition to these, there were the gifts he had already brought, the naughty boy having apparently been so sure of my answer, but when I teased him about it, he blushed and replied that he hadn't been sure at all, and that if I had broken his heart and said no, he would have thrown all his gifts for me into the sea and hoped that some mermaid would have been happy with them instead, a proposition no one could dispute as my left hand now sported a thirty carat pink diamond. And I had so many strings of pearls – black, and pink and purest ivory – and in such abundance, that I could have completely covered every gown in them from head to toe, and even these were intended only to set off the parures of sapphires, diamonds and rubies, and, from Nicky's Mama and Papa, a necklace of so many fine and enormous emeralds that its weight nearly bent me double.

This lavish gift was accompanied by a letter from Empress Minnie, whom I had addressed as 'Aunt

Minnie' while answering a congratulatory telegram from her.

Dearest darling Alix,

Sasha and I are so very, very glad that you have answered our dearest Nicky's plea with a yes. We have watched in such anguish as our poor boy's despair grew daily more terrible on receiving yet another letter from you denying his request.

All that is, of course, past now and must never be spoken of in the sunshine of your joyous coming to him at long last.

Sasha and I have sent you this token of our love and gratitude. Do please, dearest Alix, write and let me know which you prefer in terms of stones, i.e. emeralds, diamonds, etc., for future gifts. I thought the emeralds would be a lovely choice for your coloring.

I'll bid you adieu, dear girl, and ask only that in the future you address me as 'Mother Dear,' for that is what I shall be to you now and you will, of course, be my own dear child.

Best Love

Marie, Empress of Russia.

My Nicky, my "boysy," as I now called him, told his "Sunny," as he now called me, that the letter had been written to show how truly delighted his parents were at our match, delighted and surprised, as he had innocently shown me a letter from his papa that had expressed stunned amazement that I had consented to his suit.

I felt somewhat defensive on his behalf, but Nicky smiled angelically and said I need not.

"Papa is simply speaking from his heart, as he always does, Sunny darling. You see, he loves me very, very much, of course he does, and he simply worries and always has, that I will not be a very good Tsar." He leaned over and kissed my cheek when I protested. "No, darling, don't be like that. He's right – Papa, I mean – so you shouldn't take offense on my part. I certainly don't. I have never thought I'd be up to much if I ever had to become Tsar and I don't want to be one in any case. Luckily for us, Papa is still so young, and he is as strong as a bear, so it is nothing either of us needs worry about for ages. Why, we'll probably be as old as Cousin Bertie when it happens. Oh look, let's not even talk about it. It too sad a subject, don't you think, Sunny darling?"

What did I think? Well, I don't suppose I much wanted to be Empress if it meant Nicky having to be the Emperor and that would make him unhappy, and, of course, loving him as I did, I never wanted him to go through the dark and lonely misery of becoming an orphan, as I was. However, I did suppose that if we were going to get as old as Uncle Bertie and Aunt Alix before we became the rulers of Russia, we should make some sort of plan for our futures anyway.

So that is just what we did. First in Coburg, and then in Windsor, where Nicky accompanied me to visit Grandmamma, we planned and dreamed away our days. We would have six children, declared Nicky, since he had come from a family of six and thought it quite perfect. We would have seven, I countered, one more than his mama: four handsome boys for the Empire and three beautiful princesses to be friends for me.

"They won't be princesses, darling."

"And why not, my boysy of boys?"

He laughed. "Grand Duchesses, that's what our girls will be, and our boys will be Grand Dukes, all except our firstborn, poor little fellow. He'll be a Tsarevich, like me, and then Tsar one day, more's the pity, but it can't be helped."

"Where will we live, Nicky? Where will our nest be?"

His head lay in my lap as I asked that as we sprawled at the foot of an apple tree near Windsor Great Park. He looked up at me with an indescribable look of adoration, for he loved me so much, making my heart positively glow with happiness.

Being with Nicky was almost exactly like living with Ernie, they were so much the same, but with the difference that when Nicky gazed at me or held my hand, I was swept, even shaken, by feelings so utterly new and precious that they are as hard to describe as if they were snowflakes.

Nicky continued to look into my eyes with his clear blue gaze and spoke earnestly.

"Well, of course, we can live anywhere you want, my Sunbeam. There's, let's see ..." He held up his fingers to

216

try and keep count of our options while I repressed a laugh. "There's Anichkov, of course. It's been my home and it has loads of room, though I don't suppose you would want to live with Mama and Papa, would you?" My expression must have been answer enough, because he continued on hurriedly, "No, of course you wouldn't. A girl likes her own nest, doesn't she?" I nodded and smiled and he proceeded more ruminatively. "Well, there's Gatchina. It's got an awfully good park … and the old Winter Palace, oh that place is so drafty, but then we'll have to spend the season in town, Mama will insist on that, so maybe during the winter … If you don't like Gatchina, and Mama never has … I don't know why … but you'll get to decide that for yourself. Then we have Peterhof, although I always think of Old Pete as a springtime sort of palace." I nodded as if I understood, although the very idea of a "springtime sort of palace" was a novel idea to me, to say the least. "Or, you know, we could make our own little home at Tsarkoe. I do love Tsarkoe so much. I was born there and I saw my Alix there too for the first time, at the little palace, although I imagine you'd like the Catherine Palace more. It's awfully pretty and much bigger, so I –"

"Oh Nicky, could we? Could we live at that darling, precious palace, the one where we met? I know I'd love it there and it's not much bigger than the new palace, so we could make it so cozy, a little house just for us and maybe …" I trailed off, blushing.

He sat up and leaned into me, his face blazing as well.

"For us and and maybe some small ones, is that what you mean, my darling, my angel? Oh Alix, yes of course. We'll live there, or anywhere else you want. I'll build you a new palace for every day of the year, if you want, if you only promise to always love me even a millionth as much as I love you."

If the moment called for me, as a young lady, to lighten the emotional intensity of this exchange and the growing need for physical intimacy, I could not. I could only gaze at him with tears cascading down my face.

"Oh Nicky, my agoo wee one, my own heart, I will always love you with all that I can ever be, and never, ever will it make me good enough for an angel like you."

"No, it is I who can never be worthy of you," he declared, impassioned, and then, though I blush to say this, we embraced and I allowed him a most immodest kiss, and I think we were both swaying rather unsteadily when our lips pulled back.

We had three weeks of this unrivaled bliss, days of picnics and rides and hours under trees while I embroidered and he read aloud to me. Dearest Grandmamma, who understood the tender yearnings of young hearts all too well, gave us limitless stretches of time on our own, virtually unchaperoned, asking only that we not be late for dinner with her where she beamed upon us approvingly, sanctioning our love with her beneficence.

However this idyllic period passed all too quickly as Nicky was summoned home to Russia on the thin pretext that he needed to present the story of our engagement in person to his parents and to resume his duties as Tsarevich.

Nicky seemed confused as to what these duties might be, but he was a truly devoted son and did not question his parents' wishes. He left me collapsed in Grandmamma's arms, and though he did not show it at the time, he too was nearly prostrate, as I learnt from the letter he left me, telling me of his endless and enduring love and of his terrible grief at our parting. Along with the letter there was a large diamond he had entitled "Nicky's tear."

I slept with it that night under my pillow.

Chapter 14

It seemed to me that all things around me, but most especially the people, were completely changed by my engagement. This was worrisome, for I did not feel particularly changed at all. Oh, I was now engaged and a bride-to-be, but I was engaged to Nicky whom I felt I had always known, and while our new intimacy was of course different, it also wasn't. For hadn't I imagined it all in my secret young girl's heart for so many long years?

I had indeed, and I was now in possession of a jewel collection to rival that of many a ruling queen, but I still had only eight dresses altogether to display any of it on.

These truths were apparent, however, only to myself. To the rest of the world it was as though I had already become the Empress of one of the mightiest kingdoms in Christendom. Worse, within days my cousins, and even dearest Grandmamma, began to address me in French. I barely knew a word of French and was most confused as to how they expected me to respond. Grandmamma even became sharp with me when I pointed out to her that I had never learnt to speak that language.

"Alix, it is, and has always been since the time of Peter the Great, the language of the Russian court. You will be censored in Russia for this lack, for certainly you do not know how to speak their own barbaric language, a language that I have always felt is as incomprehensible as everything else about that strange land, but being unable to speak French reflects poorly upon me and upon your poor papa, and I must insist that you try harder to learn it."

Maybe I was changing too, because never before had I dared, or even wished, to contradict Grandmamma.

"Darling Grandmamma, you'll forgive me, I am certain, for saying this, but I'm surprised at your sudden enthusiasm for the French language or anything at all to do with France. I was entirely unaware that you were so fond of the place. Moreover, I speak both English and German quite fluently, and can write in both as well, and I hardly need point out that, since I am going to be the wife of the heir to the Russian throne, it might well behoove the court to learn my languages rather than I theirs, don't you think?"

Given Grandmamma's notoriously hasty temper and her positive detestation of being contradicted – an event that almost never occurred due to the fact that she was a reigning queen – I was a bit apprehensive about her reaction to my somewhat impetuous speech, but she did not look angry, only worried, contenting herself with smiling at me sadly and gesturing me towards a nearby chair with no appearance of resentment at all.

I worried I had wounded her feelings, which would have made me feel much worse than to have annoyed her, and as I reached out my young hand to her soft old one, she grasped it eagerly enough but raised her remaining hand to cut off my stammering apology.

"No, my dear, don't apologize. It is I who should apologize to you."

I was horrified and drenched in remorse. I raised her dear hand and covered it with kisses as she gazed at me with her wise old eyes.

"No, no, dearest, oh very dearest Grandmamma, please don't say such things. Haven't you been as a mother to me for as long as I can remember, and always the very soul of kindness. Please don't look sad. Can't we just forget that I said such a silly thing? I have been all at sixes and sevens since the engagement, wanting to make everyone happy, most especially Nicky, and of course you, and I'm simply a wreck. Do say I haven't made you sad."

She did not reply to my entreaty. Her eyes took on that lost and distant gaze that usually preceded one of her long reminisces of her lost Albert, and her first words did not disabuse me of this.

"I was very young when I became this country's queen, Alix, and before I could begin to learn what that meant, I had also become a wife, and it seems at times when I come to gaze back upon that, that I had become a widow before I had learned what being a wife meant, and that I had become this old woman in front of you before I ever learned what I owed to my people as their queen."

I sighed inwardly, but wanting to make up for my recent transgression, I prepared to listen patiently to her tale.

However, I was mistaken in my previous assumption. Grandmamma could still surprise me and her words that day did so.

"I made so many errors, my dear, and even though I was younger than you are, my poor Alicky, I had advantages that you do not have. I was born to my own country; you are a stranger to your new one. I was aware at a very early age that I would one day be Queen; you

223

have not been. I was raised in the court where I would become Queen; you were not. I knew what was expected of me, you see, my dear. I knew and yet ..."

This aroused my curiosity, and as I didn't want her to fall off into sleep, as she so often did when speaking to me, I prompted her, "You knew, Grandmamma, but you didn't what? What do you mean?"

She shook herself and smiled fondly at me.

"Yes, I must tell you, mustn't I? I should have had this talk with you so long ago, but then I thought possibly that you would marry poor dear Eddy and I would have the opportunity help you here. I never truly believed in a Russian marriage for you. Maybe I simply so much wished for it not to take place that I could not bring myself to believe in it. This too you will find, my darling girl, is a thing that happens to queens. Heaven knows, child, there are few enough people around us who dare to tell us things we do not wish to hear."

She smiled mischievously at me, but I could not return her smile.

"Grandmamma, what do you mean? Help me? Why do I need help? I thought you liked Nicky very much. Are you not very glad for me?"

She frowned and shook her head lightly.

"You misunderstand me, my dear. Yes, of course I like your Nicky. Who could not? He's a dear boy. That is not what I am speaking of at all, and Alix, you insult us both if you are foolish enough to think that liking someone has anything to do with marriage. It does not, or I should better say that it does not for those whom God has chosen to rule. There are matters far more important than that awaiting us. Well not me, my dear.

My race is nearly run, but yours is just beginning and I need you to hear me now and not interrupt me with girlish foolishness, which in any case is a state of mind that should be years behind you."

I felt my own temper rising, but decided to resign myself to hearing her out, both as a sign of respect and because the only thing awaiting me after this rather perplexing interview was a meeting with some odd Russian priest whom my future mother-in-law had sent to England to instruct me in the Orthodox faith, yet another thing I needed to learn all about, supposedly, along with French.

"Yes, Grandmamma, of course you are right. Please tell me what it is I need to know that will help me to be a good wife to Nicky and to avoid whatever mistakes you feel you may have made as both a queen and a wife, although of course I am sure you made neither."

I hoped that by my ending this speech somewhat disingenuously, Grandmamma would decide that I had learned all I needed to know and that we could move on to discussing something of real interest to me, such as the planning of my trousseau.

"I can see by your expression, Alix, that you are simply humoring an old woman. Well, so be it, but I'll speak anyway, for maybe one day my words will prove most useful to you. You are still young, and you are beautiful, and you are in love, and you will be a mighty Empress one day, and all of this is bound to make one a tad proud and over-confident as to one's prospects for the future. Fairytales, my dear, are for the consumption of commoners, not of royalty. We know better, and you will find that many complications will arise during the course of your, I pray, long life, and when such difficulties occur, I hope you will remember silly old Grandmamma's words and find some benefit in them."

"Yes, Grandmamma, I'm sure I will."

She sighed. "As I have told you, I became the queen of this greatest of all empires at a young age. People wanted to please me, at least the people who surrounded me did. My every utterance was greeted with perfect astonishment. They said they could not believe that one so young could be so wise. If I made a remark displaying the slightest wit, the court fell about it itself in gales of laughter. I had been raised by a sensible mother who had tried to warn me against such flattery, but to be honest, my dear, I never much liked my mother, and besides I enjoyed every moment of the attention. I had had rather a lonely childhood. Then came your grandfather ..."

"Yes, dear Grandpapa Albert. You loved him very much, I know. I love Nicky very much."

She looked at me questioningly. "Do you, my dear? That's good to hear, although, of course, it is not a bit true." She raised her hand to cut off my prompt exclamation of protest. "Oh, I know I would have said the same thing about my dear Albert if anyone had asked me at the time. In fact I did say it all the time."

She chuckled and I returned her smile, if apprehensively.

"Are you saying you didn't love him, Grandmamma?" I asked, this time with true curiosity, for I, like all their grandchildren, had been raised on the stories of the legendary love of Queen Victoria and Prince Albert.

I knew she wasn't seeing me at all when she spoke; she was far away amongst the mists of her mourned past.

"I have loved him, child. Every day since he left me, I have loved him."

"Why are you talking like this, Grandmamma? You are making it sound as if –"

"… As if I didn't love him when I had him with me, my child?"

"Yes, exactly that, and it's not true. You're not feeling well or you're trying to give me some sort of lesson that you think I need to hear and I don't, I don't need to hear this. I know I do love Nicky, so this is unnecessary."

Grandmamma's head jerked up a little and she stared at me blearily as if I had interrupted her reverie, and I hoped that it meant that she would either move on to a different subject or excuse herself for a nap.

She did neither. Instead, she began to laugh. It was terrible; she was really laughing at me. She snorted and guffawed, and even slapped her knee. I'd never even seen her chuckle before, let alone this. I felt my face redden and my fingers clench. She noted this and chortled more loudly.

Only slowly did she collect herself, and I waited stonily for her to wipe her streaming eyes before I spoke.

"I'm glad you find my true heart's emotions so amusing, Grandmamma."

She nodded happily.

"Oh I do, my dear. It makes it all easier to bear somehow, doesn't it, when one realizes that no matter how obvious and unbearable one's own mistakes were, it was all somehow inevitable, for in listening to you,

227

sweet child, I see myself as I once was and know that I would not have listened to anyone else's advice either."

"Grandmamma, I am always at your service and I am glad if I have made you feel better about some long-dead past, but I find I am very tired now and would like to rest, if you don't mind."

"I don't mind at all, my dear, but you can wait a moment more, I think. You will hear this, Alix, and then you can go and do whatever you wish. When I married your grandfather, he did not please me every moment of the day, and I was used to being pleased. He had his own ideas of what a ruling couple should be and do, and I disagreed with him, sometimes to the point of having him locked into our bedroom until I felt he was ready to give way to me."

I forgot my anger and gaped at her. She grinned wickedly back at me and I glimpsed, for the first time, the imperious young girl she had once been.

"You locked him in his room, Grandmamma? He must have been furious at you."

She shook her head, suddenly sad again, suddenly old.

"No, he wasn't. That was the worst of it. He never did get angry at me, Alicky, not when I wouldn't let him share the contents of my red boxes, or when I wouldn't listen to him about sanitation or schools or much of anything, and not when I raged at him for every disappointment, either real or imagined, in ourselves and in our children. And then, before I could fully see what sort of man he was and what sort of woman he was helping me to become, he died. Then I knew. Of course by then it didn't matter much, except to me. To me it mattered more than anything that was left to me, including my children and my crown. When I managed to raise up my head again, forty years had passed, my children were grown up and didn't like me much, and my people had nearly forgotten I existed. That's never a good thing, my dear."

My own eyes were filled with tears. Poor Grandmamma! However I knew she was wrong and wanted me to tell her so and make her feel better.

"Grandmamma, you're people love you. Why, when you had your jubilee –"

"Yes, Alicky, they came in droves. They were, I think, joyous but not too loving. We need the love of our people and of our court, Alix. You will need it far more than I ever have if you want to hold onto your throne, for the throne of the Romanovs is a troubled one."

I felt the chill of the old unspoken dreads again and looked at her, wanting … I'm not sure what I wanted.

She patted my hand.

"You're tired, child and I am too. I need to rest. I only wanted to help you. I wanted to say all that should have been taught you while you were growing up, but I've done it badly, I think, and merely frightened you. Don't be afraid, child: a queen cannot afford that luxury. I merely meant to tell you to be kind and not to bring your own wants and likes to your new country. Learn theirs instead and embrace them. You will need friends, child, and you are not good at making friends. I had great prime ministers to shield me; you and your Nicky will one day be all your people have. You must listen to Minnie despite the dislike I see in you for her. She has been where you will be and she was an obedient young wife in her time. Earn the love of your Nicky's family and of your new people. Nothing else will make you safe in that country. Adapt to them, Alix, for in the end that is what a good queen does and it makes for a happier woman. I have found both my daughter-in-law, Alexandra, and your future mother-in-law, Minnie, to be happier women than most of us in this strange business of ruling. Now go, child, go write to your Nicky, go take religious instruction, go study French, and do it all with a grateful heart, for remember that if it seems that much is asked of us, much more is given to us."

I left her, and if I did not fully agree with her advice, and if I thought her too old and somewhat at a loss to understand my own situation, then I did not discard it completely either. Indeed, over the next few days I pondered it rather deeply.

In the end I decided to discuss it with Nicky when he returned for his second visit a month later. He laughed nearly as hard as Grandmamma had done, but for completely different reasons.

"Darling Sunny, I think your granny is a charming old woman, she's been very nice to me, but she doesn't understand a thing about Russia. How could she?"

I looked down at his dear face, for I confess that his head was upon my lap as we picnicked in the gardens of Osbourne House.

"I'm so glad you say that, Nicky, but explain to me, my boysy, why is it so different? I think these days that all I know is that I seem to understand nothing at all anymore."

He smiled adoringly up at me, his beautiful blue eyes shining with happiness.

"You understand everything that is important in our world, my darling. You have made me the happiest, luckiest man alive. You've made Papa and Mama happy by saying you will be my own bride, and if we are happy, then our people, your people, dearest, are more than glad and will love you just as I do. You see, Sunny, Russia is nothing like England. In Russia, the tsars are much the same as God is to my people. All that they want in their Empress is that she be happy. Oh, and that she provide the Tsar with heirs, of course." He blushed furiously at that remark, as did I. When he could speak again he finished cheerfully, saying, "Anyway, darling, this is a silly discussion. Papa is a young man still and we'll have years and years before that terrible day dawns. You'll speak French perfectly by then, and for all I know, there will be grandsons. You will be hailed as the most beautiful Empress ever to sit on the throne of my ancestors. *Je vous adore, Alix.*"

There is nothing really that I wish to record of the following days and nights that Nicky and I shared at Osbourne. That they were perfection is really all that need be known. Any doubts I had about our future were vanquished in the light of his uncritical devotion to me and of his complete assurance that our future would be one of endless joy and ease.

Then, just as we were preparing to visit Ernie and Ducky so that I could show Nicky my own small home, he received a telegram. His papa had become ill. The imperial family, following the advice of the Tsar's physicians, was repairing to their palace in the Crimea to allow him to recuperate in a warmer climate and his parents wanted their heir with them.

He was needed at home and so we parted yet again, knowing that we would not see each other possibly for months, and maybe not until our wedding.

I didn't mind too terribly. I knew I would miss him, of course, but we had promised to write to each other every day. Then, too, I had a trousseau to order and it seemed to me that, between fittings and learning French, and maybe a little Russian along with my lessons in Orthodoxy, even a year might not be quite enough time for me to prepare for my future.

During Nicky's visit, Grandmamma and I had become quite reconciled, and as Nicky had pointed out, I did need to realize that she had become quite old and that she was filled with bitter regrets based upon the many mistakes that he and I were certainly not going to make in our turn. Unlike poor Grandmamma, with Nicky by my side, I had the utter security of knowing that I would be starting my own married life with my chosen one, and that he and I were hardly likely to end up bitter old people who wished we had done things better and who would then spend our golden years annoying our own grandchildren with tedious tales of our youthful errors.

In fact, during Nicky's stay, Grandmamma had been both amiable and filled with really good advice, even pointing out to Nicky that the longer we waited to be married, the better it would be.

"Dearest Nicky, you must understand that poor little Alicky hasn't been quite well since the passing of her dear father and that she will need a deal of rest to prepare herself for the great role that awaits her. It seems to me that you will both be much happier if she has time, a year or so, to absorb her new languages and responsibilities, rather than just being thrown into all of the new things and new people that await her."

Nicky had tried to protest that he did not feel so much time was necessary and that I would have him to turn to along with his "wonderful Mama," who was so anxious to help and guide her new daughter-in-law.

I shuddered inwardly at that, but thanks to Grandmamma did not need to say anything that might have shown that I was not particularly looking forward to being under the Empress's guidance a moment sooner than I had to be. I was wise enough, on that matter at least, to remain silent.

Grandmamma, bless her soul, blithely disregarded Nicky's comments. "No, no, my dear boy, I know too well the impetuous nature of youth, and of course you two delightful young people think that a year or so sounds like decades." She chuckled fondly, forcing Nicky to smile back at her. "Yes, I understand it all, but Nicky, you sweet child, you who love your own mama so dearly and who know that her decisions for her own children are always the right ones, must also know that Alicky's old grandmamma knows what's best for Alicky. After all, haven't I been as a mother to her since her own mama was taken? And now, since the death of her dear papa, I am nearly all the family she has. So you will agree at least that, as far as knowing what is best for her, my decisions should not be questioned."

I had to admire Grandmamma's approach to ensuring that she always got her own way in things, for if sentiment alone did not prevail, who could argue that the Queen of England knew best, and knew it no matter what the subject was.

In private with Nicky I bemoaned her stubbornness, and if he pressed me, as he was wont to do, to set a wedding date, I would allow my tears to flow and avow helplessly, "Dearest, my boysy, can he ever doubt for a second that your little girly wants to be with her manikins all the time and soonest?" Then I'd kiss his dear frowns away and finish by saying, "But I can't, darling, I can't hurt Grandmamma and go against her wishes. What sort of start would we have if it was based upon hurting the one who has always cared for me? No, we must wait for a while, my dearest, dearest Nicky, for in patience comes our lives' truest rewards. And don't you pout, naughty one. Will not a girly be with her boysy every day and ever after, to the point that you will wish only that your old bachelor days could be returned to you!"

With such sayings, accompanied by caresses aplenty, did I manage to convince Nicky that to rush into getting married would be wrong, and even if he was not wholly in agreement with me, he was helpless to figure out how to take on both Grandmamma and me at the same time, so I think that when he boarded his papa's yacht, the Polar Star, to travel to the Crimea, he was at least resigned to waiting for me, if altogether less than happy about it.

It is, I suppose, reasonable to wonder why I so readily acquiesced to Grandmamma's desire for a long engagement. After all, I was over twenty-one and I could have insisted on complying with Nicky's wishes. I could even have got Nicky to ask his parents to intervene, and if I was so sure, if I loved him so much, why didn't I want to marry him as soon as possible?

I suppose the answer is that I did not particularly like Russia. It seemed too big, and too extreme – months of darkness and killing cold, to be followed by short summers of endless light. That wasn't reasonable, unlike Europe with its perfectly normal days and nights and seasons. Then there was Nicky's family, his father a large loud boor and his mother a small biting dog. I knew we would be living closely *en famille* with them and I don't think I can be blamed for not relishing that prospect.

I liked it that I was Nicky's fiancée and was enjoying my stay with Grandmamma in the glow of my newly enhanced status in life. I realized, of course, that the reason everyone liked me so much now was precisely because I was going to marry Nicky, and I fully planned to marry him; we couldn't simply remain affianced forever. I understood all of this, and felt that, with enough time, I could accustom my mind to all the coming changes. I was not good with change but I could be brave and determined when the situation demanded that I should be.

I had begun confiding some of my less traitorous thoughts on the matter to my new companion, Mademoiselle Schneider – Catherine as I had begun to call her – a delightful little Frenchwoman who spoke perfect English. Grandmamma had engaged her long ago as a reader for her youngest daughter, my poor Aunt Beatrice. Grandmamma was hoping that if Aunt Beatrice were read to by a French *lectrice,* as the French funnily call people who read to them, she would pick up the language more easily. Aunt Beatrice, it must be kindly said, was neither very smart nor very pretty, and she took an unreasonable dislike to nice little Mademoiselle Schneider.

Grandmamma, however, did like her, and kept her on as a sort of companion. Now she had engaged her for me. This was of great fortune for me as my usual constant companion, Nanny Orchard, had become utterly disagreeable upon my engagement to Nicky and declared that she would rather go live with the "heathen red skins in the Americas" than return permanently to Russia and be at the mercy of her rheumatics in that terrible climate.

I found the little *lectrice* a charming companion from the first day we were introduced. She was rather in awe of me but I soon set her at her ease by explaining that her knowledge of that elusive, tricky language I was being forced to learn made her much more helpful to me than I ever could be to her. She had never been to Russia, so I ended up teaching her all I knew of it and she became gratifyingly excited about the country of the tsars and seemed delighted when I asked her to accompany me there when the time came.

As I did not much enjoy her reading to me in French, nor do I feel that this is an effective way to learn a foreign tongue unless one happens to be a parrot, we devised a most equable system instead. I would ask her a question about her life and she would answer partially in English and partially in French, and then I would try to puzzle out what she had said. This was a most amusing game and in no time at all I began to enjoy our little sessions and looked forward with great anticipation to our time together. Even her worshipful attitude towards me, sinful as it is to say such things, I found rather gratifying. It was in fact her open devotion to me that allowed me to speak so freely of my fears of the life in Russia that awaited me.

Catherine was quite sympathetic to my apprehension, but she was also soothing, constantly reminding me of Nicky's devotion, and assuring me she had never seen a man so in love, nor had she seen any bride-to-be who was so beautiful. In short, she expressed herself confident that all the Russian people would be beyond delighted by me when they finally saw me.

"No country has ever had such a beautiful princess, Your Highness. Why, it is like something out of a fairytale I once read."

I laughed with pleasure at her little flushed, earnest face. "I'm guessing, Catherine, that it was a French fairytale, was it not?"

She nodded and grinned slyly at me.

"As it happens, Your Highness, it was. I could read it to you if you like."

She then proceeded to read me the altogether wonderful tale 'La Belle et La Bête,' which I enjoyed mightily while teasing her forever after about implying that Nicky was an ugly beast who could only be saved by my kisses.

In this pleasant way our friendship deepened daily. All around me the world seemed almost tailor-made for my pleasure and my trousseau began to grow with the efforts of the seamstresses that Grandmamma had ordered in from London. She was paying for it all as her bridal gift to me and to honor my Nicky's preference for seeing me dressed in pink. I picked nearly every shade of that delicious color for my gowns – morning gowns, afternoon dresses, and the most sumptuous rose velvets for the evenings – and Grandmamma made me try on each newly-finished dress for herself and Catherine to admire, whereupon they would clap and exclaim in pleasure.

I do not remember ever having been so contented with my life, and then, as all my most secure moments have always ended for me, so did this, abruptly, when a telegram arrived from Livadia in the Crimea.

It was the first telegram I had ever received from anybody. Telegrams were things of novelty and of heightened importance even for Grandmamma, as I had never seen any sort of correspondence brought to her during luncheon as this telegram was. A footman entered the room rather hurriedly and whispered to the butler, Mr. Davies, who frowned mightily, and their conversation caught Grandmamma's attention, prompting her to bark at him, displeased, "Mr. Davies, if you will, what is the meaning of this? Why is my luncheon being interrupted?"

Mr. Davies blushed, mortified, and shooting the poor footman a withering glance, muttered something into Grandmamma's ear that I could not hear, although I did not have to wait long to find out what all the commotion was about.

"A telegram?" Grandmamma exclaimed, startled.

"Yes, M'am, a telegram," stuttered poor Mr. Davies.

"Hand it to me immediately, then. What are you waiting for? Who is it from? Oh never mind, hand it here."

Mr. Davies stared in horror at Grandmamma's outstretched hand.

"Oh but, Your Majesty, I can't … Well, I mean … I …oh dear. You see, Your Majesty, it is addressed to Princess Alix, so I thought … I mean, I wondered if –"

Grandmamma's face purpled alarmingly.

"*To Princess Alix?* You have brought a telegram for my granddaughter? Someone has sent her a telegram and you interrupted my luncheon merely for this?"

Poor Mr. Davies appeared on the verge of collapsing and I was too busy trying to stifle my giggles with my napkin to even wonder why I had received a telegram. Besides, Grandmamma was quickly working her way to the bottom of this outrage all on her own.

"Tell me, Mr. Davies," she all but shrieked at him, "did you decide all on your own to interrupt my luncheon to deliver a telegram which, since it was addressed to my granddaughter, can only have to do with something like the arrival of a new dress?"

Before Mr. Davies could answer, the young footman who had started all the trouble in the first place, volunteered, "It wasn't Mr. Davies's idea, M'am, to bring in the telegram. It was mine."

Grandmamma affixed him with gimlet eyes and asked slowly, "I see, Mr. …?"

"Gansley, M'am."

"Then please explain yourself, Mr. Gansley. Cook will now have to reheat the entire meal as my fish is cold."

Mr. Gansley nodded, less contrite than I would have expected him to have been, to the point where I shuddered for him.

"Certainly, M'am. I brought it in, and I am most sincerely sorry for interrupting your luncheon –"

Grandmamma waved aside his attempts to apologize with an impatient hand accompanied by a ferocious glare.

" … It was on account that I recognized that it had been sent by the Emperor of Russia, which is why I took it upon myself to bring it here to Mr. Davies, who, if you don't mind my saying so, looks much worse for wear than your fish does now, M'am, and probably requires a certain amount of heating up himself."

Grandmamma made a dreadful noise which it took me a moment to realize was a choking laugh. Poor Mr. Davies did indeed look much the worse for wear and had to be ushered away by Mr. Gansley to the safety of the servants' quarters and at least a chair, to be promptly replaced by another attendant who efficiently saw to the rescuing of our poor dead fish.

It was not until the remnants of our luncheon were cleared from the table that Grandmamma returned to the matter of the telegram as respite from all the previous commotion.

Her face grew very serious.

"Alix, this telegram is addressed to you from Nicky."

Still in a delighted mood from our entertaining lunch, I smiled with polite interest.

"Thank you, Grandmamma, and what does he say?"

She shook her head.

"I'm sorry, my dear, it is not good news. I think it would be better if you were to read it yourself."

My mouth went suddenly too dry for me to speak and I could only shake my head in fear, wordlessly declining Grandmamma's suggestion.

Grandmamma nodded her understanding and proceeded to read it out loud.

Dearest Alix. Stop. Papa is terribly ill. Stop. I need you near me. Stop. Please come immediately. Stop. Nicky. Stop.

Grandmamma laid the telegram onto the table beside her and sighed. "I'm sorry, my child. I feared this might happen."

"You feared?" I asked, confused.

"Yes, Alicky. I have been receiving regular dispatches from our ambassador to Russia, naturally, and then too Ella has written to me. It seems that Tsar Alexander's condition was always much worse than the doctors were willing to admit. Now his physical deterioration has become too obvious to deny. I believe he is dying, Alix. I'm very sorry, my dear, sorrier than you'll ever know."

"But I … I … Grandmamma, do I have to go? Oh no, I didn't mean … I only meant … I mean, I'll only be in the way if the Emperor is ill and I can't imagine how I could –"

"He is not ill, Alix, he is dying, and Nicky has summoned you. You do have to go, my dear. You must, unless –"

I seized on that word, "Unless what, Grandmamma? Oh yes, it is better if I don't go, isn't it? That is what you think too, isn't it? You think I'd just be in the way, and to go all that way only to stand around and be awkward … and the wedding isn't for months yet, maybe a year … and my trousseau –"

Grandma shook her head and redirected her attention to the window, avoiding my imploring eyes.

"You won't need your trousseau, Alix. Ask Ernie to send your mourning dresses on to meet your train as it crosses Germany. And no, my dear, I meant that the only way for you to avoid going to the Crimea immediately is to end your engagement to Nicky."

"*End my engagement?* But I love Nicky. Why would I do that?"

Grandmamma nodded, still looking away from me.

"Then there is no question at all, is there? He has summoned you. He says he needs you. His father is dying. You must go to him. I think Mademoiselle Schneider will agree to accompany you, and of course you will have your maid. I'll wire Ella to meet your train and to accompany you from there. I am afraid you will have to take a regular passenger train, my dear. This is hardly the time to impose upon the imperial family. I imagine that poor Minnie is beside herself. I remember when Albert –"

"Grandmamma, won't you look at me," I sobbed.

She turned towards me and I wished she hadn't. Her eyes were black with pity.

"Let us not, Alicky, let us not be sentimental and afraid. Nicky needs you and you must be strong for him. In time …" She trailed off.

I tried to master myself but my voice and hands were still shaking badly.

"In time, Grandmamma? But I don't understand. I mean, of course I'll go. Nicky needs me and I do want to be with him. I didn't mean what I said before. I was just shocked. But you make it sound as though I won't be returning, and I will be. It cannot be long, no matter what happens to the poor Tsar. I will go and I will try to help, and then I will come home, home to you, here or at Balmoral or at Windsor. I have to visit Ernie and Ducky too, and I –"

"Alix, you tire me. Stop this and pull yourself together. Go and order your maid to pack your things and wire Ernie for your mourning attire. Do not try to predict the future, it is a fool's game. I will wire Nicky and Ella and tell them you are coming. I will arrange for a coachman to see you to the station in the morning. You cannot delay. Any delay will be looked upon most unfavorably by Nicky's family, your family now, Alix."

She rose and tottered out of the room without throwing me another glance. I did not follow her for a while. I couldn't rise and wire my brother for mourning clothes or tell my maid to pack. I found that I could only sit in the room stiffly until the shadows lengthened across the fading carpet. Only then could I rise wearily, feeling older than Grandmamma ever had, I think, and making my slow way up the stairs to follow her instructions.

Chapter 15

In the end I chose two maids, my own dear Tudelberg and one of Aunt Alix's maids who had expressed a lively interest in visiting Russia, so there were the four of us, as my delightful little *lectrice* Catherine had naturally chosen to accompany me on what I imagined would be a visit of no greater length than a few weeks.

My two maids naturally traveled in fourth class along with my single trunk of old black dresses, the ones Ducky had helpfully made certain would meet my train *en route*. I kept Catherine with me in my first class carriage, although it must be stated that a first class carriage still provides a perfectly lamentable excuse for travel. The food was atrocious, the berth was uncomfortable, and the temperature alternated between freezing and steam-heated purgatory.

The trip took us five days and by the third day, when we had gained Warsaw, I began to regret having kept Catherine with me. It was not that she was lacking in kindness or attention to my needs – on the contrary, she remained the soul of mindfulness – nor did she flag when I asked her to read aloud to me throughout my long sleepless nights in the jolting narrow berth. It wasn't her behavior that began to depress me, it was that there grew in her an almost imperceptible, but still noticeable, sort of awed horror at the endless wasteland passing by our train window. I watched her watch the cities vanish, and then the outlying houses and villages, and then the vast nothingness began and she seemed to become smaller and more shriveled.

In truth, I felt as though I was shrinking along with her, but her widened, dazed eyes and her skin's assuming the color of the frigid landscape that surrounded us had the effect of dampening my own spirits until I insisted that she stop staring outside and invited her to draw the curtains. Nevertheless she had aroused my own nerves to such a degree that I was actually glad to see Ella when she joined me at Kyvl on our fourth day.

My relief, however, was rather short-lived.

Ella, whose arrival held up the train for two hours to allow for the loading of her trunks, was the only member of the imperial family not already in attendance at Livadia. After embracing me and staring around my compartment in horror, she quickly brought me up-to-date with developments on the situation in the Crimea. Sergei, who had immediately traveled to Livadia upon hearing of his brother's condition, had kept in constant contact with her, so her information was fresh.

The Emperor's condition had so deteriorated that he was now reduced to breathing pure oxygen and had been unable to eat or to dress for over a week. Minnie, the Empress, was on the verge of a complete nervous collapse. Nicky, at least according to Sergei, was in an equally bad state and spent his time wandering around the small palace wringing his hands and telling anyone who encountered him that he would be fine as soon as "Papa gets better and Alicky arrives."

I didn't much like hearing this as I feared that he was creating in his mind the possibility that my arrival would somehow cause his father's fortunes to rally, a vain hope according to Ella, who agreed with Grandmamma that it was only a matter of time before the Emperor left this world, and a very little time at that.

Ella, though, being Ella, gave me only a few moments to absorb all this, moments I sorely needed in order to gather my thoughts and to plan what to say to Nicky, to the Empress, and to the apparently endless hordes of Grand Dukes and Grand Duchesses who were there at this most solemn of death watches.

Instead she chose to unnerve me further by discussing my wardrobe of all things! Clad in a beautiful dark-green suit, she finished her breathless recitation of recent events in Livadia and then gazed at me, seemingly horror-struck.

"Alix, is that a black gown? Oh no, no, say it is navy. Oh, my dear, what were you thinking?"

Given that my dress was quite obviously black, I did not bother to dignify such a stupid question with an answer but merely sighed and asked her why my gown being black should surprise her, since I believed it was she who had suggested to Grandmamma that Ernie be wired to send on my mourning clothes.

"Forgive me, Ella, should I be wearing one of my new pink trousseau dresses to show, possibly, what ...? Would that please everyone, do you think, that I should add a little gaiety to proceedings? Yes, yes that would send a strong message, wouldn't it?" Not giving her time to answer, I allowed my anger and scorn to show in my voice as I finished. "Why would you even raise such a matter as my clothing at this time? I am going to become, whether I like it or not, the Empress of the Russian peoples much sooner than I had anticipated, so you see, Ella, differently from you, a Grand Duchess,

247

and apparently one of a dozen or so of you, people will indeed be looking to me to set the tone in this solemn affair and I hardly think an appearance of frivolity is called for just now."

I felt myself relax inwardly. Maybe I had needed just this, someone to allow me to release the emotions that had been building up inside of me. Furthermore, it was past time that Ella recognized the nature of our new relationship. I was no longer her poor little sister, and the sooner she realized this, the better, as far as I was concerned.

Ella did not respond at first. Clearly she was abashed. However, when she did speak, her words robbed me of all my poise.

Her eyebrows raised, her perfect forehead creased, her beautiful hands fluttering, she presented the very picture of shocked innocence.

"Alicky, how can you speak to me like this?" She wiped at an invisible tear and peeped at me to see how her antics were affecting me. As they weren't affecting me at all, she straightened in her seat and fastidiously adjusted some lace at her cuff.

"I'll certainly be the first, and the gladdest, to kiss your hand and bow my knee when you do become Your Imperial Highness, but I hope that even when that glorious though, you will hopefully agree, sad day – given present circumstances – arrives, you will still recognize that I am your older sister and one who loves and cares for you with every fiber of my being."

Her words pained me. She was right, and even if she were not, she was all I had left to me of home in this rickety train, in this disconcerting land.

I reached out impulsively for her hand and she rewarded me with a smile that at least gave the appearance of warmth.

"There now, aren't we perfect friends and sisters, Alicky?"

I nodded, my own eyes filling with tears. Her smile deepened and she patted my hand before leaning back more comfortably in her berth.

"I began badly, didn't I? Of course you must have thought I was being the silliest girl in the world to speak of dresses at such a tragic time, though if Sergei is to be believed, I would speak of clothes on Judgment Day itself, if I were left to my own devices."

She waited for me to laugh and continued.

"Well, there you are, you agree and I'm sure it is true, but this time, darling, you must really hear me. You cannot wear black, Alicky, not even a scrap of black, until official mourning begins, and of course, well, the Emperor, he is still –"

She seemed at a loss as to how to continue, so I leaned forward helpfully.

"Alive is the word I think you are searching for, Ella dear. You are saying it would make for a bad show if I were to wear black whilst he continues to breathe, is that right?"

Ella looked appalled.

"Well yes, I suppose, but I would never have put it quite so plainly. It is an easy mistake. We were basically raised by dear Grandmamma, and at her court mourning has always been deemed appropriate attire at all times since the death of her beloved Prince Albert, hasn't it?"

We laughed together for a moment, overcome with memories of dearest Grandmamma and her relentless crêpe drapings.

Ella continued. "You see, dear sister, hers is the only court where it is allowed, that is all I meant, which means that you, princess, will need to change pretty rapidly into something else. We will arrive there in a little over an hour, you know. Shall I ring for your maids to bring your trunks?"

I couldn't answer her for a moment. Her words, "a little over an hour, a little over an hour, a little over…" No, I couldn't, I couldn't possibly step off this train, a place that a few moments ago had seemed an uncomfortable, even prison-like, conveyance but had now suddenly been transformed into a small, safe, familiar haven in the world, a place where nothing was expected of me and all was known to me.

A little over an hour, and then what?

"Alix, Alicky, what is it? You have grown all white. Are you ill?"

I shook my head and replied through numbing lips, "No, not ill. I'm simply … Oh, I'm worried, I suppose. I –"

"About your dress, dear? Oh no, don't be. We have plenty of time for you to change. I don't suppose there's a chance of finding an iron on this silly train, but I don't think anyone will even notice a few wrinkles under the circumstances."

I shook my head and thought of telling her, asking her, to help me, really help me, to say something comforting, but I didn't. I felt something come over me, or maybe I heard something from deep inside myself, a voice, one I knew I needed to heed. *Don't tell Ella you're frightened; don't tell anyone anything, not now, not ever. Wait for Nicky.*

I listened to my inner voice and I felt calmer.

I smiled at Ella.

"I'm sorry – terrible woolgathering. Yes, certainly, I'm simply terrified as to what I should wear now. In fact," I shrugged and laughed, "I only have my terrible old blue traveling suit, the one I wore from Osbourne to the train. Grandmamma said I should send for black, so I did, and I have nothing else suitable with me. I cannot wear my traveling suit, obviously, but thank heavens you're here, my Ella, and thank heavens twice that you have packed enough for a whole season."

I reached up and rang for Tuttles in her compartment. She must have been waiting eagerly for my summons, as she arrived within a minute. Perhaps there was no heat at all in fourth class; it was scant enough in first.

She curtsied cheerfully to me, and even more so to Ella whom she was obviously delighted to see again.

"Miss Ella, I mean Your Highness. It is so fine to see you again, it truly is."

Ella inclined her head in a regal manner. I noted this and decided it was time for me to adopt a similar pose.

I interrupted Tuttles's flow of words.

"Tuttles, we haven't any time at all. I need you to confer with Grand Duchess Ella's maids and have them identify which of her trunks is the one that might contain a suitable suit for me to wear upon arrival." I smiled at Ella. "Believe me, it will hardly matter to me which suit of yours I borrow, as I'm certain they are all entirely appropriate, and if they are even half as pretty as the one you are wearing, I should be quite presentable."

Ella stared at Tuttles and me in outright horror.

"Alix, I must speak with you privately … about the trunks –"

I waved away her appeal.

"Oh, don't be silly, Ella. Tuttles has known us since forever." I turned to Tuttles, laughing. "You see, Tuttles, the Grand Duchess is trying to spare me from being embarrassed in front of you, as if you were not all too aware that we are facing a rather grave dress shortage due to our lack of preparation for this sad journey."

Tuttles chuckled and addressed Ella.

"Oh, certainly, Your Imperial Highness. I'm sorry, Miss Ella, I hope I am addressing you correctly. These Russian titles have me in quite a spin. But I'll get to the task right away. As I was saying, Miss Alicky, I mean Your Highness … Oh I'm in a state, I am … please forgive me. We don't have any formal clothes for Princess Alix that aren't black, except that terrible old blue suit which is in no fit state for anyone to wear, if you'll pardon my saying so, Your Highness."

I began to laugh so hard at Tuttles's attempts to explain our predicament that it was a moment before I could wipe my eyes and gasp out that no apologies were necessary. It wasn't until then that I noticed that, though Tuttles was grinning back at me, Ella still looked terribly upset.

"Ella, what in the world is wrong with you? I'm hardly in a position to judge your taste in clothes, which in any case is beyond compare. Are you afraid that poor Tuttles won't find the right trunk? Maybe you could accompany her to the baggage compartment. I know it is a great deal to ask of you, but desperate times ..."

Ella shook her head, her lips pressed into a line.

"Alix, even if I or my maids could begin to find the right trunk, there is not a garment in there that would be suitable. I didn't want to say this in front of a servant," Tuttles looked affronted at the word "servant" but it did not deter Ella, "but similarly to you, I packed a great deal of mourning wear for should the worst occur, and as for the rest of it, I hardly know what is in the trunks myself. They are mostly things Sergei sent for."

I inclined my head, my laughter far away now.

"Forty trunks of items that Sergei sent for, things Sergei might want to, say, wear during his brother's illness, is that what you are telling me, Ella?"

I didn't give her a chance to finish. I reached up, unpinned the first button at the neck of my black gown and turned to Tuttles. "Tuttles, go and fetch my blue suit, please." She goggled at me. "This moment, please."

My newly-adopted tone of authority allowed no room for hesitation and she left with a confused curtsey towards both Ella and me.

Ella stared at me, looking relieved.

"Well, I suppose it doesn't matter what you wear so long as it's not black, and soon enough you'll be in black, and so will I, and after that –"

"It does indeed matter what I wear, Ella. Everything I do from now on will matter greatly, and I am not wearing that old blue suit, you are. Please disrobe and hand me your skirt and jacket. This blouse will do just fine."

253

For the second time on that strange day, my sister's white forehead creased.

"What? You cannot be serious?"

I continued slowly to unbutton my jacket.

"Disrobe, Ella, and give me your suit."

"You've run mad, Alix. I'm certainly not going –"

I held out my hand. "But you will, and you will now."

When Tuttles reentered the compartment a few minutes later, her own face turned nearly as white as Ella's to see Ella standing there in her blouse and petticoat, and shivering.

Tuttles looked at me aghast as I fumbled with the green skirt's fastenings. I turned to her.

"Tuttles, please assist me with these garments and then help the Grand Duchess into the blue suit. It's too cold in here to be half-undressed."

Tuttles did as she was told and within a few moments I was dressed and smoothed into Ella's beautiful dark-green ensemble and she was wearing my dusty old garment. I was a few inches taller than her, but as I cheerfully commented, it merely gave the skirt a nice swing when I moved.

The whistle blew and the train shuddered to a cautious halt.

The conductor's voice echoed down the cars.

"Sebastopol. All disembark for Sebastopol."

Ella, shaking, tried to step around me hastily, but stumbled on the dragging hem of my old suit. I sidled around her effortlessly.

"I will alight first, Ella."

She nearly spat out her words at me. "That you won't, you miserable creature. In Russia, a Grand Duchess still precedes a princess, no matter how rudely attired that Grand Duchess might be."

She tried to edge around me again. I raised my hand and pushed her in the chest hard enough to make her stumble back.

"Maybe so but the future Empress precedes all, and besides, look ..."

Ella's angry eyes followed my gaze to the window. There he was, Nicky, my Nicky. At the sight of him, her eyes fell and she sat down abruptly.

"After you, Alix."

I didn't feel triumphant, only vindicated, and so it was with a straight spine and a haughty chin that I disembarked from the train and stepped onto the soil of Russia for the first time as its future Empress. I did not look back – for what would have been the point?

Chapter 16

The so-called palace at Livadia was a small, dark house filled with so many royal personages that it resembled a dank seaside boarding house in Brighton I once traveled to with Irene during the winter. That was an ill-fated, somewhat rheumatic, sort of trip, where in addition to our being offered cramped and poorly-decorated, damp rooms, we also found ourselves surrounded by rather down-at-heel people, the sort who could only afford to visit seaside resorts in the off-season, amongst whom, to be fair, we could be counted at that time.

My introduction to the imperial residence of Livadia made much the same distressing impression upon me, although there were, I suppose, differences; it was just that one had to look very hard to find them.

At a rundown resort, there is a sort of pathetic and desperate attempt at gaiety of the kind where people exclaim, "Ah, a shingled beach in the rain. We really must have a plate of winkles and ignore the weather," or, "Ah, we are on holiday and we must wear our best clothing."

Here in Livadia I naturally discovered no forced gaiety, given the circumstances, rather piety contests as to who was most submissive to the will of God and who had best served the Emperor and the imperial family.

Nor was I the only one to be anxious about my wardrobe, as it was obvious that the Romanov women, while owning countless sets of clothing and vast quantities of jewels, were limited in what they had on hand to wear that would appear suitably sober without actually tipping them over into mourning apparel. Attics had been raided and old dresses had been unearthed, either that or they had all gained many pounds in weight within a few days. Nevertheless, they looked less ridiculous than the Grand Dukes and court officials who were all stuffed into, or had hanging off them, a bizarre collection of much-decorated uniforms, with ornamental swords swinging from their hips that threatened at any moment to trip them up, or possibly someone else who might pass too close by them.

They clanked and they rustled and they stunk of mothballs, and little Xenia, still merry despite her tearstained face, observed, grinning, "Isn't it odd that they are all crashing about in what look like ancient uniforms? I mean, Papa has been a great peacemaker, so it is a funny way to honor him now, isn't it?"

Nicky, though, attributed their attire to my presence. "You see, darling, you see how they honor their future Empress. Even Papa does, and he is so very sick ..."

Nicky, who had been virtually mute since our first meeting, was referring to my arrival two days previously. When he met me at the train, I was shocked by how pale he was, and then yet more taken aback by his greeting. With eyes reddened with tears and shaking hands he stared at me and then proceeded to clutch me in front of Ella for the entire three hour carriage ride from the station to the palace at Livadia, without his really saying anything beyond murmuring my name in an unnervingly prayerful way.

He didn't even tell me what to expect until we arrived at the gates, when he said, "Papa will be waiting. We'll go directly to Papa. He'll be waiting now. He has been

258

waiting for you, darling, we all have, Nicky most of all. You'll see how it is now."

I was too upset at his appearance to attach much meaning to his disjointed words. I have learned that at times of great stress it is best for me to remove myself mentally from the immediate situation, even if I cannot do so physically, and this stratagem almost served to erase my awareness of Nicky's hand painfully grabbing mine and helped to keep me from flinching at the awful sounds of his sobbing for the entire length of that terrible journey.

I was in fact so benumbed and far removed from my reality that I was able, I think, to maneuver gracefully through the throng of extraordinarily dressed people who were gathered outside the old wooden palace to await our carriage and to manage to incline my head in acknowledgement as they addressed me in either French or Russian, I could not tell which. Nicky's sweating hand at that moment felt better than it had in the carriage, for at least it was tugging me through that crowd of roiling strangers.

As soon as we reached the palace doors, he began pulling at me even harder, so I did not notice at the time the ugly dark-red wallpaper or how narrow the hallways were. In fact, we did not pause once in our haste until he ushered me rather pressingly through the door of a small, dimly-lit bedroom that reeked of sickness.

Oddly, that calmed me. It smelt like Papa's room after he got sick and that made me realize that, mighty emperor or not, it did not matter: Here was simply a man and a family in distress, and it was in this more quiescent frame of mind that I was able to kneel in front of the poor Emperor.

They had, for no reason I could ascertain, forced his bent frame out of bed and into a chair. That was how I found him; a shrunken old man propped into a chair by pillows and dressed in the uniform of a Russian colonel.

I knelt wordlessly in front of him. He did not speak; I do not think he was even capable of speaking by then. His eyes were already gazing into that other world, the one we must all anticipate, whether sovereign or serf, and I felt strongly that he was at peace with this realization.

Later, when Nicky and I were alone in an ugly little parlor downstairs, I tried to share this feeling with him. He did not seem to be able to hear me, though. As soon as we entered the room and I had sat down, he leapt upon me, burying his face in my skirt and sobbing while clutching my legs, which had by then begun to pain me considerably.

He spoke like a broken man.

"Did you see, Alicky, did you see, darling, how sainted Papa got all dressed up for you? It was just for you, he said. Mama told me he said that was the only way to greet the next Tsarina of Russia. Everyone was dressed for you, but then it is all so silly, isn't it, Alicky? I mean, Papa is going to rally because he has to, because if he doesn't, well then it will be all up with us, you see."

I closed my eyes and drew from a growing well of strength inside me that seemed to have rather miraculously appeared since I crossed onto Russian soil. I believe it was the divine beginning to work in me.

I gently stroked his feverish head and parted his sweat-soaked hair.

"Dearest Nicky, be calm, my boysy, my precious. This is God's will, not ours, not even your dearest papa's. But I do know that if he could speak, he would tell you to be strong and embrace the place which providence has chosen for you and you alone. You must honor him now and more so when your papa sits by the even greater King in Heaven. Come, sweet one, do sit up. I will ring for some tea and we will think it all out, shall we?"

The effect of my words also seemed to be miraculous. It was as though I, little Alix of Hesse, was divinely inspired, because as soon as I spoke, Nicky sat up and stared at me with an expression that can only be described as rapturous.

"Alicky, yes, yes, darling. Oh my Sunshine, tea, yes of course! Why, you must be so exhausted and worn down, and yet just look at the way you are sitting here, as cool and beautiful as an angel, and taking care of your own boy. My darling, all that you say is true. It is God's will, at least I –"

Then he began to sob again, my new-found wisdom dissolving into a feeling of impatience. I wanted tea, I wanted to be told where my room was, I wanted to be alone.

I stroked his swollen face.

"No, dearest, don't start all that again. People will be looking to you for strength and we must show them that strength even when we are not feeling strong. You are your papa's dear son and all around us is confusion and fear. You must not give way to your feelings of despair."

261

He stared at me with the helpless, innocent expression of, I could not help thinking, a calf about to be slaughtered.

The next two days passed in much the same manner. Nicky veered between delight at my presence and utter devastation at his father's rapid decline as the death watch around the Emperor tightened in that tiny chamber where the poor Emperor himself was reduced to making only the occasional enfeebled gestures to no one in particular. Nicky's mother, the Empress, presided over her husband's bedside, as was only right, and from her sad perch she decided who she could and could not bear to have near her.

I did not take it personally that I was not selected to number amongst this select group. The Empress was in great pain and terror at the terrible loss awaiting her, and besides we did not know each other. She had greeted me distantly, if correctly, upon my arrival, and subsequently I saw very little of her, save when Nicky insisted I be with him in his father's room, and those times I dreaded. The Empress wanted Nicky to herself. Only in his presence did she feel able to set aside her iron sense of dignity and permit herself to cry.

I could hardly bear to be with them. It is not that I lacked understanding of their terrible grief, for I had so recently lived through this ordeal with my own papa, nor was I untouched by the poor invalid's sufferings, for indeed I was, but these were not yet my people and this was not my loss, and I felt as though I were intruding. Worse, to get to and from the Emperor's room, one had to jostle through the imperial crowd of watchers, or more precisely, of waiters, for they were all waiting in an atmosphere of great tension.

Nicky's uncles had positioned themselves along that narrow corridor in order to have access to him. Some urged that Nicky pull himself together in the hope of discerning some element of the dying Tsar in his son, or if that were not possible – and Nicky's precarious emotional state seemed to suggest that it wasn't – to be able to assess how his weakness, which was now apparent to all, would affect them in the coming reign, for good or for ill. Amidst this grotesque charade it was becoming eminently apparent to me that I could not expect to be left alone, for their scheming wives had begun to follow me around, adopting a falsely ingratiating air, one made entirely pointless by the fact that we shared no language in common.

I therefore came to the necessary conclusion that if Nicky were to discuss private matters with anyone, it had better be with me, for I loved him truly and had no agenda beyond concern for his well-being. In respect of matters of state, I urged him to speak to the doctors privately and to summon his father's ministers to Livadia to obtain appropriate and coherent advice as to the proceedings to come, by which I meant, but did not say directly, the funeral.

I am, of course, only a woman, but even I knew that certain arrangements would become immediately necessary upon the death of a mighty ruler, and one who was dying far from his capital. I knew that some things would need to be done, but I did not know what they were. Nicky did not seem to know either, or even to wish to know, but rather would only stare at me terror-stricken when I suggested he summon those officials who would.

"Darling, I can't. Papa is the Tsar, and besides, what could I say to them? I don't know how to talk to the ministers, I never have. I wouldn't know what to say. We don't know each other at all."

Oh what his words did to me! How could it be like this? I longed to escape to the peace of Hesse-Darmstadt, which even under Ducky's reign seemed so simple and desirable, or to Grandmamma at Windsor or Osbourne. I longed to be little Alicky again, but unlike Nicky, I could feel the iron handcuffs of my future tightening around my wrists, and while I did understand Nicky's dread, I knew that giving in to it was no way out of it. I had been wrong on the train when I thought Nicky and I could share our fears. I would always have to hide my fears from him hereafter or we would all be lost.

I poured all the love I bore him into my smile.

"Precious Boysy, I love you so much but, darling, what you say is funny. You don't need to know the ministers. They are there to serve you, as they have dutifully served your papa. Surely you can't be afraid of them?"

His eyes met mine squarely.

"But I *am* afraid of them, Alix, I am afraid of them, and of my uncles, and of Mama, and I was afraid of Papa too, always, always … I mean until now." He choked on yet another sob and I saw that it was only with great difficulty that he was able to continue. "I never wanted to be Tsar. I don't think anyone else wants me to be Tsar either. If they do, they have certainly never showed it. I suppose Papa thought he'd live a long, long time and it would not matter if I did not amount to anything, but now –"

I gazed at him seriously. "... But now, Nicky, now all of that cannot matter. Now you are going to become Tsar, whether you like it or not, whether anyone likes it or not, and now you must show them all that they were wrong if they failed to have faith in you. For remember, God chose you for this role and –"

He interrupted me. "Alix, do you know the day of my birth?"

"Yes, of course, darling, May 6th, but I don't see –"

"Job's day, Alix. I was born on the Day of Job!"

"So you were, my darling, and what greatness thereby awaits you and your people. For did not Job face, and then overcome, his trials to become beloved of God?"

Nicky shook his head in tearful discomposure

"But I won't, I'm not going to. Oh, you don't know, Alix, you don't. We will all fall. It is all that can come. I am the lamb, the sacrificial lamb!"

I scowled. "Stop this, Nicky. Stop this now. You are the Tsarevitch, you will be Tsar, and you will be a great Tsar. You are scaring yourself and me too with these fancies. It makes me feel as if I do not matter. Do I not matter to you, Nicky? Does my love and faith in you mean nothing? Is it all written in the stars that nothing but loss can come from your reign and that God has chosen you in error? If so, maybe I have too. Is that what you mean?"

His skin went ashen and he fell dramatically to his knees before me.

"Marry me, Alix, marry me today, and I'll be everything you believe I can be."

I stared down at him in horror. If my shock was mixed with repugnance, I shall not own it, even to myself.

I stared at him and all possibilities flashed through my mind: I could leave, I could return home to Darmstadt, to Ernie and Ducky; I could become a maiden aunt to their children; I could travel to see Grandmamma who was old and would not always be there; I could travel between my sisters as the inconvenient girl who could have been a queen twice over but wasn't. Then I recalled Ella's face when I had obliged her to remove her jacket on the train …

I saw everything and I fell to my knees so that we were face-to-face. Then I held out my hands, which he grasped eagerly. There I espied his whole, clean, pure soul in his beautiful blue eyes, and beyond that purity, I saw his love. I could love him too, love him and guide him and help him carry his heavy burden. For maybe it was not Nicky who was the golden calf of sacrifice; maybe it was I who had been chosen to save Russia or at least to save the man who would rule her.

"Yes, darling, yes, I will marry you the minute you say."

My statement was rewarded with the first smile I had seen from him since my arrival in Russia, and in spontaneous joy he rose to his feet, lifting me to mine in one graceful movement and laughing aloud.

"I'll send for Father Yanishev. He can instruct you in our faith here, darling."

I laughed too.

266

"I don't think so, boysy. It will take me forever to learn. Can't we be married if –"

"... If you're not Orthodox, darling?" He shook his head and grinned playfully. "No, the next Tsarina of Russia, her Imperial Highness Alix of Hesserdornova, can hardly not be Orthodox. But never mind, all you have to do is to repeat what he says. In your voice it will become sacred anyway." His face became serious. "Thank you, darling, you honor me. All of my life I will spend trying to show you how much, how grateful, how –"

I stilled him with a very improper kiss. I did not want this lightness of the moment, of my lifting heart, ended with tears.

Eagerly he returned my embrace and, pulling me to my feet, he proposed, "A dance, Your Majesty?"

I curtsied, eyes blazing.

"Yes, Your Majesty, yes please."

He began to lead me across the room in step, and for a moment I was so happy, simply so glad to be with him, that I did not even feel my sore legs or detect the rustling and murmuring behind us. It was not until Nicky, my hand raised high in his, had made the requisite turn in that small parlor that we realized that we were no longer alone.

Clustered in the doorway were his uncles and Ella, and they were watching us with grave and censorious eyes. Nicky, blushing, quickly dropped my hand and we both faced them with reddening faces.

I could hear what would be said of us in the future. "They danced as he lay dying."

His Uncle Vladimir shouldered his way through his brothers into the room and came to a stop in front of us, before kneeling at Nicky's feet.

He did not need to say a word; Nicky's reign had begun.

Chapter 17

It might have seemed to the world, and, yes, to myself as well, that one should be entitled to expect to be allowed a moment or two of simple joy following one's decision to wed, but to assume so in my own case would be to be badly mistaken. Looking back, of course, it is impossible to know whether my acquiescence to Nicky's request of me, to his need of me, made things better or worse, but it surely seemed worse in my eyes for it became yet another source of contention, and heaven knows we were not short of those!

The Tsar was dead. The Tsar was Nicky. The dead Tsar needed to be buried.

"You cannot bury the late Tsar at Livadia, Nicky," advised the uncles and the ministers. "The Tsar must rest at Peter and Paul's with all the other dead tsars. Why don't you know this, Nicky?"

The Tsar was beginning to smell, so what should be done? Worse, no tea had been brought to Aunty Miechen, and Uncle Vladimir could be heard bellowing about this and about the dreadful state of his brother's corpse all through the corridors. Minnie had rung for smelling salts as she and the other ladies were all on the point of fainting, but none was brought to her. Where were the maids, the servants, the coachmen? Oh horrors, they were hiding and crying in their rooms and the stables. Why was this so? Who was in charge of this madhouse? Why, it must be the new Tsar, but where was the new Tsar? Oh horror of horrors, he too was hiding and crying in his room.

A storm arose over the Black Sea. The skies darkened, the winds howled, the outdoor furniture was swept off the balconies, the seabirds screamed in unison with the wailing women and the bellowing uncles, and the dead Tsar was turning black.

Now what?

Sergei opined gravely to me, when he and Ella visited my room, that it seemed to him that this storm would make it impossible for a ship to come and transport his brother's body back to St. Petersburg. I stared at him stupidly. I could not even bring myself to ask the question as to why this particular option was the one he had chosen to focus upon, but I didn't, I couldn't, blame Sergei, for there was so much confusion around the household that to stay sane one simply had to focus upon something.

I myself spent those two days of the storm closeted in my room with nice old Father Yanishev, trying to learn the alien words to the Orthodox rites. Uncle Vladimir concentrated upon his lack of tea, nearly achieving success when one of Minnie's ladies-in-waiting volunteered that she thought she could figure out the intricacies of a samovar if only someone, anyone, could solve the puzzle of how water was to be delivered to it. Aunt Miechen threw open all the windows, thereby letting in the rain and wind, in a vain attempt to drive out the odor of the late Emperor, and this made all the ladies look more insane than ever when their hair began to loosen as badly as the morale of our shipwrecked crew.

Then there arose a hero in our midst. Sandro, little Xenia's new husband, organized a small crew of men, Nicky amongst them, to remove the Emperor's corpse to one of the outbuildings. It didn't really solve any of the other problems, but we were all able to breath and that enabled a few servants to creep back into the palace and serve tea. With these small, heady triumphs, a renewed vigor arose in Nicky, who came to my room, accompanied by Sandro, while I sat with Xenia and my by now constant companion, Father Yanishev.

Nicky appeared flushed and windswept. Sandro only appeared windswept. I smiled at Nicky and he returned my smile wholeheartedly.

"Darling, it is done. I have done it, with Sandro's help. Sandro spoke to me too, he really did, and he made me understand that all will be well. I simply have to be obedient to God's will and —"

Sandro interrupted him sharply while rolling his eyes at Xenia, who glanced down uncomfortably as he spoke.

"Nicky, you know that is not exactly what I said. What I said was that, whether you like it or not, it is apparently the will of God that you be Tsar, so you really have to accept your situation and begin to —".

Nicky cursorily wave him to silence and sat down beside me.

"I've come up with the most wonderful idea, darling. I think we should get married tonight, here, while Papa is still in the house, well near the house anyway. It will be as though he will be giving us his blessing. Good old Father Yani here can marry us, can't you, Father?"

He turned to address poor Father Yanishev who appeared as stunned as I was by Nicky's words.

Father Yanishev swallowed and fidgeted for a minute, before finally mumbling, "If Your Majesty wishes it, then of course, although Her Highness has yet to take her vows in the Orthodox faith, so we will need to attend to that first, and –"

Nicky, coming as close to rudeness as I had ever heard him, replied, "Then do it now, Father. How long can it take? After all, young children go through this ceremony each day and –"

It was Xenia's turn to interrupt Nicky, which she did in a shrill and protesting tone.

"Nicky, how can you? Oh, oh ..."

She began to sob and Sandro rushed over to her and pulled her against him while staring reproachfully at Nicky who looked more irritated by his sister's outburst than in any way repentant.

"Xenia, are you so selfish that you cannot even wish for me the same comfort and happiness that you have in your Sandro, especially now that Papa is gone and I am all alone and have to be Tsar. I need Alix, why can't you understand that?"

This was a question Sandro took the opportunity to answer resolutely over his sobbing wife's head.

"Nicky, I don't think Xenia means to be selfish and of course she understands, we all understand, that you wish to be married as soon as possible. I think she is simply trying to say that maybe now is not the best moment. There is your father –"

"Papa is dead, Sandro, and besides he gave his express consent for our wedding and –"

"Yes, we all know he is dead, Nicky, but your mother isn't, and –"

Nicky shot me a triumphant glance before answering Sandro.

"I have spoken to Mama. I did so before I came in. I went and saw her and told her we had moved Papa outside, and I asked her if she would mind if I married Alix without delay, and she said –"

Xenia raised her white face from Sandro's shoulder. "You asked Mama about a having wedding today? Oh Nicky, why are you –?"

Nicky glared at her and I shifted uncomfortably in my seat, wishing I could vanish, wishing they all would vanish.

"Yes, I did, Xenia. Mama at least understands that I must have Alicky as my wife immediately if I am going to be able to manage."

This declaration made, he resorted to sobbing again. Sandro and I averted our eyes. Xenia didn't.

"I see, and so she gave her consent, then, did she?"

Nicky reached for my hand. His was sweating and he gripped my limp, cold one so hard that I winced, but he didn't notice. He was only intent on his struggle with his sister now.

"She said it did not matter to her. And no, don't look at me like that, Xenia. You know Mama always says that when she means yes. You remember when we would want a second desert or to go out, and if she said, 'It doesn't matter to me,' it meant yes, and so you see –"

Xenia looked as though she was going to leap at Nicky's head and I watched in dumb horror as Sandro was obliged to restrain her.

It was Sandro who spoke next.

"All right, Nicky, Xenia, let us try to remain calm. God knows, someone has to. If we all go mad, we will have to do so in competition with the uncles, and that is a battle we cannot possibly win. Listen, maybe it is Alix's opinion we should all be asking. She is the bride, after all, and should we not hear her feelings on the matter?"

Nicky and Xenia both chuckled weakly, and I could have loved Sandro right then for his calmness and strength, if only he had left me out of it, for I could not say what my real feelings were. I could not say that Nicky disgusted me at that moment and that I thought the so-called palace at Livadia was the ugliest house I had ever seen. I could not say that it seemed to me that if none of these mighty Romanovs could even bury a man, they could hardly be expected to run a country, and that the whole idea of Nicky being Tsar was almost as preposterous as the bizarre grin that had formed on the dead Emperor's rotting corpse.

No, I could not say any of that, so I said only this: "I cannot say what it is best for us to do. I am a stranger here, so I will do whatever everybody, and especially the Tsar, wishes."

At that I bowed my head and I too began to cry, whereupon all of them grew immediately solicitous towards me. Nicky patted my shoulder and murmured endearments; Father Yanishev sighed sympathetically; Xenia said she thought I should rest; and Sandro said under his breath that he thought I was the only one in this Bedlam who had any sense.

In the end I was judged for my choice not to make a choice as harshly as if I had. The uncles, upon hearing of Nicky's plan, declared he was an idiot and that he had to get married in St. Petersburg as every tsar was and that, speaking of tsars, could somebody please plan to bury the dead one before they married off the living one? Minnie just cried and refused to voice any further opinion on whether Nicky and I should marry, and Ella told me later that the entire family believed that it had been my idea to wed Nicky while still at Livadia, such was my greed for the throne. Only Sandro defended me, but no one listened to him as he was not well liked by the Empress. He had, after all, stolen her favorite daughter away in marriage. Nicky crumbled under the opprobrium and said that maybe it would be best to marry in the St. Petersburg after all, but still as soon as possible.

I think we all would have remained there gossiping and fratching amongst ourselves forever if wise Grandmamma had not had the foresight to understand that with the demise of Tsar Alexander would come the death of any leadership. So, upon receiving confirmation of the Emperor's death, she immediately dispatched Uncle Bertie and Aunt Alix, the latter to comfort her sister Minnie and the former to take charge of proceedings. They arrived post haste and by the day following their arrival our entire deranged household, complete with imperial corpse, was herded onto the family's private train and set out for St. Petersburg.

This is not to say that all went smoothly from there. We had to stop constantly and unload the poor Emperor's body in local churches so that the peasants could kiss his blackened, bloated remains, and the family had to join in the proceedings as well. This disgusting scene lasted for three days in Moscow alone, but at last, at endless last, we arrived in St. Petersburg where I was allowed to accompany Sergei and Ella to their palace where I was to remain for the next week until the final funeral rites for the Tsar were completed and I could marry Nicky.

While I could not speak a word of their language, I fancy I heard the people in the streets as Sergei, Ella and I drove by, declaring, "There she is. There goes the funeral bride."

Made in the USA
San Bernardino, CA
26 May 2016